CHAPTER 1

Six Weeks Ago

"Hey, lady!" a guy yells as I race by him with a tray of dirty dishes. "I need the check!"

"Be right there!" I say, trying not to drop the tray as a little boy runs in front of me.

I pass through the door to the kitchen, set the tray down, and take a moment to catch my breath.

"You okay?" my boss Martin asks as he flips burgers on the grill.

"I'm just tired." I walk over to him. "Is that cheese melt almost done?"

"Right here." He hands me the plate.

I thank him before returning to the dining area and delivering the cheese melt to the woman at table six.

She holds up her glass of iced tea and tersely asks, "Could I get a refill?"

"Sure," I say. I notice the couple at the next table giving me dirty looks, likely because I haven't taken their order yet.

"Be there in a minute," I say with my most endearing smile.

As I get the lady's iced tea, Jenna comes up to me. "Table seven is waiting to order. You want me to do it?"

"No, I will," I say.

Jenna's always offering to help me. She's a great friend. She not only got me this job but also gave me a place to stay when I got evicted from my apartment last year.

I drop off the iced tea and hurry over to the guy waiting for his check. I hand it to him. "Sorry for the wait."

"You should get a different job," the guy says with a snort. "One you can actually do."

Why do people have to be so mean? Maybe if this guy knew my situation — how even this simple job is hard for me — he wouldn't be so harsh. Then again, he seems like the type of guy who wouldn't care.

I race over to the couple who had been giving me dirty looks.

"Sorry, it's a little crazy today," I tell them. "What can I get you?"

"We're leaving," the man says, glaring at me as he and the woman exit the booth.

"But I was just about to—"

"Forget it," he says. "We'll go somewhere else."

"Miss?" the woman at table eight yells, waving me over. "I need my check."

I hurry to her table and give her the check.

"Where's my side of fries?" a man yells, and I realize I forgot to put the order in.

"They're coming!" I say, racing back to the kitchen. "Martin, I need a side of fries. I forgot to put the order in."

"Grace, you gotta write it down," he says, sounding frustrated with me.

"I know. It just got really busy, and I didn't have time."

He shakes his head as he scoops up the fries and dumps them in a paper-lined basket.

I take the basket of fries to the guy. "Sorry for the wait. Need anything else?"

"No, I'm good."

Behind Closed Doors

ALSO BY ROWEN CHAMBERS

The Surprise Party
Behind Closed Doors

BEHIND CLOSED DOORS

ROWEN CHAMBERS

JOFFE BOOKS

Joffe Books, London
www.joffebooks.com

First published in Great Britain in 2025

© Rowen Chambers 2025

Cover art by Cherie Chapman

ISBN: 978-1-80573-225-9

PROLOGUE

A gust of wind slams into me, and I stumble back, my hands frantically feeling around for anything to grab onto. But there's nothing. No railing. No support beams. Nothing.

"Please," I beg, my gaze darting down to the knife. "Don't do this."

I glance behind me and see I'm frighteningly close to the edge. One more step. That's all it would take before I tumble off the side of the building and fall hundreds of feet to my death. I can already see it in my head. Images of my mangled body on the street. Strangers gathered around me, staring in horror, wondering how it happened.

Would it be ruled an accident? Suicide? Would anyone ever find out the truth?

My heart thunders in my chest. My entire body trembles with fear. How did this happen? This was supposed to be one of the best nights of my life. A celebration. A night I'd always remember.

When I woke up this morning, I couldn't believe all this was real — that I'd found such a wonderful man. And not only had I found him, but I'd soon be marrying him!

Never in my wildest dreams did I think it would end this way. I should've known it was all too good to be true.

"I'm sorry," I say, my voice trembling. "Please, just let me go. You don't have to do this."

"Unfortunately, I do. And you have no one to blame but yourself. If only you'd listened to me."

Our eyes meet, and I search for any hint of compassion. Or just a tiny shred of doubt that could save me. But all I see is anger. Pure rage.

"You're right," I blurt out, desperate to say anything that might stop this. "I should've listened to you. I should've done what you wanted."

"But you didn't. And now it's too late."

"It's not too late! I could—" My voice cuts out as the knife rises in front of me.

It hovers dangerously close to my face, and I instinctively go to take a step back. I stop myself, though, remembering how close I am to the edge.

"No," I say, my heart racing so fast I can barely breathe. "I'm begging you! Don't do this!"

But it's too late. Nothing I say will stop this.

What was supposed to be one of the best nights of my life is going to end with my death.

I'm not. I'm exhausted, and my feet hurt. But I still have three hours left in my shift.

"Want me to get table five?" Jenna asks as I go behind the counter. "He's really hot, and I don't see a ring."

Looking over, I see a guy in a suit. She's right. He's really good-looking, with dark wavy hair, tan skin, and a very handsome face.

"I've got it," I say, heading toward him.

The guy's even better-looking up close. I'm sure he has a girlfriend. Guys like him always have girlfriends.

"Can I get you something to drink?" I ask.

The guy's texting someone on his phone. "I'm sorry, what was that?"

"A drink. We have soda, iced tea, coffee."

"I'll have a—" He stops, gasping when he sees me.

What's that about? Do I have something on my face? Or maybe I spilled something on myself. I glance down at my uniform. It looks clean.

I look back at him. "Is something wrong?"

He stares at me, still not saying anything.

"If you need more time to decide, I can come back."

"That won't be necessary." He smiles a little. "Please, you'll have to forgive me. You look like someone I used to know."

"Who?"

He shakes his head. "It doesn't matter. What's your name?"

"Grace."

"That's a beautiful name."

"Is it?" I shrug. "I guess I never thought about it."

"It fits you."

"How so?"

He leans back in the booth, gazing at me, lips slightly upturned. "A beautiful name for a beautiful girl."

I laugh. "Yeah, okay. So, did you decide on a drink?"

"Water is fine. I assume you have sparkling?"

Sparkling water? At a diner? Is he serious?

"Sorry. All we have is regular."

A smile breaks out on his handsome face. "I was joking, Grace. You looked like you could use a laugh."

"You're right. I could definitely use a laugh."

"Rough day?"

"Yeah, we're busier than usual."

"I see that," he says, looking around. "I don't know how you do it. I wouldn't be able to keep up."

"Miss?" I glance over at the counter and see a woman holding up her empty glass of soda.

"Go help her," Suit Guy says. "I need a minute to decide."

"Okay. I'll be right back."

"What's he like?" Jenna asks, coming up beside me as I refill the lady's soda.

"The guy? He's nice." I smile as I say it.

"Did he ask you out?"

"No." I laugh. "You think a guy like him would ask me out? He probably works on Wall Street and is engaged to some high-society girl."

"Then why would he be at a diner in New Jersey?"

"Maybe he was driving through town on his way to the city."

She takes the soda glass from me. "I'll finish this. You go find out where Suit Guy is from and what he's doing here."

"I'm not asking him that. It's none of my business."

I return to Suit Guy's table and take out my order pad. "Did you decide what you want?"

He sets his menu down. "What do you recommend?"

"The cheeseburgers are good."

"I'll have one of those, then."

"Anything else?"

"That'll be it." He smiles at me, and my pulse quickens.

I smile back. "It shouldn't be long."

"What time is your break?" he asks.

"Not for an hour. Why?"

"I have some time to kill." He arches his brows. "Maybe you could join me?"

"Oh, I'm not supposed to sit with the customers."

"Even during your break? You should be able to do whatever you'd like. It's your break, after all."

"I guess you're right. It's not really a rule. It's just not something I've ever considered. I usually sit in the break room and look at stuff on my phone."

"What do you think?" He smiles a little. "Would you mind keeping me company for a few minutes?"

"Um. Sure," I say.

I can't come up with a reason not to unless he has a girlfriend, in which case I should leave him alone. But if he had a girlfriend, he wouldn't be flirting with me. Maybe he's not flirting. Maybe it's like he said, and he's just killing time and wants some company.

"I should introduce myself," he says. "I'm Evan. Evan Sinclair."

"Nice to meet you." I motion to the kitchen. "I'll go put in your order."

When I get to the kitchen, Jenna rushes over. "So? What did he say?"

"He asked me to sit with him during my break." I tear the order off the pad and add it to the ones hanging above the grill.

"He asked you out?" Jenna asks like she never in a million years thought that would happen.

"He didn't ask me out," I say. "He's just killing time and didn't want to sit there alone."

"What are you two talking about?" Martin asks, putting a plate holding a grilled cheese sandwich and fries under the warmer.

"There's this really hot guy out there," Jenna says, "and he just asked Grace out."

"It's not a date," I say, rolling my eyes. "I'm just going to sit with him during my break."

"Who is he?" Martin asks. "What do you know about him?"

"Would you leave her alone?" Jenna says. "This is her chance to finally meet a guy."

"You make me sound like a loser who can't get a date," I say.

"Well, you have to admit you've been in a dry spell. When was your last date? A year ago?" She crosses her arms and arches a brow.

"Jenna, your order's up," Martin says before I can counter her argument. He adds a plate to the two already under the warmer.

"Yeah, got it." She takes the plates and leaves the kitchen.

"Don't be going out with his guy until you know more about him," Martin says.

I lean against the counter. "You know I'm twenty-eight."

"Yeah, what about it?"

"I'm an adult. You don't have to worry about me."

"Age doesn't mean anything. My daughter's thirty and got involved with a guy who took off and left her with nothing. If she'd listened to me, she never would've dated him."

"You don't like any of the men your daughters go out with."

"Because they're liars. Back in my day, men didn't hide who they were." He puts a beef patty on the grill. "There were a few bad apples, but for the most part, we were good, honest men. Now you got all these imposters online, pretending to be something they're not."

"Not every guy's like that."

Martin flips the burger, then waves his metal spatula in front of my face. When our gazes lock, he says, "You be careful, you hear me? You're a nice girl. You're better off alone than with some jerk."

It's sweet that Martin feels the need to watch out for me. I've only worked here six months, and he already treats me like one of his daughters.

Maybe he's right, and I'm better off alone. But I wouldn't mind having a man in my life, especially if it's the right man.

CHAPTER 2

"How was the burger?" I ask Evan.

My break started a few minutes ago, but I stopped at the restroom to freshen my makeup and let my hair down from the tight ponytail it was in.

"It was good," he says. "Thanks for the recommendation."

"You can't really go wrong with a burger," I say with a nervous laugh.

Why am I so nervous? This guy isn't interested in me, though he did invite me to sit with him. Does that mean he's going to ask me out? Why me? Jenna is far more attractive, with her bleached blonde hair and curvy figure. I have dark hair, a flat chest, and barely-there hips. I've always been thin, but I lost weight after the accident.

"What is it?" I ask. Evan is staring at me. "Do I have mustard on me? I thought I got it all off but—"

"It's your hair," he says. "You look different with it down like that."

"Oh." I do that nervous laugh again.

"I like it. It looks good." He leans back. "You're a very beautiful woman, Grace."

"Um, thanks," I mumble. He's probably only saying that to be nice. I'm average-looking at best. Definitely not what most people would consider beautiful.

His brows rise. "You don't believe me?"

"Not really."

"Why would I lie about that?"

I shrug. "Maybe so I'll go out with you?"

"I wasn't planning to ask you out."

"Oh."

I look down at the table, my face heating. Of course, he wasn't going to ask me out. He's way out of my league. Why did I let Jenna make me think this guy might be interested in me?

"Your order will be right up," I hear Jenna say to the people in the booth behind me.

Evan watches her as she walks off.

"She's single," I tell him. "If you were wondering."

"I wasn't." His gaze returns to me. "What about you? Are you seeing anyone?"

"No. I've kind of taken a break from dating."

"Why is that?"

"I haven't felt like it."

A few months after the accident, I went on some dates, but I just wasn't into it. Maybe it was the guys I went out with, or maybe it was me. Either way, something wasn't working, so I gave up trying.

"Are you still on this 'dating break'?" he asks.

"I don't know." I tuck my hands under my legs and glance around the diner. "Could we talk about something else?"

"You're nervous," he says.

I look back at him. "I'm not nervous."

"You are." His lips rise to a slight smile.

"Okay, maybe I'm a little nervous," I say, since I obviously can't hide it.

"Can I ask why?"

"Because I don't know what this is. I don't know why you wanted me to sit here with you."

"You seemed like a nice person, and I wanted someone to talk to," Evan says.

"That's it? You just wanted to talk to me?"

"Is there something wrong with that?" Evan clasps his hands and rests them on the table.

"No, but it's a little odd. I mean, if you were trying to kill time, you could just look at your phone."

"I spend far too much time on my phone. I need a break from it. Besides, whatever's on the phone isn't nearly as interesting as you."

"I'm not that interesting," I say.

"I find you very interesting."

"Why?"

"Because I know nothing about you, which makes me curious to know more."

"What do you want to know?" I shift in my seat, suddenly unable to sit still.

"Whatever you'll tell me." Evan takes a sip of water, then pats his mouth dry with a napkin he takes from the dispenser. "Let's start with why you chose to work at a diner."

"I didn't choose to do this. I just needed a job. I'm not very good at it, but I've lasted here for six months, which is longer than any of the other jobs I've had since—"

I stop myself. I just met this guy. He doesn't want to hear my life story.

"Since what?" he asks.

"Nothing," I say, shaking my head. "Forget it."

"Grace, what is it?" he asks. "What were you going to say?"

"I was in a car accident. It damaged the nerves in my neck, and now I get these really bad headaches. Sometimes they're so bad,

I can't work and have to go home. My other jobs fired me for it, but my boss here doesn't make a big deal if I have to leave. So even though this isn't the greatest job, I'm kind of stuck here."

"Unless another opportunity presents itself."

"I don't see that happening," I say with a laugh. "I don't have people knocking down my door to hire me."

"It's not always about a job. Opportunities can come in many forms."

What opportunities? The only way I'm leaving this job is if a better one comes along. One that won't fire me for missing work when I get one of my headaches. I doubt that job exists, at least around here.

"Are you from the area?" Evan asks.

"Not this town. I grew up an hour south of here."

"Is that where your family is?"

I pause before answering. Even though it's been a while, it's still difficult for me to talk about it.

"My family is gone," I say.

"Oh." Evan's brows furrow, and his lips turn down. "I'm sorry to hear that. Can I ask what happened?"

"My brother died a few years ago from a drug overdose. And my parents . . ." My voice cracks, and I take a breath, trying to compose myself. "They died in the accident."

"The one you referred to earlier?" he asks.

I nod.

"My dad was driving. My mom was next to him, and I was sitting in the back. A car swerved into our lane, and we went off the road. The car flipped and . . ." I clear my throat. "My parents didn't make it."

"I'm sorry, Grace," Evan says, putting his hand on my forearm. "I can't imagine how horrible that must've been for you."

"It was awful. I still have nightmares of the crash."

"When did this happen?"

"It's been almost two years. I spent a few days in the hospital, and when I got out, I had to figure out how to plan a funeral." I wipe the tears from my eyes. I'm embarrassed I'm getting this emotional with a total stranger, but I can't help it. I miss my parents so much.

"That must've been a very difficult time," Evan says, his hand still on my forearm.

"It was the worst. Looking back, I honestly don't know how I made it through. It helped that I left town. Coming here got me away from all the memories."

"Why here?"

I shrug. "I got a job. I applied all over and told myself wherever I got hired would be where I'm meant to go. A store at the mall hired me, but they let me go after two weeks. I had four more jobs before I finally ended up here."

"I admire your perseverance," Evan says, leaning back in the booth. "Many people wouldn't be able to move on after a loss like that."

"I didn't have a choice. I needed to make money. The small amount my parents left me went to pay for their funeral. And then I had medical expenses, which left me so broke I couldn't pay rent, so I got evicted from my apartment and then couldn't get a new one because my credit's so bad. If Jenna hadn't let me stay with her, I'd probably be living in my car and—" I stop, again realizing I'm telling this guy way too much about myself. "Sorry. I didn't mean to tell you all that."

"I'm glad you did," he says with a slight smile. "You're exactly what I'm looking for."

"What do you mean?" I say, getting a strange feeling from his comment.

Evan laughs a little. "That was poorly worded. What I meant is someone who's as open as you and honest about their past. It's refreshing. It's not often I meet someone like you."

"I don't usually share that much," I confess. "I almost never talk about the accident. It brings up too many bad memories."

"I'm sure it does." He gives me that slight smile again. "But I'm very glad you told me. And again, I'm sorry for your loss."

He seems sincere, and yet . . . I have this uneasy feeling in the pit of my stomach. Maybe it's the way he's smiling like there's something vaguely sinister behind it. Like he's hiding a secret.

I'm being paranoid. The guy's trying to be nice, expressing sympathy for me, and I'm reading something into it.

"That's something we have in common," he says, looking down at the table.

"What do you mean?"

"The loss of a parent." His eyes rise to mine. "I lost my father when I was just a young boy. He had a sudden heart attack while he was at work. I saw him that morning, and by evening, he was gone."

"I'm so sorry," I say, feeling more of a connection to him now that I know this. A lot of people can't understand what it's like to lose a parent until they experience it themselves.

"It was a huge loss for me," Evan says. "And I only lost one parent. I can't imagine enduring the loss of both parents, as well as your brother."

"Yeah, I haven't quite gotten over it," I say, feeling a lump in my throat. "I don't think I ever will."

"That's completely understandable."

"I'm going to start crying if we don't change topics." I take a breath, then force out a smile. "So where are you from?"

"California." He sets his hands on the table, his fingers interlaced, reminding me of my high school guidance counselor. He always put his hands on his desk like that when we'd meet to discuss my future. We'd decided I'd be a nurse. Obviously, that never happened.

"Where in California?" I ask.

"San Francisco."

"I've heard it's really nice there. I've always wanted to visit, but I haven't made it past Pennsylvania."

He smiles. "Not much of a traveler?"

"I'd like to be. I just don't have the money. So why'd you move to New Jersey?"

"I don't live here. I live in New York. As of now, it's only temporary. I haven't decided if I'll be staying."

"When you say New York, you mean the city?" I say since it's just across the bridge.

He nods. "I was hired to do a consulting project for a company in Manhattan. I was looking for a change from California, so the timing couldn't be more perfect."

"How do you like New York?"

"The city itself is great, but I'm having trouble meeting people. Everyone's in such a hurry. It's not as easygoing as California. I've been here for several weeks and haven't been able to get anyone to slow down long enough to even have a conversation. That's why I asked you to sit with me."

So, he really isn't trying to ask me out. He's just lonely and wanted someone to talk to.

"If you live in the city," I say, "how'd you end up here?"

"When I need to think through a problem at work, I go on a drive. It helps me find the solution. I drove all morning until it finally came to me. I wasn't ready to return to the city, so I decided to stop and have lunch. This diner just happened to be where I ended up."

I check the time. "My break's almost over."

"It was nice meeting you, Grace."

Evan looks me in the eye with an intensity that makes my heart race. I can't tell if it's attraction I'm feeling or something else, though I don't know what that something else would be.

"Nice meeting you, too," I say, scooting out of the booth. "I hope everything works out with your job."

"Thank you." He smiles. "And thank you again for spending your break with me."

I kind of wish we had more time. I like hearing him talk. He has a smooth, deep voice that's very appealing.

"You're late," Jenna announces as I hurry back to the kitchen.

"By like two minutes," I say, glancing in Martin's direction to see if he heard her. But he's not there. He must've gone out back for a smoke.

"So?" Jenna watches as I tie my apron around my waist. "What happened?"

"Nothing. He was just bored and wanted someone to talk to."

"Really?" She scrunches up her nose. "That's weird."

"It's not weird. He's from California and doesn't know anyone. He moved to Manhattan for some kind of tech job."

"Then why is he at a diner in New Jersey?" Jenna asks.

"He was driving around and decided to stop for lunch." I pull my hair back up into my regular ponytail, then retrieve my order pad from the counter.

"Are you going to see him again?"

"I doubt it. I never go to the city, and if I did, it's not like I'd run into him." I turn to Jenna. "How old do you think he is?"

She shrugs. "Thirty-four? Thirty-five? It's hard to tell. When a guy wears a suit, I always think he's older." She smiles. "Why do you care?"

"I'm just curious."

"I'll go ask him." She takes off.

"Jenna, no!" I jump in front of her. "Don't talk to him. I don't want him thinking I'm interested."

"Why not? It's the truth, isn't it?" She crosses her arms, but a knowing smirk tilts her lips. "I haven't seen you blush like that the whole time I've known you. And what was with the laugh?"

"What do you mean?" I stuff my order pad in my apron pouch, avoiding her gaze.

"You sounded like a teenager with a crush. Like you were nervous or something."

"Why were you watching us? You should've been working, not spying on me."

"I thought you might need some help. When you go that long without dating, it's hard to get back into it."

"It wasn't a date," I say, rolling my eyes. "We were just talking."

"I still think that's weird. What guy asks a waitress to sit down and talk to him? Old retired guys, sure. We might be the only people they see all day. But that guy out there is young and really hot. And from the looks of that suit he's wearing, he has money."

"Yeah? What's your point?"

"You really think some young, hot, rich guy can't find a girl to talk to him? In a city as big as New York?"

"Maybe he can, but that doesn't mean he can't talk to me, too." I take off, quickly moving through the kitchen.

"I'm not saying he can't," Jenna says, nearly stumbling to keep up. "I'm just saying it's odd. Customers don't usually ask the server to sit down and chat, especially city guys who should be at work."

"I think you're reading too much into this."

"Why did he keep looking at you that way?"

I stop mid-pace, jerking around so fast that I end up almost nose-to-nose with Jenna. I step back and ask, "What way?"

"He was staring at you, almost like he knew you."

"He doesn't know me, but he did say I looked like someone he knew."

"What are you two yapping about?" Martin yells. "You should be working."

"Yeah, we're going," Jenna yells back.

"Don't say anything to him," I tell Jenna as we go through the door to the diner.

"I can't. He's gone."

When I get to Evan's table, I pick up the money he left for the check. It's a crisp hundred-dollar bill. The total for his lunch wasn't even twenty dollars.

Evan is either rich, or he *really* wanted to thank me for talking to him. It's too bad he left. I kind of wish we'd exchanged numbers. I'd like to see him again.

CHAPTER 3

It's been a few days since Evan came into the diner. I keep checking the door to see if he'll show up. I don't know why he would. If he wants a greasy burger and fries, he can easily get it in Manhattan. He doesn't need to drive all the way to New Jersey.

The door chimes jingle, and my eyes dart over yet again to see who's coming in.

"It's not him," Jenna says as I wipe down the counter.

"I don't know what you're talking about."

She glances at me as she fills a glass at the soda machine. "You've been looking for Suit Guy since that day he came in here."

"His name's Evan, and I wasn't looking for him."

"Then why do you check the door every time someone comes in?"

I shrug. "I didn't know I was doing it."

"Yeah, right," she says with a laugh. She finishes filling the glass and walks over to me. "If you're looking to go out with someone, I know the perfect guy."

"Thanks, but I don't want to date anyone right now."

"So, if Suit Guy came in here and asked you out, you'd turn him down?"

"No. I mean, maybe."

"I knew you liked him. But since he's never coming back, what do you think about going out with my cousin Tony? He moved here last weekend." She smiles, gets her phone out, and pulls up a picture. Tony has thick black hair, green eyes, and a deep dimple in his chin. "What do you think?"

I shrug. "He's okay."

"Why don't we all go out tonight?" She slips her phone in her pocket. "You could meet him."

"I don't know. I'd feel weird dating your cousin."

"It's not weird. And tonight isn't a date. It's just three people having dinner. And Tony's paying, so you can't use money as an excuse not to go."

"Thanks, but I'm gonna pass." I go back to wiping the counter.

"Why?" Jenna folds her arms. "You keep saying you need to get out more."

It's true. All I do is work and sleep, mainly because I don't have money to do anything else.

"Okay, I'll go," I tell her. "What time?"

Jenna squeals and claps her hands. "He's picking us up at seven. Tony's a great guy. I think you'll really like him!"

On my way to the break room, I get excited about tonight. It'll be good to go out and do something. I'm not thrilled about being set up with Jenna's cousin, but maybe it won't be that bad.

"I'll see you at home," Jenna says when our shift ends at five.

"Yeah, see ya," I say, filling my travel mug with soda. I'm exhausted and need the caffeine and sugar to keep me going.

"Grace?"

Turning around, I almost spill my drink when I see Evan standing there.

"Hey." I smile. "What are you doing here?"

"I was in the area and thought I'd stop by and say hi." He smiles, and my heart starts beating faster.

"I wish you'd shown up sooner," I say, pressing the top on my travel mug to lock it in place. "I was just getting ready to leave."

"Then I came at the perfect time. I was going to ask if you'd like to have dinner."

He wants to take me out? Like on a date? I thought he wasn't interested in me.

I'm definitely interested in him. He looks really good, even better than last time. He's dressed casually today, or what's probably casual for him. He's wearing light-colored pants and a blue button-up shirt with the sleeves rolled up, showing off toned, tanned forearms.

"Is that a 'yes'?" he asks, and I realize I was too busy staring at him to give him an answer.

"I'd love to," I say, somewhat sheepishly, "but I already made plans with Jenna. My roommate. She works here. You saw her the last time you were here. Blonde hair. A little shorter than me."

"Yes, I remember. Do you think she'd be open to changing your plans to another night? I realize I should've given you more notice, but I didn't have your number, so I wasn't able to call in advance."

"Sorry, but I wouldn't feel right canceling on Jenna," I say. "Her cousin is going, and she really wants me to meet him."

"Him?" Evan asks, his brows rising. "So this is a date?"

"No. I mean, Jenna wants me to date him, but I haven't met him. I don't know if I'll like him."

"But you agreed to go out with him," Evan says. "I assume that means you're no longer taking a break from dating?"

I'm surprised he remembered that. Most guys can't remember anything I tell them.

"I'm open to dating, but I don't know if Tony's the right guy. Guess I'll find out," I say, forcing a laugh.

Evan isn't laughing. He's not even smiling. Is he jealous? He can't be. We just met.

"Maybe we could have dinner some other time," I say. "I'm free this weekend."

His lips purse for a long moment, then break into a smile. He says, "This weekend would be perfect. How about tomorrow?"

I pause to think what day it is. "Oh, tomorrow's Friday! Yeah, that works. I'll be done here at two-thirty. I'm guessing you work until five?"

"My schedule is flexible. I could be here at three if that works best for you."

"It does, but I'm not sure what we'd do. This town is kind of boring."

"We don't have to stay here. Would you like to go to the city?"

"Are you kidding?" I say, unable to hide my excitement. "I'd love to! I never go there because it's too expensive."

"Don't worry about the cost. It's my treat. I'll plan the evening," Evan says. "All you need to do is be ready when I pick you up. I'll need your address, and, of course, your phone number."

My excitement plummets as I feel a sudden sense of unease. Should I be agreeing to this? I know almost nothing about this guy, and suddenly I'm willing to let him pick me up and take me to the city?

"Is something wrong?" he asks with concern.

"No. It's just . . . I don't know you very well," I say. I'm tempted to say more, but I just leave it at that.

Evan sighs, rubbing his jaw as he shakes his head. His eyes meet mine. "I'm sorry. I wasn't thinking. I made you uncomfortable. Please, forgive me."

"No, it's fine. I just think going to the city and spending that much time together is a bit much when we don't really know each other."

"You're right. It is. I shouldn't have been so forward. It was very inconsiderate of me." Evan sticks his hands in his pockets and eyes the tile floor between us.

"Don't worry about it. I'm just cautious," I say in a hurry. "It's not like I think you're dangerous. I'd just like more time to get to know you."

He nods, and his eyes slowly come back to mine, a tentative grin on his face. "I completely understand. We'll go somewhere in town. You can pick the place, and I'll pick you up here. Or you could meet me at the restaurant if that would make you more comfortable."

Maybe I'm assuming the worst of Evan when I really have no reason to. He seems like a nice guy. He's polite. He dresses well. He has a good job. Maybe I'm being too cautious. I really would like to go to the city. Plus, Evan said it was his treat. I wouldn't have to pay for anything.

"I changed my mind," I say.

He looks at me with concern. "About dinner?"

"About the city. I'd love to go!"

Evan's face lights up, and he smiles. "Then I'll pick you up here at three."

"Sounds good." I check my phone. "I need to go. Tony's picking us up at seven, and I need to get ready."

Evan's smile sags a little, but he says, "I'm glad I caught you before you left."

"Me too," I say. "I'll see you tomorrow!"

As I leave, my excitement for tomorrow night builds. A very handsome, sophisticated, and presumably wealthy man is taking me to Manhattan for a night out!

Things like this never happen to me. I usually have horrible luck, especially with men. But maybe that's about to change.

CHAPTER 4

"What do you do around here for fun?" Tony asks.

When we got to the restaurant, Jenna grabbed the seat next to me so I'd be forced to sit directly across from her cousin.

"I don't really do much," I say. "Other than work."

Jenna nudges me. "Maybe you could show Tony around town. He's free tomorrow night."

"I can't. I already made plans." I turn my attention to the single-page laminated menu in front of me.

"What plans?" Jenna sets her beer down and faces me. "What are you doing?"

"Going out with a friend." I give her a look to let it go. I don't want to talk about Evan in front of Tony.

"What friend?" she asks, clearly not getting my message.

"It's not anyone you know," I say.

"Maybe you could show Tony around on Saturday," she interjects, brows up. "I'm sure he'd be happy to take you to dinner as a thank you."

I ignore her efforts at matchmaking and look back at Tony. "Tell me about your new job."

"I'm doing construction for a new apartment building," Tony says.

"It's the one we drove past last week," Jenna pipes up. "Remember when I pointed out the sign?"

I do, but I didn't know she was doing it because her cousin was working there. I thought she was hinting that I should move out. I was only supposed to stay with her for a few weeks, but I've been living with her for a year.

"How long have you been in construction?" I ask, trying hard to keep my attention on Tony.

"Since high school, but I've had other jobs. I even tried selling insurance once, but I wasn't any good at it. I'm not an office guy. I need to work with my hands."

Jenna pops up from her chair. "Grace and I need to use the restroom. We'll be right back."

"I'm good," I tell her. "You go ahead."

"Are you sure?"

I roll my eyes but get up from the table. When Jenna and I get to the restroom, she grabs my arm, her face lit up.

"So? What do you think?" she asks.

"About Tony? He's nice," I say. "Is that what—"

"That's it? 'He's nice'?" Jenna frowns. "You don't like him."

A frustrated sigh escapes despite my best efforts. "I like him, but I don't know if I want to date him."

"Why not? You don't have to marry him. Just go on some dates. Get to know each other." Her eyes narrow. "Hey, were you making that up about tomorrow night? You're not really going out, are you?"

"Actually, I am. I'm going into the city."

"With who?" Jenna asks.

I hesitate, not sure I should tell her now that she's so eager for me to date her cousin.

"Grace, tell me. Who is it?"

"Evan." I sigh. "That guy who came into the diner. The one in the suit."

"You said he didn't ask you out."

"He stopped in today, right after you left, and asked if I'd have dinner with him tonight. I told him I was already going out with you, so we decided to go tomorrow instead."

She huffs. "Now I get why you don't like Tony. You'd rather go out with a rich guy."

"It's not a date. Evan and I are just going as friends."

"Yeah, right." She rolls her eyes. "If a guy asks a girl out, it's a date."

"It doesn't have to be."

"Is he paying?"

"Yes, but only because I told him I can't afford to do anything in the city."

Jenna grins, a triumphant look in her eyes. "He's paying because he thinks it's a date."

"Or he's just bored and wants someone to do stuff with."

"Yeah, because rich, handsome guys have such a hard time finding friends," she says sarcastically.

"What's with all the negativity?" I finally say, at the edge of my patience with my friend. "When you first saw Evan, you wanted me to go out with him."

"I was just kidding around. I didn't think you'd actually date the guy. I mean, think about it, Grace. It doesn't make sense."

"What doesn't make sense?"

"Nothing. Forget it." She motions toward the door. "We should go. Tony's going to think we left."

When we get back to the table, I see our food has arrived.

"Perfect timing," Tony says, smiling at me.

"Sorry we took so long," Jenna says, putting her napkin on her lap. "I was messing with my hair."

As we're having dinner, Tony talks about his family and where he grew up. Jenna pipes in now and then, adding stories about Tony from their childhood. Hearing them talk makes me miss my family more than ever. We were really close. On weekends, we always did something together, like bowling or seeing a movie. And my mom insisted we have dinner as a family almost every night. When my brother and I were teenagers, we'd complain about having to spend so much time with our parents, but we secretly liked it. Our parents were loving and kind, and they would do anything for us.

"I need to go," Jenna says suddenly, getting up. Her plate is barely half-empty. "Thanks for dinner, Tony. Would you mind taking Grace home?"

"You're leaving?" I say to Jenna.

"I need to run some errands. I'll see you later!" She takes off.

"Sorry about that," Tony says, probably knowing just as well as I did that Jenna made up an excuse to leave so we'd be alone together. "She's taking this matchmaking thing a little too far. I'll take you home now if you want."

Tony covers the check, and as we're leaving the restaurant, I get a text from Evan. *I'm looking forward to seeing you tomorrow, Grace. I have a lot planned so our evening might run rather late. I hope that's acceptable.*

"Everything okay?" Tony asks.

"Everything's fine," I say to Tony.

I fire off a text to Evan. *I work early on Saturday but I can miss out on some sleep.*

He immediately texts back, *How did your date go?*

That's strange. I wasn't expecting him to ask about Tony.

Could we talk tomorrow? I'm not home right now.

You're still out with him?

Why does he care? I text back, *I'll see you tomorrow.*

I put my phone away, my heart beating faster than normal.

"You okay?" Tony asks as he opens the car door for me.

"I'm fine," I say, forcing a smile.

Tony takes me back to my apartment building and walks me to the door. "I had a good time tonight. I'd love to take you out sometime, if you're interested."

"Um, maybe," I say, my mind going to Evan. All night, I've been thinking about him, which isn't fair to Tony. I shouldn't go out with him when I'm clearly interested in someone else. "Actually, I think we might be better as friends."

"That's fine," he says with a shrug. "You've got my number, so you can call if you change your mind. Goodnight, Grace."

When I get up to the apartment, Jenna's on the couch, watching TV.

"I'm home," I say, getting her attention.

She looks over at me. "Why are you back so soon?"

"Because I'm not interested in him. Tony's a nice guy, but I don't want to go out with him."

"Why? I thought you guys were perfect for each other." She gets up and comes over to me. "It's because of that guy, isn't it? The rich guy. You'd rather date a guy with money so you didn't even give Tony a chance."

"I did, but I didn't feel anything."

"But you felt something with the rich guy?"

"More than I did with Tony. Evan texted me on the way here and said he has a lot planned for us tomorrow."

"You didn't think it was odd he texted you when you're on a date with someone else?"

"He assumed I was home."

"Or he was checking to see if you were still out with Tony. That's the real reason he texted you. He wanted to see how your date was going."

"That's not what he was doing."

"Did he ask about the date?"

"Yeah, but why is that a problem?"

"What did you tell him?"

"I said we'd talk tomorrow. Jenna, I know you want me to date Tony, but I can't force myself to feel something for him. If it turns out Evan is the guy for me, I need you to be okay with that."

"You don't even know him, and you're already thinking he might be the guy for you?" she says like I'm crazy for even considering it. "You have nothing in common with him. He's some rich guy who has no idea what it's like to not have money."

"You don't know that. It sounds like Evan made his own money. I don't think he grew up with it."

"I bet he did. Just watching him, seeing how he carries himself, he seems like someone who's always been rich."

"I'm not talking about this," I say, walking away. "I'm really excited about tomorrow, and you're ruining it by saying all these bad things about Evan."

"I'm just being realistic," she says, following me to my room. "What could you possibly have in common with a guy like him?"

"I don't know." I face her, my hands on my hips. "I guess I'll find out tomorrow. Now would you leave so I can go to bed?"

"Grace, don't be mad at me. I just don't want you getting hurt by this guy."

"It's part of life. You can't avoid it. Trust me, I've been hurt enough times to know."

"Okay, well, goodnight." She leaves, shutting the door behind her.

Maybe I shouldn't have been so quick to turn Tony down. Jenna's right. He's one of us, while Evan's several income brackets above us. But why should that matter? I still want to go out with him, even if it's just as friends. And who knows? Maybe it'll turn into more.

CHAPTER 5

"You're meeting him in the city, right?" Jenna asks as I'm putting on my makeup.

We're in the employee restroom, which is barely big enough for the two of us and only has a tiny mirror that's cracked down the middle. The lighting is terrible, making it a bad place to do makeup, but it's my only option. Employees aren't supposed to use the restroom the customers use.

"He's picking me up." I swipe on another coat of mascara. "That's why I'm getting ready here."

"You're letting a guy you just met pick you up in his car? Grace, he could kill you!"

"He's not dangerous. You saw him. Did he look dangerous?"

"You can't tell if someone's dangerous by how they look." She grabs my arm and turns me toward her. "Call him and tell him you'll meet him."

"It's too late. He's probably already here." I check my phone for the time. "I gotta go. How do I look?"

She takes a step back, her eyes moving over me. "You look like you're going to a funeral."

"What do you mean?" I ask, panicking because that was not the look I was going for. I'm wearing a long black dress, which is the only thing I have that's appropriate for a nice restaurant, assuming that's where we're going. Since Evan didn't tell me what we're doing, I wanted to be prepared for anything. And given how well he dresses, I couldn't show up in jeans and a sweater.

"Never mind," Jenna says, waving her hand around. "You look great. Don't listen to me."

"You really think this dress looks like I'm going to a funeral?" I ask, frowning.

She shrugs. "Only because it's black and covers everything. I can't even see your legs." She leans down, pretending to look for them. "Are they under there?"

"This is the only dress I have. And now that it's September, the nights are getting cold. It'll be good to have my legs covered."

"Whatever." She opens the door. "Let's go."

"Stay here," I tell her, dropping my cell phone in my clutch bag before leaving the room.

"No way. I need to meet this guy," Jenna says, following me.

"Not now. You can meet him some other time," I say as we pass through the kitchen.

"Sorry, but it has to be now. I need to get a good look at him so I can describe him to the police in case he kills you."

"He is not going to kill me, Jenna," I say through gritted teeth.

"Hey!" Martin yells from behind the grill. "Where are you going all dressed up?"

"She's got a date," Jenna tells him.

"It's not a date," I say.

Jenna nearly runs into me when I stop and spin to face them.

"Who's the guy?" Martin asks as he flips burgers on the grill.

"You don't know him. And I don't have time for this. He's probably already out there waiting for me. I need to go."

"He's picking her up," Jenna says. "And taking her to the city."

I glare at Jenna. "Would you please stop talking?"

"How well do you know this guy?" Martin asks.

"I'll be fine. I have to go." I walk through the kitchen and out to the diner. I look back and see that Jenna has followed me. "What are you doing?"

Jenna just shrugs. "I told you I have to meet him."

"Jenna, please," I say, holding up my hands. "Just leave him alone."

"Grace."

Evan's deep voice comes from behind me. I turn to see him coming toward me, a big smile on his handsome face.

"Hi," I say, my heart racing as he stops in front of me.

Every time I see him, he seems to look even better than the time before. Tonight, he's wearing black pants and a crisp white dress shirt with a light blue tie that looks very expensive. I don't know for sure since I've never bought a tie, but the one Evan's wearing doesn't look cheap.

"I wasn't sure if you were here," he says. "I asked around and the busboy thought you had left."

"I was just in the back getting ready," I say.

"Hi, I'm Jenna," she says, extending her hand to Evan.

"It's nice to meet you, Jenna," he says, shaking her hand. "You're Grace's roommate?"

"I'm also her best friend." She puts her arm around me. "I'd kill anyone that hurt her."

"Good to know," he says. I see his lips twitch up.

"She's kidding," I say, yanking away from her. "She's always kidding. Aren't you, Jenna?"

"Not always," she says, her eyes still on Evan. "So, what time will you have her home?"

"Jenna!" I scowl at her, mortified she's acting like this.

"It'll probably be after midnight," Evan responds. He looks at me. "Unless you decide you'd like to end the evening before that, of course."

"We'll see how it goes," I say, smiling at him. "We should get going."

"It was a pleasure meeting you, Jenna," Evan says to her. "I promise to take good care of her."

"You better," I hear Jenna mutter as Evan and I leave.

We go out to his car, a shiny silver Mercedes.

"You look beautiful," he says, opening the door for me.

"Thanks. I wasn't sure what to wear." I rub my hands down the front of my dress, feeling my cheeks warm.

"What you have on is perfect," he says as I get into the car. It has that new car smell, and the leather seats feel buttery soft.

Evan gets into the driver's side, looking at me as he puts on his seatbelt. "How was your day?"

"It was okay. How was yours?"

"Good. Very productive."

"What is it you do again?" I ask. "I know it has something do with computers."

Evan pulls out of the parking lot, pointing us toward the road that leads toward the city. Only once we're on our way does he answer.

"I create software. I'm currently working with a financial company to create software for their investment division."

"That sounds difficult. You must be really smart."

He glances at me and smiles. "I wouldn't necessarily say that, but education has always been important to me. I'm an avid reader."

"Oh, I like to read, too," I say, pleased we have something in common.

"What type of books?"

"Romance, or sometimes I read fantasy. It depends on my mood."

"You only read fiction?"

"Yeah. Why?"

"I prefer nonfiction. Something that will advance my knowledge in a subject."

Is he insulting the types of books I read? I'm sure he doesn't mean it that way. I'm probably being overly sensitive.

"What else interests you?" Evan asks. "Do you have any hobbies?"

"Not really. I took a painting class a few years ago, but I wasn't any good at it." I laugh at the memories that emerge. "My final project turned out terrible. My mom couldn't even tell what it was supposed to be."

"Perhaps you could try again. It takes some time and a lot of sustained practice to learn a new skill," Evan says.

"I don't have time. I'm always working." I look over at him. "Hey, sorry about Jenna. She wasn't trying to be rude. She's just really protective of me."

"There's no need to apologize. She seems like a nice young woman. Well, except for her comment about wanting to kill me."

I cringe. "Sorry. She obviously didn't mean it."

"It's fine. I understand why she said it. She probably wants you to be with her cousin, and now you're out with me. I'm sure that doesn't please her."

"I told her you and I are just friends," I say, deciding I need to get to know this guy before I agree to date him.

He nods. "I see."

I look over to see his grip tighten on the steering wheel.

"Is something wrong?" I ask.

"Not at all." He glances at me. "I like your dress. It looks nice on you."

"Thanks! It's the only one I have."

"Perhaps I'll have to fix that," he says with a smile.

"Hey, about what I said, about us being friends." I rub my hands together, then swallow to wet my suddenly dry throat. "You're okay with that, right?"

"Of course. Why wouldn't I be?"

"I wasn't sure if you thought this was a date."

"I would've liked for it to be, but I understand you have someone else." Evan pauses. "I assume you're seeing him again?"

"Um, no. I don't think so."

He stops at the next intersection and looks over at me. "Can I ask why not? Did you decide you didn't like him?"

I glance at the car beside us. I need a moment to figure out whether Evan is genuinely curious or if he's digging for a particular answer. I finally say, "He was okay. We just weren't a good match. He felt more like a friend than someone I'd want to date."

"Which is how you feel about me," Evan says as he continues down the road. "You don't see me as a romantic partner. Is that correct?"

"No. I mean, I'm not sure how I feel about you. You're not my usual type."

"And what is your usual type?"

I shrug. "Guys who are more like me. Grew up without money. Always struggling to pay their bills."

"Is that what you want?" Evan asks, the confusion clear in his voice. "Someone more like yourself economically?"

"I just want a guy who treats me well. What about you?" I ask, desperate now to shift the attention away from me and my financial struggles. "What do you look for in a partner?"

"Someone who enjoys doing things as a couple. I'm not one of those men who wants to spend weekends on the golf course with other men." Evan glances my way a few times before he continues. "If I'm in love with a woman, I want my time to be spent with her."

I stare out at the passing scenery. "Most guys I've dated want to hang out with their friends more than me."

"I don't see the appeal of that. I'd much rather enjoy a romantic evening with a beautiful woman than spend time with a group of men."

"What else do you look for?" I ask.

"Someone who's open to experiencing new things. Going to new places. Traveling."

"I'd love to travel, but I can't afford it."

"Where would you go?"

"Maybe Paris? Everyone makes it sound so romantic."

"It can be, depending on where you go."

"You've been there?"

"Many times. I've been all over the world," Evan says.

We reach the George Washington Bridge that will take us into Manhattan. I try to look everywhere at once, even though there's not much to see beyond the steel beams of the bridge and the snarl of traffic ahead of and behind us.

"Do you travel for work?" I ask.

"No, for pleasure. Traveling is something I enjoy."

"I'd love to hear about all the places you've gone," I say, wistful and wanting to take in Evan's every word now. "I'm sure I'll never go anywhere myself."

"Why is that?"

I laugh. "I can barely afford rent. I don't think traveling is in my future."

"It could be. Anything's possible."

That may be true for some people, but not me. It feels like I was born under a dark cloud. Bad things are always happening to me. I keep hoping that'll change, but it hasn't so far, which makes me doubt that it ever will.

CHAPTER 6

"Dinner was amazing," I say, leaning back in my chair. "But now I'm stuffed. How many courses was that?"

"Six." Evan smiles. "I hope you don't mind that I planned the menu ahead of time. I wanted you to be able to try a little of everything. I assume you've never had some of those dishes?"

"No." I laugh. "I couldn't even pronounce some of them. I grew up eating hamburgers and fries. Pot roast. Spaghetti and meatballs. Stuff like that. My mom was a good cook, but she never made anything fancy. What about you? What did your mom make when you were growing up?"

"Lobster. Braised duck. Rack of lamb. My mother made what appealed to her, not me. She didn't believe in catering to a child's taste preferences. I don't remember ever eating things like hotdogs or macaroni and cheese."

"What's your mom like?"

He smiles a little. "I think we could find a more interesting topic of conversation than my mother. Tell me about your roommate. How did you two meet?"

"I want to know more about your mom," I say. "Where does she live?

"Northern California. About an hour from San Francisco."

"Does she live by herself?"

He cocks his head to the side. "Why are you so interested in my mother?"

I shrug. "I'm just curious."

He checks his watch. "I didn't realize it was so late. We need to get going."

"Why? What are we doing?"

"I'm taking you to a show. I hope you like musicals." Evan stands and comes around the table, guiding my chair out as I get to my feet.

"I love musicals. Is it on Broadway?"

"It is. It's very popular and has excellent reviews."

"I've always wanted to see a Broadway show. Jenna's going to be so jealous. She loves musicals." I retrieve my phone from my clutch. "Just a second, I'm going to text her."

"Could you wait until we're outside?" Evan says. "The restaurant discourages cell phone use. I don't want someone coming over and scolding us for it."

"Oh, uh, okay."

I put my phone away.

I've never been to a restaurant that scolds you for using your phone, but maybe that's normal for fancy places like this. It's so expensive they didn't even have prices on the menu. I guess if you have to know what something costs, you're too poor to eat here. But I snuck a peek at the bill and saw the total was over $800! That's what I pay Jenna for a month of rent!

Outside the restaurant, a limousine is parked on the street. The driver gets out and walks up to Evan. "Mr. Sinclair?"

"Yes," he says. "You'll have the service take care of my car?"

"Of course, sir." He smiles at me. "Right this way."

We're taking a limo to the theater? This is incredible! I've never been in a limo, not even for prom. As I get in, I'm thinking this must be a dream. Is this really happening?

"Did you drop something?" Evan asks, noticing my eyes darting around.

"No, I've just never been in a limo." I look at him. "Couldn't we have just taken your car?"

"I've been drinking. I feel fine, but I'm not going to risk it."

I wasn't thinking about that, but I'm glad Evan did. The driver involved in the car accident that killed my parents had been drinking. He wasn't legally drunk, but he'd had enough that it impaired his driving and caused him to swerve into our lane.

"Oh! I need to text Jenna," I say, once again pulling out my phone. I let her know I'm riding in a limo on my way to see a Broadway musical. I assume she'll text right back to share in my excitement, but she doesn't.

"What did she say?" Evan asks.

"Nothing. She's probably watching TV and not checking her phone," I say.

But I know it's not true. Jenna is always checking her phone. Disappointed, I tuck the phone away and hold my clutch in my lap.

"After the show, I'd like to take you out for a drink," Evan says. "I know of a place that has wonderful views of the city."

"I'd love to, but I should probably go home. I have to be up early tomorrow."

"I understand. But I would like to see you again." He smiles a little. "Would you be open to that?"

"Um, yeah, I just . . ." I pause, chewing on my lip.

"Just what?" he says.

"I'm not sure why we would. Tonight's been great, but we don't really have much in common. I don't know why you'd want to go out with me when you could go out with someone else."

"I'm not looking for someone else." He turns to me and tucks a strand of my hair behind my ear. "I'm very selective about who

I spend my time with, and I'd like to spend it with you. There was something about you that intrigued me from the moment we met."

My cheeks flush. I don't know what to say to that. No other man had ever said something like that to me before.

Evan takes my hand, and my chest warms from his gentle touch. "When you came up to me at the diner, I immediately felt your warmth and compassion. I could tell you were having a hard day, and yet you didn't let it get to you. You greeted me with kindness and a genuine smile, and you gave up your break to sit with me."

"A lot of people would've done that," I say, ducking my chin to try to hide the worst of the blushing.

"No, most people wouldn't." Evan lifts my chin until our eyes meet again. "You're an amazing person, Grace, and I don't want tonight to be the last time I see you. I want us to go out again, even if it's only as friends."

"I'd be okay with us doing something again," I say, thinking I should give this a chance. Why not? The worst that could happen is it doesn't work out.

Evan smiles. "I'm very pleased to hear that."

The limo pulls up to the theater. Moments after we stop, the driver opens the door for us. We get out, and Evan puts his hand on my lower back as he ushers me inside.

"What do you think?" Evan asks after we take our seats. They're in the second row, centered in front of the stage.

"These seats are incredible. How'd you get seats this close to the stage at the last minute?"

"Money has a way of making things happen. I tried to get the first row, but those seats were reserved for a charity that brings the arts to foster children. I was obviously not going to take their seats."

"It's nice there's a group that does that. What's the charity?"

He tells me the name, then says, "I'd never heard of it, but after I learned more about it, I decided to make a donation."

I smile at him. "That was kind of you."

"I'm happy to donate to a worthy cause. I do it as much as I can."

It's clear from what Evan's spent tonight that he has a lot of money, but that doesn't mean he has to give it away. A lot of people wouldn't. I'm glad Evan isn't one of those people. It makes me like him more.

"Can I get you anything?" Evan asks. "A glass of wine? Something to snack on?"

"No, I'm good, but thank you for offering."

It's yet another thoughtful gesture. He's been asking all night if I need anything, offering to get it for me if I do.

Evan's really surprised me tonight. I thought someone like him would be more self-centered. Growing up, my parents had a pretty negative perspective about wealthy people, saying they were greedy and cruel and looked down on people like us. I felt the same way until I met Evan. He's proof that people with money can be generous and kind.

The show begins, and I'm completely mesmerized — by the sets, the costumes, the talent of the performers. I've never seen anything like this. The few musicals I've gone to were high school productions. I had no idea what to expect tonight, but this is better than I could've imagined. When it ends, I'm still in awe as we leave the theater.

"How did you like it?" Evan asks.

"It was the best show I've ever seen," I say, raising my voice so he can hear me above all the noise.

He points to his ears. "It's too loud in here. Let's talk in the car."

The car? I thought his car was still at the restaurant.

I wait until we're on the street where he can hear me again and say, "Your car is here?"

"I had it delivered so it'd be waiting for us after the show."

It must've taken him a lot of time to plan tonight. He thought of every little thing. It's really sweet he did all that.

"It should be on the next block," he says. "Are you cold? I could give you my jacket."

"No, I'm fine."

Evan had a suit jacket in his car and put it on before we went into the restaurant. I didn't used to like men in suits. I thought they looked stuffy or snobby. But I don't feel that way about Evan. I think he looks sexy. His suit fits him perfectly like it was made for him. It probably was.

"Are you sure you don't want to stop for a drink?" Evan asks once we're in the car.

"Not tonight. Maybe some other night," I say, trying to hide my yawn. It's been a wonderful evening, but I'm tired.

He gives me a slight smile. "So, you haven't changed your mind? You're open to seeing me again?"

"Yeah. I had a really great time. I'd love to do this again." I laugh. "Not this exact night. I meant something simpler. We could maybe walk around Central Park. Get a hot dog. It doesn't need to be anything extravagant."

"But you enjoyed tonight," he says as he carefully pulls into traffic and drives away from the theater.

"Well, yeah, but I don't expect a night like this every time we do something."

"Grace, I have the money. Let me spend it on something I enjoy. What good is it if it just sits in a bank? I'd much rather use it to put a smile on the face of my very beautiful friend."

It's odd to think of money that way. To me, money is a lifeline, a way to survive. I've never thought of it as something to use for pleasure. I've never had that luxury. I wasn't raised that way. My parents struggled for their entire lives, sometimes unable to pay the electric bill or put food on the table.

"Did you grow up like this?" I ask. "Having money?"

"We had what we needed," he says.

I'm guessing that means he didn't come from wealth, but he also wasn't raised in poverty.

"I've been very successful in my career," he explains. "I've created software programs that have proved to be very lucrative to my clients, and they've rewarded me for it by letting me share in the profits."

"This was back in California?"

"Yes, in San Francisco. I went there after college and immediately found work at a large tech firm. I was only there a few months when I realized I could make a lot more being on my own, creating specialty software for clients."

"How many clients have you worked for?" I ask, thinking it must be a lot, given his wealth.

"I'm not sure. I haven't kept track." Evan's hands tighten around the wheel, but his voice is light when he says, "Let's change topics. My employment history will put you to sleep."

I was hoping he'd tell me more, but maybe he doesn't like talking about work when he's trying to relax. I'm the same way. When I'm not at the diner, I try not to think about it. It didn't even come to mind tonight when I was out with Evan. In fact, the past few hours, I felt like I was living someone else's life. Someone with money who can go to nice restaurants and ride in a limo and see Broadway shows.

But unfortunately, that's not my life. Tomorrow, I'll go back to reality.

CHAPTER 7

"How was your date?" Jenna asks when she arrives at the diner for her shift at nine. I've already been here for three hours. To say I'm exhausted is an understatement.

"It wasn't a date," I say, pouring a cup of coffee as Jenna puts on her apron.

"Then what was it?"

"A night out with a friend."

"Yeah, okay," she says. "When's the last time a friend took you out for a fancy dinner and a Broadway show? That's something a guy only does when he's trying to date you."

I bring the coffee to the old man sitting at the end of the counter. It's slower than usual today, maybe because the weather is lousy. It's a cold, rainy September day. It feels like fall has finally decided to show up after weeks of hot weather.

"How was the show?" Jenna asks, coming over to me as I'm wiping down the counter.

"It was great! Our seats were right in front of the stage. Didn't you get my text last night?"

Jenna skips right over that question. "What about Evan? Do you still like him?"

"Yeah, as a friend." I turn to face her. "That's all we are. I haven't decided if I want us to be more than that."

"Are you going to see him again?" she asks, one hand on the counter, the other on her hip.

"Probably, but I don't know when. We didn't make plans," I casually say. I don't tell her that Evan definitely wants us to see each other again.

She doesn't say anything, but I can tell that she wants to.

"What is it?" I say. "Just tell me."

She shrugs. "I just don't know why you're getting involved with someone like Evan when you could be with a great guy like Tony."

"Someone like Evan? What's that supposed to mean?"

"Someone you could never be with. Seriously, Grace, you really think a guy like him would end up with someone like us? He probably grew up in a mansion, going to private school and spending his summers at the country club."

I roll my eyes and turn away, fiddling with the condiment bottles in front of me. "He didn't grow up like that. I asked him about it last night."

"All I'm saying is that Tony makes sense. Dating this Evan guy doesn't. Even if you go out with him, it's not going to last."

For the rest of the morning, I avoid Jenna. She doesn't even know Evan. If she did, she'd see he's not like other rich guys. He's polite and considerate, and I think he really cares about me. But if I told Jenna that, she wouldn't believe me. She's determined to make him the bad guy.

When my shift ends at three, I'm getting my stuff from the break room when Evan calls.

"Hi, Evan," I say, answering his call.

"Hello, Grace. How was work?"

I'm amazed at how even just his voice makes me all tingly inside.

"Busy, but I'm done now. I'm heading home." I sling my purse over my shoulder and leave the break room.

"I just wanted to call and tell you what a lovely time I had last night."

I smile when he says 'lovely'. Guys my age don't typically use that word. Evan's older than me, but still, it's not how guys talk, at least the ones I know. But I like that about him. I like that he's different than what I'm used to.

"Last night was great," I say, walking out to the parking lot. "I'm still thinking about the show. It was amazing. Something I'll never forget."

"I wish we'd had more time. There was so much more I wanted to do. Perhaps we could go out again this week? Are you free tomorrow?"

"No, I have to work. I'm off Monday and Tuesday, but by the time you're done at your job, it's kind of late to go out."

"I could take the day off. I've been working nearly every day since I moved here because I've had nothing else to do. I think I've earned a day off, and I'd love to spend it with you, if that's something you would like."

Part of me thinks it's too soon to see him again. But we're not dating. We said we were friends, and if a friend invited me out, I'd say yes. So why am I overthinking this?

"Um, yeah, we could spend the day together," I finally say. "Maybe on Tuesday?"

"Let's say Monday. And don't worry about getting here. I'll pick you up."

"What are we doing?" I say as I get in my car. "Where are you taking me?"

"You'll find out later," he says. I can practically hear the smile in his voice. "Goodbye, Grace."

I'm a little annoyed that he wouldn't tell me what we're doing. Does he want it to be a surprise? If so, I'd rather he just tell me. I'm not a fan of surprises. I guess it doesn't matter. Whatever he's planning will be better than sitting at home all day, which is what I'd be doing if he hadn't invited me out. And I'm sure he'll spend a lot of money on me again.

I've never been one of those girls who wanted to date a rich guy. Still, I have to admit, it was nice going out last night and not having to think about what things cost. I felt like a different person. For those few hours I was with Evan, I wasn't worrying if I'd have enough money to pay my bills. I wasn't counting how many hours were left before I had to go back to work. I was too immersed in Evan's world to think about those things.

He took me places I'd never been and introduced me to foods I'd never tried. It was fun and exciting. I felt alive in a way I haven't since my parents died. Part of that was probably due to the hustle and bustle of Manhattan, but even so, it was good to feel that way again.

Unfortunately, last night was just a fantasy. The real world is the one I'm in now, the one where there's never enough money. I never thought I could escape that world, but what if I could? What if I could have a life where I didn't always have to struggle? What if Evan could offer me that?

As if it would ever get to that point. Why am I even thinking about this? Evan and I aren't even dating, and here I am imagining a future with him. But, hey, a girl can dream, right?

* * *

On Sunday, my morning shift flies by because I'm completely distracted by Evan. I can't stop thinking about him and about our date Friday night. I guess it wasn't really a date, but it was an evening I'll never forget. It was so extravagant, unlike anything I ever thought I'd experience.

"Where is he taking you tomorrow?" Jenna asks as we go into the break room.

"I don't know. He didn't say."

"And that doesn't bother you?" Jenna says as she sits down on the lumpy couch across from the employee lockers.

"Why would it bother me? I'm sure whatever he plans will be great." I join her on the couch and stretch my legs out.

"It seems odd he wouldn't tell you."

"He wants to surprise me."

"You hate surprises," she says, hauling herself off the couch. "I'm going to see if Martin will make me a sandwich. I skipped breakfast and I'm starving."

Moments later, she returns, holding a vase overflowing with flowers. "These just came for you. Some delivery guy dropped them off." She hands me the vase.

"For me?" The vase is heavy, and I don't want to drop it, so I set it on the small end table next to the couch. "Who are they from?"

She pulls out the card and turns it over. "I don't know. The card's sealed. But from the size of that bouquet, I'd say they're from the rich guy. No one else we know could afford something like that. I bet those flowers cost a hundred dollars."

"Evan wouldn't send me these," I say, snatching the card from her. "I told him we're just friends."

"He obviously wants to be more than that. Open the card."

I slide a finger under the flap and carefully peel it open. The card inside reads, *I wanted to brighten your day with some flowers. Evan.*

"Was it him?" Jenna asks.

"Yes," I say, putting the card back in the envelope. "He said he wanted to brighten my day."

"That's code for he wants to date you," she says, a smug grin on her face. "What are you going to tell him?"

"Jenna!" Martin yells from the kitchen. "Come get your sandwich!"

She leaves, and I take my phone out and text Evan. *Thanks for the flowers. They're beautiful.*

Seconds later, my phone rings — it's Evan.

"Hey," I answer. "I love the flowers, but you didn't need to send me anything."

"I wanted to," Evan says. "I thought you'd enjoy them."

"I'm not sure how I'll get them home. I might need Jenna to hold them in her lap so they don't spill all over my car."

"I would've sent them to your apartment, but I didn't want them being left outside your door. So about tomorrow, would eight o'clock be too early for you?"

"Eight in the morning?"

"Yes. I know a wonderful place where we could have breakfast, and then I thought we'd do some shopping and go to a museum."

I'm not a fan of museums, but I'd love to go shopping at some of the iconic department stores in New York. I can't buy anything, but it's still fun to look around.

"I can be ready by eight," I say.

"Great! I'll pick you up then. Enjoy the rest of your day," Evan says in an upbeat tone.

"I will. Bye, Evan."

As I end the call, I admittedly feel a little unsure about tomorrow. Is it too soon to spend the entire day with a guy I just met? Is this supposed to be a date, or are we just going out as friends?

I like Evan, and I'm open to dating him, but there's something holding me back. Something I can't figure out. I don't know what it could be. He seems like the perfect guy. He's smart, ambitious, polite, handsome.

Maybe that's my issue with him. He's *too* perfect, and I'm not. I'm a mess, and so is my life. So why is he interested in me?

CHAPTER 8

"I'm exhausted," I say to Evan as we sit across from each other at the table. "I don't think I've ever done that much in one day."

He chuckles. "I wasn't sure if you'd come back, so I wanted to fit in as much as I could."

It's just after seven, and we're having dinner at a trendy restaurant near Central Park. We went all over Manhattan today. Evan taught me about the history of the city, the landmarks, and the museums we went through. For someone who grew up in California, Evan knows a lot about New York. He knows a lot about everything. I could come up with any random topic, and he seemed to know something about it.

"I'll come back," I say. "Assuming you want to show me around again."

"I'd love to." He smiles. "I had a wonderful time. The other night, and even more so today."

When the server appears, Evan orders a bottle of wine. I don't usually drink wine, but that's because the kind I can afford isn't very good. I'm sure Evan ordered a very expensive bottle.

"Have whatever you'd like," he says as I look through the menu. "It's on me."

I've lost track of how much Evan's spent today. He paid for all my meals, bought us tickets for another Broadway show — the matinee this time — and got me a dress and shoes to wear to dinner tonight. I changed clothes at the store and put what I was wearing in the shopping bag. The dress cost over $300. I told Evan it was way too much, but he insisted I get it, saying how good I looked in it.

"I appreciate you taking me out," I say, "but it's too much. You've paid for everything today."

"I was happy to. You sacrificed your day off to spend it with me. I owe you for that."

The server reappears with the wine Evan ordered and two wine glasses. Evan casually waves her away, then fills both glasses halfway.

"You don't owe me," I say, smiling at him. I follow his lead and swirl the glass around a bit. "I wanted to do this. It was better than spending all day in my apartment."

"What are you doing tomorrow?"

"I'll probably run errands. Do laundry. Nothing too exciting."

"What would you think about spending the day with me again?"

"Here? In the city?"

"If that's what you'd like, then yes. There are so many things we still haven't done."

He takes a sip of his drink, and again, I mimic his motion. The wine is crisp against my tongue and goes down smoothly. It's way better than any wine I've ever bought.

"I don't know, Evan. I don't want to take up all your time. Shouldn't you be working?"

"I'm not an employee who has to report to the office. I'm a consultant. I set my own hours."

"But you already took today off. I'd feel bad if you took tomorrow off, too."

"Why would you feel bad?" Evan leans back in his seat. "I want to take it off. We could go to a museum. Walk around Central Park. Whatever you'd like."

"If you're sure, then . . . okay. Let's do it."

I'm excited I'll be spending another day in the city, but I feel a little awkward knowing I can't pay for these activities. When Evan pays, it seems like we're dating. Is that what today was? Did Evan think it was a date? He didn't say he did, but taking me to restaurants with dim lighting and soft music and ordering a bottle of wine doesn't seem like something you'd do with a guy who's only a friend.

"I think I've lost you," Evan remarks. "Your mind seems to be somewhere else."

"I was just thinking," I say before taking another sip of wine. "About what?"

"Today. It kind of felt like a date."

He leans back in his chair, his eyes on mine. "What if it was? How would you feel about that?"

I take a moment before answering. Do I want to date Evan? Part of me would love to, but the other part — the one stuck in reality — doesn't think it would work between us. We're from two different worlds. We're nothing alike.

"You're not giving me an answer," Evan says. "Does that mean you're not interested?"

"It means I don't know how this would work." I sigh before continuing. "We're so different. I'm a waitress at a diner, and you're a successful businessman."

"I'm a tech consultant," he says with a slight smile. "I know very little about business. As for us being different, I see that as a benefit. We can learn from each other. Expose each other to different things. And in doing so, we'll grow closer."

I hadn't thought of it that way. I hadn't even considered our differences could bring us closer, but maybe he's right. Maybe it's my own fears holding me back from this relationship. Maybe I'm reluctant to be with Evan because I don't think it'll last. I have a long history of things not working out, and I don't want to add Evan to that list. But that mindset could also mean missing out on a great guy.

"What do you think?" Evan asks, reaching over to hold my hand. "Could we give this a try?"

I smile at him. "I guess we could."

"I was hoping that would be your answer." His smile is bright even in the restaurant's dim lighting. "I didn't want to pressure you in any way, but I feel a real connection between us, Grace. I'd like to at least explore it and see where we might end up."

I'm not sure I feel this connection he's talking about, but that's probably because I was thinking of him as a friend. Now that we've agreed to date, maybe I'll start to feel differently.

"Thank you for dinner," I say as we leave the restaurant. The food was too fancy for me, and the portions were ridiculously small, but I didn't want to complain, knowing the meal cost a fortune.

"You're welcome," he says, holding my hand as we go down the street. "I'm sorry you didn't enjoy it."

"What do you mean? I enjoyed it."

He stops and turns to me. "Grace, be honest."

"Okay, maybe it wasn't the best, but I'll eat most anything. Growing up, I had to eat whatever we could afford, which wasn't always good," I say, a bit sheepish.

"I can afford to get you whatever you'd like, so I need you to tell me if you're not happy with something. I'll do what I can to correct it."

That's nice of him to say, but I still feel like it's wrong to speak up when he spent so much money on dinner. I was raised to be grateful for whatever I was given, even if I didn't like it.

"What would you like, Grace?" Evan asks. "Name it and it's yours."

"Pizza sounds good," I say, embarrassed to admit I'm still hungry after just having dinner.

"There's a place just down the street, a block from my apartment. We'll go there."

"Your apartment is on this street?"

"It's two blocks away," he says, leading me down the busy sidewalk.

Did he plan this? Did Evan purposely take me to a restaurant close to his apartment with the intent that we'd go back to his place after dinner? I hope he doesn't think something will happen tonight. I'm not ready for that. I didn't even agree to date him until an hour ago.

He takes me to a little Italian restaurant that sells pizza by the slice. It's delicious and takes care of the hunger I was feeling after having such tiny portions at dinner. But now I'm feeling a little sick knowing we're going to his place. When we reach the front of his building, I stop suddenly.

"Evan, wait," I say.

"What is it?" he asks, facing me, concern on his face.

"I'm not ready for this. It's too soon."

He cocks his head to the side. "You think I'm expecting something? Grace, I wasn't even thinking of that. I just thought you'd like to see my apartment, but if you'd rather not, I'll be glad to take you home."

Relief washes over me as I realize his intentions weren't what I thought. I shouldn't have assumed anything, but when a guy invites you up to his place, it's usually because he wants something.

"Let's go inside," I say, tugging on his hand. "I'd love to see your apartment."

"Are you sure? Because we certainly don't have to."

"I'm sure. I promise."

Evan's apartment is on the third floor of an old building that's been renovated to look modern and new. It's a large two-bedroom with floor-to-ceiling windows and furniture that looks like it was just purchased.

"Is all this new?" I ask, running my hand along the back of a leather couch.

"Yes. I had everything delivered before I moved in. It would've been far too much work to move my things from California."

"Is everything from your old place in storage, then?"

"No, it's in my house."

"You have a house?" I ask.

"In San Francisco." He points to the couch. "What do you think of this color? I'm thinking black would've been a better choice than brown."

"I like the brown." I turn to him. "Why didn't you tell me you had a house?"

"I thought I did. Why does it matter?"

"I think it's odd you never told me. Does that mean you're moving back there?"

"It means I haven't decided. I told you my job is only temporary."

"Then why are we even doing this? Why would we start dating if you'll be leaving soon?"

"I won't be leaving soon, and I don't know if I'm moving back." He cups my face between his hands, and his eyes soften. "As for us, I don't know what's going to happen. However, if this turns into something, I can assure you, I won't be going anywhere."

"How do I know you're not just saying that?" I ask.

"Grace, I'm not someone who goes out with a woman simply because I'm bored or because I find her attractive. I only go out with women I feel a true connection with, someone I could see myself being with in the future."

Is he saying he could see us getting married someday? That can't be right. It's way too soon for that. He must mean he could imagine me becoming his girlfriend.

"How long have you had a house?" I ask.

Owning a house makes him seem more mature and responsible. Not that I didn't think he was those things before, but this makes me feel more certain about it.

"I've had it for about five years," he says.

"Could I see a picture?"

"I don't have one." He walks over to the chair next to the couch. "Do you think this chair is too big for the space? I'm considering exchanging it for something smaller."

"I don't think it's too big."

"Perhaps I need more time to get used to it." He smiles at me. "Would you like to see the rest of the place?"

"Sure."

I follow him down the hall to the bedrooms. One is set up as an office with a long desk and three large computer monitors. I'm still not sure what exactly Evan does. Every time he explains it, I end up more confused. But I've never understood tech stuff. I can figure out my phone, but that's about it.

"That's a really big room," I say, standing outside his bedroom. It's at least three times the size of mine. There's a king-size bed, two nightstands, and two large dressers. Why does he need two dressers in addition to a walk-in closet? What guy has that many clothes?

"You're welcome to go in and look around," he says. "The bathroom is very well done. It's one of the reasons I chose this place. It has an extra-large shower and two sinks on the vanity."

Why does he care about having two sinks? He's only one person. He can't use two sinks at the same time.

"Is this what your house looks like?" I ask. "I mean, the style. Is it similar to this?"

He smiles a little. "Why are you so curious about my house?"

I shrug. "I'm just wondering what it looks like. I've never dated a guy who owns a house."

He chuckles. "I'm thirty-four. It's not unusual for someone my age to own a house."

"It is for the people I know." I look around the bedroom once more. "Most of my friends can barely pay their rent."

"Yes, well, I've done fairly well for myself. Besides, the house is an investment. Even if it's just sitting there empty, it's an asset that's appreciating in value."

That's another thing I like about Evan. He talks about things like assets and investments. People in my world don't use words like that. We don't need to because we have nothing to invest.

I think what Evan said earlier is right. I could learn a lot from him, and maybe he could learn something from me. Maybe it's good we're so different from each other.

Maybe this could work after all.

CHAPTER 9

"You're going out with him *again*?" Jenna asks when she joins me for breakfast. "You've seen him almost every day for two weeks."

It's hard to believe I've only been going out with Evan for two weeks. It feels longer than that, probably because we spend so much time together. He comes here and takes me out, or we go into the city. He keeps asking me to stay with him overnight, but I haven't yet. We've slept together, but when it's over, I ask him to take me home. For some reason, it feels too soon to be staying at his place.

"He's picking me up after work." I pour milk into my coffee.

I'd normally be at the diner, but Martin finally hired someone to fill the open waitstaff position, and the new person took the early morning shift. It's good I won't have to work so much. Of course, it also means I won't be getting overtime anymore.

Jenna takes a box of cereal from the cupboard. "Don't you want a break from each other?"

"Why would we want a break? We just started dating. It's not like we've been together for years and are sick of each other." I take a long sip of my coffee.

"I'm just saying, it seems excessive." She fills a bowl with some cereal. "Doesn't he have anyone else to go out with? Like some guy friends?"

"Why do you care how much I see him?" I smile. "Do you miss me?"

"Yeah, I do. You're never around anymore." She takes her cereal and sits on the barstool next to the counter. "Let's go out tomorrow. We'll have a girls' night."

"I can't. I already made plans with Evan."

"Cancel them and go out with me," she says, chomping on her cereal.

"I'm not doing that." I sit beside her. "I want to go out with him. He's taking me to a new Italian restaurant. You know how much I love pasta."

"So does Tony. He can make his own from scratch. He's a really good cook, which you would've found out if you'd dated him."

"How's he doing?"

"Tony? He's good." She finishes what's left of her cereal and goes to put her bowl in the sink. "He asked about you."

"What did he say?"

"He wanted to know how you're doing. I told him you're seeing someone."

If I were dating Tony instead of Evan, I'd probably be going to fast food places instead of fancy restaurants and discount movies instead of Broadway plays. It's strange to think how different my life is with Evan compared to how it would've been with Tony. Still, even if Evan had never walked into the diner, I just didn't connect with Tony.

"It's not too late." Jenna grabs a soda from the fridge, facing me as she cracks open the top.

I lift a brow. "Too late for what?"

"To date Tony instead of the rich guy." She gulps her soda, then says, "I'm telling you, Grace, there's something not right about that guy."

Jenna walks off and goes into her room. I'm tempted to follow her and demand what she meant by that. I'm thinking she's just saying it, so I'll go out with Tony. Frustrated, I storm into her room. Jenna's on her bed reading a magazine, but she looks up at me as I walk over to her.

"What's wrong?" she asks.

"What you said about Evan. What did you mean?"

She shrugs, then turns her attention back to her magazine. "I just get a bad feeling from him. I can't explain it."

"Are you saying this because you want me to date Tony?"

"It has nothing to do with Tony." She throws her legs off the bed and stands, a frown marring her usually cheerful face. "Why do you care what I think? You're the one who has to date him."

I care because her comment has me concerned. Is there something about Evan I'm not seeing? Something I should be worried about? If so, what is it? Since Jenna can't seem to tell me, I'm thinking she made it up because she doesn't want me dating him.

"Why do you hate Evan so much?" I say. "You don't even know him."

"I don't hate him. I just don't like that he's taking up every free moment you have. It's not normal. No guy wants to spend all his time with a girl he just met."

"We didn't just meet. And he spends all his time with me because he likes me. Why is that wrong?"

"Think about it, Grace. He doesn't want you spending time with anyone else. That's a huge red flag. He's isolating you from your friends."

"That is not what he's doing," I say, getting angry. "Why are you being so negative about him? Why can't you just let me be happy? *You're* the one who pushed me to talk to him in the first place."

"Grace, I'm not—"

"You know what, I don't want to hear it. I can't talk to you right now. I need to calm down."

I go to my room and slam the door shut. A crushing pain pulses through my skull, signaling the onset of a headache. They tend to show up when I'm under stress or really tired, and right now, I'm both of those things. I've been getting home late from my dates with Evan and not sleeping enough. Combine that with the stress of fighting with Jenna, and I know this headache isn't going away anytime soon. I'd take one of my pills, but I'm out. I've been out of them for weeks, unable to afford to buy more. Even if I could afford them, I don't think I have any refills left on my prescription, and I don't have money to see a doctor.

I shut the blinds on my window and crawl into bed, hoping my headache will go away on its own. But hours later, I'm still in agony, the pain so bad I feel like I might get sick.

"Grace," Jenna says, knocking on my door. "You're gonna be late for work."

I check the time and see my shift starts in ten minutes. I'm not ready. I haven't even showered. How am I going to work when my headache is this bad? All the noise — on top of being on my feet for hours — will make it even worse.

"I don't think I can go," I say, opening the door.

I must look even worse than I feel because Jenna steps back when she sees me. "What's wrong? Are you sick?"

"It's my head. It's really bad today," I say, stumbling back to bed.

"Did you take one of your pills?"

"I don't have any. I've been out for weeks."

"Why didn't you—"

"I didn't have the money."

She frowns. "Grace, why didn't you tell me? I would've given you an extension on the rent. Or I could've loaned you the money."

"I didn't want you doing that. Taking money from friends never turns out well. And I thought I was getting better. I've only had two headaches this month and they weren't that bad."

"You want me to take you to the emergency room?" Jenna asks.

Is she kidding? I just told her I couldn't even afford my medications. An emergency room visit would probably bankrupt me. I turn my back to her and curl into a ball, my head throbbing.

"What can I do?" she asks quietly.

"Just go to work. Tell Martin I'm sick and can't make it in today."

"Yeah, okay. I'll check in with you later." She gently closes the door.

Martin's not going to be happy I'm missing work, but hopefully he'll understand. He knows about my headaches and knows I'd fight through the pain and show up to work if I could. But I can't today. I haven't had a headache this bad in a long time.

Around three, my phone rings, the high-pitched sound feeling like a lightning bolt slicing through my head. I blindly search the nightstand for my phone and answer before it rings again.

"It's not any better," I say. "It's actually worse."

"What are you talking about?" a deep voice says.

It's Evan.

"Sorry," I say. "I thought you were my roommate."

"What did you mean just now? When you said it's not any better? Is something wrong?"

"It's just a headache," I say, trying to make it sound like it isn't a big deal.

"Are you at work?"

"No, I couldn't go in. I was dizzy and sick to my stomach."

"I'll be right there."

"Wait — what? Evan, no. You don't need to—"

He doesn't respond, and when I look at my phone, I see he ended the call.

Is he really coming here? I don't want him to see me this way. I look awful. My hair's a mess. I haven't showered. I'm wearing baggy sweats and an oversized T-shirt. I'd clean myself up, but I'm in so much pain I don't think I could stand the feel of the water hitting my head.

When Evan arrives, he softly knocks on the door. Just minutes before, I managed to drag myself out of my room and unlock the door before collapsing on the couch.

"It's open," I call out.

"Grace?" Evan says.

"On the couch," I mumble.

He comes over and sits beside me. "How are you feeling?"

"Bad," I say. I can't hide this from him. If we're going to keep dating, he needs to know how serious my headaches can be. "It hurts to move."

"I stopped at the drugstore on my way over." He hands me a plastic bag. "Maybe one of those would help?"

Inside are a variety of painkillers, some ice packs, and a heating pad.

"It's really sweet of you to buy all this," I say before laying back and throwing an arm over my eyes, shutting out the harsh light coming through the blinds, "but unfortunately none of it will do anything. The only thing that works is the meds from my doctor, but I'm out."

"Then I'll get you more. Call the pharmacy. I'll go pick them up," Evan says, getting to his feet.

"I can't. My refills ran out." I close my eyes and let out a shaky breath. "I just need to wait and hope it goes away."

"Do these headaches happen a lot?"

"It depends. Sometimes I'll get one every day, and then I'll go weeks without one. I get them more when I'm tired or stressed."

"I can't watch you suffer like this," Evan says. "I'm taking you to see a doctor."

I shake my head, then stop when the pain spikes a level higher. Tears burn my eyes. "Evan, I can't. I don't have insurance, and I can't afford—"

"I'll pay for it. Let's go."

He carefully lifts me into his arms and heads for the door. I'm in too much pain to argue with him, and I think I really do need medical help at this point. I've never had a headache this bad last for this long.

Evan takes me to the emergency room and waits with me for hours until I'm finally able to see a doctor. I'm given a new prescription for pain meds, but the doctor says it may take a while for them to kick in. Evan insists I stay at his place the rest of the day so he can keep an eye on me.

He's such a great guy. When he called me earlier, he could've told me to get some rest and that he hoped I felt better. Instead, he showed up at my place and immediately jumped in to make sure I got the medical attention I so desperately needed.

I'm really lucky I met him. I had my doubts about us being a couple, but today, Evan has proven he wants to be with me, even with my health issues. He's shown me I can count on him and that he'll be there for me when I need him.

I haven't had that kind of stability in a long time — not since before my parents died. I forgot just how much I'd missed it. It's too soon to say if Evan and I have a future, but I can already see it in my mind. I could see myself marrying him someday.

CHAPTER 10

"How are you doing?" Evan asks, sitting beside me on his bed.

His voice is gentle, and his fingers brush my hair from my face. I slowly open my eyes and breathe a sigh of relief. "It's gone. My headache's gone."

"I'm glad to hear that." He smiles at me. "Would you like some breakfast?"

"Breakfast? What time is it?" I ask, stretching my arms over my head.

"Almost ten o'clock."

"What day?"

"Sunday. Those pills you took knocked you out. You've been asleep since yesterday."

I slowly sit up. "I feel really groggy, but at least the headache's gone."

"You want to go back to sleep?"

"No, I should get up." I look at Evan, suddenly panicked. "Oh no! Did you tell Jenna? She's going to be—"

"Yes, I called her. I told her you were staying here."

"What did she say?"

She better have been nice to Evan, especially after what he did for me. This should prove to her Evan is a good person and not some selfish rich guy.

"She was relieved to hear that you received medical care." Evan holds my hand. "I assured her I'm taking good care of you and will continue to do so."

"That's really sweet, but you've done enough. I have to get home. I work at the diner this afternoon." I try to move around him so I can get out of bed.

Evan chuckles, his hands on my shoulders, stopping my movement. "You're not working today. I spoke with your boss and told him you wouldn't be coming in."

"You talked to Martin?"

"Yes. I explained the situation and he was very understanding." Evan squeezes my shoulders a bit. "He wants you to get better. We all do."

"But I *am* better. My headache is gone. I'm tired, but once I shower and eat something, I'll be fine."

"Grace, you need to rest. You'll stay here with me for a few days, and then we'll decide if you're able to go back to work."

"A few days?" I say with a laugh because he's delusional if he thinks that's actually happening. "Evan, I can't stay here. I have to be at work. I already missed a day." I try once more to get out of bed, but Evan holds onto my upper arms, stopping me.

"You're not going back to the diner," he says in a stern tone. "I already worked it out with your boss. He'll have the new person cover your shifts until Friday. You can return after that, and only *if* you're feeling up to it."

Friday? Is he serious? It's Sunday. I can't go all week without working.

"You already decided this?" I say, angry he talked to Martin behind my back. "You did this without even talking to me?"

"Grace, you can't do that job in your condition. It's far too demanding."

I try to ignore the uneasy feeling I'm getting from Evan. This is not the same Evan who cared for me at the hospital.

"I'm fine." I look around the room. "Where's my phone? I need to talk to Martin."

"Your phone is put away. I didn't want it going off and waking you up."

"I'm awake now. I want it back. I'm calling Martin and telling him I'll be coming into work."

"Grace, you are not going back there. You could barely stand up yesterday. Do you really think you're ready to wait tables for eight hours?"

"Maybe not, but I have to do it anyway. I can't take time off. I need the money."

"I'll give you the money. Whatever you would've made, I'll give you twice that if you stay here and rest."

"I don't want your money. You've already spent way more on me than you should have." I shove the covers off and get out of bed. "I appreciate it, I really do, but I can't stay here. I need to go to work." I start heading to the bathroom.

"I spoke with the doctor," Evan says.

His words bring me to a stop. I face him and say, "What doctor?"

"The one at the ER. He believes your headaches may be caused by something more serious than stress or a lack of sleep. He advised that you see a neurologist and have some tests performed."

I walk back over to him. "Why did he tell you this and not me?"

"Because you weren't coherent enough to understand. He asked to speak to someone in your family, so I . . ." Evan looks down, then back up at me.

"You what?"

"I told him you're my fiancé." Before I can say anything, he adds in a hurry, "It was the only way he'd tell me about your condition. I explained that your parents are gone and that you don't have any other family."

I'm not sure how I feel about this. Should I be angry that Evan lied to the doctor to get him to tell him about my health? Maybe he was just concerned about me and didn't know what else to do. I just don't see why the doctor didn't tell me this himself. While it's true I wasn't comprehending everything he said, I still think he would've told me about a possible problem with my brain.

"What does he think is wrong with me?" I ask.

"He didn't know. That's why he recommended you see a specialist. In the meantime, he told me to make sure you take it easy, meaning don't be running around a diner all day."

"He said that? He said I can't work?"

Evan lets out a slow breath, almost as if I'm trying his patience. "He recommended you don't until you have tests run to rule out anything serious."

"But I can't. You know what those tests would cost? I don't have the money for that. I can barely pay my rent and keep gas in my car!"

"I'll pay for it." He puts his arms around me. "You're more important to me than anything else, Grace. I'd pay any amount to make sure you're healthy. I'll call a neurologist first thing tomorrow and make you an appointment."

This is all too much to take in. Being told I can't work? Finding out I might have some kind of problem with my brain? Staying here with Evan? This wasn't supposed to happen. I was supposed to see a doctor, get some pills, and go home.

"I need my phone," I mumble, pulling away from Evan. I open the drawer in the nightstand and find there's nothing in it but an earbuds case. "Where did you put it?"

"Grace, stop it," Evan says, yanking my hand from the drawer and slamming it shut. "Didn't anyone teach you it's not polite to search through someone else's personal items? Your phone is in the other room. I'll go get it for you."

I watch him leave, concerned by his reaction. I'm his girl-friend. I should be allowed to open a freaking drawer without being scolded for it like a child. He's been this way before when I've come over. He doesn't like it when I look for something without asking. Last week, I wanted a spoon, and he got upset when I took one from the drawer. I keep telling myself it's just one of his quirks, something about him I should learn to overlook, but it bothers me.

"Here," Evan says when he returns, handing me my phone. "Perhaps you should shower before you look through it. You were exposed to a lot of germs in the ER. Why don't you go clean up while I change the sheets?"

Change the sheets? Is he that disgusted by me? I know I haven't showered in over a day, but I don't smell. Maybe I'm overreacting. Cleanliness is another one of Evan's quirks. I mean, I guess it's better than him being a slob.

I take my phone into the bathroom and see several missed calls from Jenna, along with some texts, plus two missed calls from Martin.

"You okay in there?" Evan asks, knocking on the door.

"I'm fine," I say. It's been all of ten seconds.

"You need help getting the shower running?"

"I can figure it out."

I was going to call Martin, but I'll have to do it later. I don't want Evan standing outside the bathroom door the whole time, listening in or telling me to hurry up.

After I shower, I wrap myself in one of Evan's large, luxurious towels, then remain in the bathroom and call Martin.

"Hey, kid, how are you feeling?" he says almost as soon as he answers.

"A lot better, but I don't think I'll make it in today."

"Yeah, your boyfriend called and told me you'd be out."

"I'll take today to rest and be back tomorrow."

"Tomorrow? Evan said you'd be out all week," Martin says. "He said you were seeing a specialist about those headaches of yours."

"Maybe," I say, not sure if I really need to. "I don't have an appointment yet. But even if I go, I don't need to be off all week."

I went to a lot of doctors in the months after the car accident. They all said my headaches were brought on by stress combined with nerve damage in my neck that happened when the car was hit. They never said there was anything wrong with my brain, so I don't know why the doctor told Evan that. And if the doctor really believed something was wrong, why didn't he run tests when I was at the hospital?

"I don't want you coming back here until you've got a clean bill of health," Martin says. "Evan made it sound like this was serious. Something about pressure on the brain. You can't mess around with something like that, Grace. You go see a doctor and make sure everything's good."

"Okay, but I'll still have a job, right? You won't hire someone to replace me?"

"You think I'd find someone in a week?" he says with a laugh. "It took me three months to find Kara, and who knows if she'll stay?"

Kara, the new girl, is twenty-one and lives with her parents. She told Jenna this is her fifth job in three months, which tells me she probably won't last long at this one.

"I'll try to get back there as soon as I can," I say.

"Keep me posted on how you're doing."

"I will. Bye, Martin."

The door swings open. Evan looks between me and the shower stall. "What are you doing? Why aren't you in the shower?"

"I'm done. I was just drying off."

"Hurry up and get dressed, then come out to the kitchen. I'm making you breakfast." He takes off, leaving the door open.

I was going to call Jenna, but I'll have to do it when Evan's not around. He's being really clingy. If I'm going to be staying here for another day or two, I need some space. I can't have him hovering over me all the time.

Why is he acting like this? Is it because he's worried about me? Or am I seeing a side of him I didn't know existed until now?

CHAPTER 11

When I return to the bedroom, I find the bed has been made, and all the pillows are back in place, including the black-and-gray decorative throw pillows. I guess I won't be going back to sleep.

"I got you some clothes," Evan says, coming into the room holding a stack of neatly folded items.

"You didn't have to do that." I look around. "Where are the clothes I was wearing before? Did you put them in the wash?"

"I threw them out. They were beyond saving. Did you know those pants you were wearing had a hole in them?"

"Evan, they're sweats. I wear them to bed. It's not like I wear them in public." Though I *have* worn them to run to the store. The hole is really small, though. It's not like anyone would notice it. Well, other than someone like Evan.

"If that's all you have to sleep in, I'll get you something else. Now get dressed. Breakfast is waiting."

As he leaves, I look through the clothes he brought me. There's a pair of dark gray pants made of a soft sweater-like material and a matching V-neck top. It's not like anything I own or would even pick out for myself. It's nice, sure, but not my typical style.

After I get dressed, I go out to the living room. It's open to the kitchen where Evan is making something on the stove, his back to me.

"What do you think?" I ask.

Evan turns around, smiling when he sees me. "You look nice. Do you like it?"

"Yeah, it's really soft. It feels expensive. Does this mean we're going out?"

"Grace, you're supposed to stay in and rest. That's why I got you something comfortable to wear."

"I'm supposed to lay around in this?" I say, thinking it probably cost hundreds of dollars. There's no way something this nice was cheap.

"It's loungewear," Evan says. "It's meant for lounging around the house. It's much better than those sweats you were wearing."

I liked my sweats, but maybe it was time to toss them. I would've been fine with a new pair of sweats, especially for just lying around. What I have on feels too fancy to hang out in. I'm worried I'll snag the fabric or spill something on it.

"Come over to the table," Evan says. "The eggs are done."

He turns back to the stove while I sit at the table that's just off the kitchen. There's only one place setting, and in the middle of it is a dish of plain yogurt topped with fresh berries and walnuts.

"Is this for you?" I ask because Evan knows I don't like yogurt.

"No, it's for you. Go ahead and start."

"I don't eat yogurt, remember? I'll just have the eggs."

He brings over a plate with two over-easy eggs. He knows I prefer scrambled, so why didn't he make them that way? I bite back my irritation. Evan sets the plate in front of me before taking his seat.

"Aren't you going to eat?" I ask.

"I already did. I was up at six, had breakfast, and went to the gym. Then I went to a store down the street and got your clothes. I left you a note, but when I returned, you were still asleep."

I take a bite of the eggs, trying to ignore the runny texture. I really wish he'd made them scrambled, but I don't want to complain since he was nice enough to make me breakfast.

"Try the yogurt." He pushes the bowl toward me. "It's good for you."

I dip the spoon in it and take a bite. I almost spit it back out. Despite what he thinks, I know what I like to eat. And yogurt — even topped with berries and walnuts — isn't it.

"It's too sour," I say, making a face. "But I'll eat the berries."

Evan's mouth twitches before he looks away. He seems frustrated with me, even a little angry, but he knows I don't like yogurt.

After breakfast, Evan cleans up while I go sit on the couch. I pick up the remote and turn the TV on.

"Grace, turn it off," Evan says.

"I can't watch TV?"

He comes over, takes the remote from me, and turns off the television. "The noise will give you a headache."

"I'll keep the volume low." I reach for the remote.

"I don't want the noise. Find something else to do. Perhaps you could read a book."

"I need to dry my hair," I say, getting up. "Do you have a hairdryer I could use?"

"It's under the sink."

He returns to the kitchen while I go to the bathroom. I usually let my hair air-dry, but I needed an excuse to get away from Evan. He's driving me crazy with all his rules. He's not usually like this.

When I'm in the bathroom, I shut the door and call Jenna. She answers on the second ring.

"Grace, are you okay?" she says in a rush.

"I'm fine. Sorry if I worried you. I didn't have a chance to call. I fell asleep on the way to Evan's place. What time did you talk to him?"

"I didn't. He called the diner and talked to Martin. That's how I found out you went to the hospital. I'm really mad Evan didn't call me. I'm your roommate and your best friend. I should've been the first to know."

Evan told me he called Jenna. Why would he say that if he didn't actually do it?

"He said you're staying there all week," she says.

I sigh and lean back against the sink. "It won't be all week. I can't miss that much work. I'd lose my job."

"Martin wouldn't fire you. He treats you like a daughter."

"Yeah, but still, I can't be gone that long. I need the money. Evan wants me to see a doctor tomorrow about my headaches, but after that, I'll make him bring me home."

"He's not gonna do it. He'll find some reason to make you stay. Or he'll force you to."

"He can't force me to stay." I roll my eyes even though she can't see me.

"I'm just saying he seems like someone who doesn't take no for an answer."

"Why are you still so negative about Evan? After everything he did for me yesterday, I thought you'd finally see that he's a nice guy. He's paying my ER bill out of his own pocket, and he paid for my pills and bought me some new clothes."

"A guy spending money on you doesn't make him a good guy. Evan is rich. Whatever he spent on your hospital bill is probably nothing to him."

"Why would he do it if he didn't care about me?"

"To get you hooked on him and his money so that you can never leave him."

"That is not what's happening here. Evan knows I don't care about his money. I'm with him because I like who he is as a person."

"You know almost nothing about him," Jenna argues. "He never tells you anything."

"He tells me stuff," I insist.

But, honestly, there's a lot Evan hasn't told me. Whenever I ask about his past or his family, he changes the subject. I know his mother lives in Northern California, but he hasn't told me much else about her. And he doesn't talk about his childhood. It seems to upset him when I ask, so I've just stopped bringing it up.

"I don't need to know every little thing about Evan to know that he cares about me," I say. "He's taking me to see a specialist about my headaches. He's even going to make the appointment and pay for it."

"Of course he is," she mutters.

"Jenna, why are you being like this? Why can't you be happy for me?"

"Grace?" Evan opens the door. "Who are you talking to?"

"Jenna. I'm almost done. I'll be out in a minute."

He leaves but doesn't shut the door.

I sigh and say to Jenna, "I have to go."

"Why? Because your boyfriend told you to?"

"Because I need to go. I'll talk to you later." I end the call before she can respond.

I remain in the bathroom to dry my hair. Under the sink is a small hairdryer with the cord neatly wrapped. It's in its own clear container next to other clear containers containing extra bottles of shampoo, soap, and other supplies. Everything is organized and labeled, and all the containers are arranged so that the edges align. I've never met someone so committed to being tidy.

"Did you find what you need?" Evan asks, startling me.

"Yes," I say, taking out the hairdryer.

He joins me in the bathroom. "What did Jenna have to say?"

"Not much. She just wanted to make sure I'm okay."

"Why wouldn't you be?" Evan smiles, but something about it seems off. "You're with me. Doesn't she know what good care I take of you?"

"Yes, of course," I answer. That's a lie. There's no way Jenna trusts him to care for me, which I think is really unfair. If Evan hadn't shown up yesterday, who knows what would've happened to me? "She just wanted to know if I was feeling better."

"Did she call you?"

"No, I called her. I didn't want her to worry."

"Why would she worry? I already told Martin you were doing much better."

Why is he asking so many questions about my call with Jenna? Why does he care?

"Jenna said you didn't call her," I say. "She said you only called Martin."

He pauses, then nods. "Oh. Yes. That's right. I had planned to call her, but then realized I didn't have her number."

Then why didn't you tell me that? Why did you say you talked to her if you didn't?

"I still need to dry my hair," I say, changing the subject. "I'm getting cold with it wet."

"Yes, fine. Go ahead, then meet me in the living room."

He leaves, and I notice my heart's pumping faster. I'm on edge, and I'm pretty sure it's because of Evan. He seems different today. He's treating me like a child. Telling me what to eat. What to wear. What to do.

Maybe it's Jenna making me think this way. She's said more than once that she thinks Evan is controlling. But it's not true. Evan's not controlling, although since I woke up this morning, he's done nothing but tell me what to do.

After I dry my hair, I find Evan in the living room, looking at his phone. I sit beside him on the couch.

"What are you doing?" I ask.

"Just waiting for you to finish your hair." He sets his phone down and then looks at me. "Have you ever considered wearing it shorter?"

"I tried short hair in high school. It was not a good look on me."

"It was probably the style, not the length, that you didn't like." He picks up a chunk of my hair and lifts it to just below my chin. "Yes, this is much better. It shows off your face."

"Evan, that's way too short," I say with a laugh. "I'd never wear it like that."

He releases my hair. "Are you saying you wouldn't even try? You do know that hair grows back, don't you?"

"Yes," I say, annoyed by his condescending comment. "But I told you, I already tried it short. I didn't like it."

"But *I* would like it that way. Doesn't that count for anything?"

"What's wrong with the way it is now?" I cross my arms. "You're always saying I'm beautiful. Were you lying?"

"Of course not." He brushes his hand over the side of my face. "You're beautiful no matter what. I'm just suggesting you try something new. And think how much easier it'd be to do your hair if it were shorter. I'd be more than happy to pay for you to go to a professional salon here in the city."

I back away from him and stand up. "What's going on here? Because whatever's happening, I don't like it."

"I don't know what you mean." He seems genuinely shocked by my reaction. "I was only making a suggestion."

"You were telling me what to do. You've been telling me what to do since I got up this morning, and I'm tired of it. Why are you being this way?"

"Grace, I'm sorry if you feel that way, but that was not my intention." He reaches for my hand. "Please. Sit down. Let's talk about this."

He waits until I'm sitting next to him, then says, "I care about you, Grace, more than you know. And when I saw you in so much pain yesterday, it frightened me." There's truth to that statement. I can see it in his eyes. Evan rubs my hand. "I don't want *anything* to happen to you. That's why I'm being this way. I'm honestly not trying to tell you what to do. I'm just trying to help you."

I notice the deep concern etched on his face and hear it heavily in his tone. Maybe I misjudged the situation. I still don't like that he's been so demanding with me today, but I can understand why he's been doing it. When someone you care about is sick or in pain, you want to do whatever you can to help them. Evan may have gone a bit overboard, but his intentions were good. I let out a sigh and feel my shoulders drop.

"I wasn't going to tell you this yet," he says, "but I need to, so you'll understand why I'm being this way. Why I care so much about what happens to you."

"What is it? What do you want to say?"

Evan looks into my eyes. "I love you, Grace."

CHAPTER 12

Evan loves me? We've only been dating for a couple of weeks. How could he love me this soon?

Do I love *him*? I definitely care about him, but I don't think I love him — not yet. I'm not saying I never will, but at this point, I'm still getting to know him.

"It's too soon, isn't it?" Evan says, looking down. "I shouldn't have said it. I knew I shouldn't, but it's rare I feel this strongly for someone. I didn't want to go another second without telling you." His eyes rise back to mine. "But I can see by the way you're looking at me that I should've waited."

"Evan, no, I'm glad you said it." I grip his arm. "It's just . . . sooner than I expected."

"It's because I almost lost you. It made me realize how much I love you."

"You weren't going to lose me. I've been having headaches for years."

"But that was the first time I saw you like that." He grips my hand. "It scared me, Grace, more than I can describe. That's when I realized I love you. I never want you to have to suffer like that again, not if it's in my power to prevent it."

I look down, feeling terrible I can't say it back, but I don't want to say it if I don't mean it. I'm not someone who falls in love easily.

I'm not even sure I've ever been in love. I've had a few boyfriends, but I don't think I loved them. Wouldn't I know if I did?

"You don't have to say it," Evan tells me like he's reading my mind. "I didn't expect you to. In fact, I admire that you're cautious with your heart. I tend to be more open with mine, which can be to my detriment sometimes."

I look back at him. "Are you saying you've been in love before?"

"Yes." He smiles a little. "Why does that surprise you?"

"It doesn't. It's just that you've never talked about anyone else."

"Because I'm with *you* now. It's the past. It doesn't matter." Evan leans over and kisses me. "What matters is you. And our relationship."

It's sweet he's being vulnerable with me and expressing his feelings, but I don't think I'm ready to hear this. I know I told him I was, but the more he talks, the more I realize I'm not. It's happening too fast. I'm still getting to know him. There's so much he hasn't told me, like about his past relationships.

Who was he in love with? And why aren't they still together?

I move back on the couch, away from him. "I want to know."

"Know what?" he asks, his brows drawing together.

"About your other relationships. When you were in love."

"Grace, that's completely inappropriate," he scoffs. "And disrespectful to you. I'm not discussing other women with you."

"But I asked. I want to know. It's not disrespectful if I'm asking."

"Why is this important to you? Why do you need to know?"

"Because it's your past. It tells me more about you and who you were before I met you."

"Why does it matter who I was?" Evan tilts his head, a slight smile on his face. "What's important is who I am now."

"Okay, but I still want to know. We've dated for weeks, and you've hardly told me anything about your past."

"The past isn't relevant," he says.

"It is to me. It's part of getting to know you. I'd feel closer to you if you opened up to me about things like this, but every time I ask, you change the subject."

"Fine." Evan folds his arms over his chest and presses back into the couch cushions. He clearly doesn't want to talk about this, but I want answers. I'm tired of him avoiding the topic of his past. "What do you want to know?"

"How many women have you been in a relationship with?"

"That depends on how you define a relationship."

I sit up straighter, annoyed he's making this so difficult. Why can't he just answer the question? "Someone you've dated for a few months," I say.

He pauses, his jaw muscle tensing. "I'm not sure of the exact number, but it's probably around three or four. Maybe five. I really don't remember."

"Were any of them serious? Serious enough that you considered getting married?"

"Yes. But it was years ago."

"Are you saying you were engaged?"

"Only for a brief time."

Evan was engaged? I'm not surprised. He's a good catch. A lot of women would want to marry him.

"When were you engaged?" I ask.

"Grace, I'm really not comfortable talking about another woman when I'm with you. It's wrong."

"It's not wrong. And I want to know. When were you engaged?" I say. I'm not letting him out of this conversation that easily.

He hesitates, then finally says, "It was in my early twenties. I don't remember my exact age."

How is that possible? How could he not remember how old he was when he asked a woman to marry him? That seems like the kind of moment in life you wouldn't forget.

"What happened?" I ask. "Why didn't you get married?"

"It just didn't work out. Honestly, looking back, we were far too young to get married."

"How'd you meet her?"

Evan shakes his head. "I'm not answering any more questions. I've told you more than enough. I didn't even want you to know."

"Why? I actually like you more now that I know this."

"Why is that?"

"It shows you're not afraid to commit. A lot of guys are, especially in their twenties." I pull my feet up and face him.

Evan clasps his hands loosely in his lap. "I've always seen myself married. The single life isn't for me. I don't enjoy being alone. It's not that I can't be, but I'd prefer to have a partner."

He gives me a slight smile, and I find myself matching it. "We've talked enough for now," he says. "I need to do some work in my office since I'll be taking time off this week."

My smile drops and I straighten my spine. "About that. I can't stay here. I need to go home tomorrow."

"Grace, no. You can't. The doctor made it clear that you should rest."

"They always say that. They don't realize that some of us have to work, or we can't pay our bills. I can't miss a whole week at the diner. I'm already short on money this month, and I'm not going to get overtime now that Martin hired another server."

"I'll pay your wages for the week," Evan says. "That way you can rest without worrying about money."

"Evan, I don't want your money. I want to work. I'll be bored just sitting around all week."

"You hate working at the diner. You're always saying how tired you are after being on your feet all day."

"I know, but some parts are okay. I like working with Jenna. Martin gets cranky sometimes, but he's still a good boss. And

I like some of my customers. This one old lady always brings me baked goods."

"You don't have to work at the diner to see those people. You could go visit them whenever you'd like."

"Visit them?" I frown, not sure what he means. "Why would I visit them? I see them all the time."

"You wouldn't if you quit."

I almost choke out a laugh. "I'm not quitting the diner. It's not the greatest job, but it's better than most I've had."

"Think about it, Grace," Evan says, clasping my hand. "Wouldn't it be nice to no longer have to wait tables?"

"Sure, but that's not how life works. I have bills to pay."

"You wouldn't if you moved in with me."

I gape at him, thinking he must be joking. But he looks serious. "Move in with you? We just started dating."

"We've been seeing each other for weeks now. We've spent more time together than apart," Evan says matter-of-factly.

"Yeah, but it's still too soon for me to move in."

"Why?" His grip tightens around my hand. "If you had the chance to not work so hard, to actually have time to enjoy your life with someone who truly cares about you, why wouldn't you at least consider it?"

"Evan, it's too soon. We're still getting to know each other. Just today, I found out you were *engaged*." I try to pull my hand away, but Evan won't let go. And I'm sure there are other things I don't know about you."

"All you need to know is that I love you and want to be with you," he says. "That's all that matters, isn't it?"

"I'm sorry, Evan, but the answer is no."

"I understand." He drops my hand, his jaw tight, his shoulders stiff. "I'll be in my office." He gets up and goes down the hall.

He's upset with me for not giving him the answer he wanted, but I'm not ready to move in with him. I wasn't even considering it. The thought hadn't even crossed my mind. A month ago, I didn't even know Evan. How could he think I'd be ready to move in with him? I don't know if I should be flattered or concerned by his request.

If I had to pick one, I'd go with concerned.

CHAPTER 13

"You're back!" Jenna squeals, running up to me as I come into the diner. She gives me a hug. "Is Evan here?"

"No, he dropped me off at home so I could change into my uniform."

It's Tuesday, and I'm back at work. Evan wasn't happy about it, but it wasn't his decision. I wanted to come back. I was bored at his apartment.

"Let's go in back," Jenna says.

As we walk through the diner, I see it's not very busy. I hope it stays this way. I feel better, but I'm still a little tired, so I'm really hoping I don't have to race around too much today.

"What happened with the specialist?" Jenna asks when we get to the kitchen.

"He said the same thing all the other doctors have said. There's nothing wrong with my brain. It's the nerve damage in my neck combined with stress causing my headaches."

When I left the doctor's office yesterday, I wondered if Evan lied when he said I needed to see a specialist. The ER doctor would've talked to me about that, but he never did. I was out of it that day, but it's not like I was unconscious. I think Evan made it up because he was worried about me and wanted to make sure I was okay. Or maybe he did it so I'd stay with him longer. It's possible none of that is true, but something about his story seems off.

"Hey!" Martin yells as he comes out of the break room. "Is that my favorite waitress?"

"Martin!" Jenna huffs. "What about me?"

He laughs. "You stopped being my favorite when that loser boyfriend of yours tried to steal from me."

"That was one time! And he wasn't my boyfriend."

"Then why were you making out with him in the storeroom?"

"Okay, again, it was one time." She points at Martin as her cheeks flush. "And you promised you wouldn't bring it up again."

Watching them interact, I realize how much I've missed this place. Well, not the diner, but the people. Jenna and Martin are like family to me. It feels good to be back with them.

"So, how are you doing?" Martin asks me. "You feeling better?"

"Yes. I went to the doctor, and he said everything's fine."

"You up for going out tonight?" Jenna asks. "I met the bartender at that sports bar near the mall. He said if we show up tonight, we'll drink for free."

"Why would this guy give us free drinks?"

"He's her new boyfriend," Martin says as he puts a burger on the grill.

"He's not my boyfriend," Jenna gives Martin an annoyed look before looking back at me. "I've only been out with him twice."

"Really?" I say. "Why didn't I know this?"

"Because you're never home. And even when you are, you're in your room talking to Evan."

It's true. I'm always either with Evan or talking to him on the phone. I've been neglecting my friendship with Jenna. I'm overdue for a night out with her.

"Okay, let's go out," I say. "I want to meet this guy."

"You better not bring him here," Martin says to Jenna. "If you do, I'm locking up the meat cooler."

She sighs. "Seriously, Martin, it was one time. You need to get over it."

He nods toward the dining room. "You gonna get out there and work or stand here talking all day?"

"I was talking to *you*!" She throws her hands up. "I swear, I can't win."

She takes off and goes out to the diner.

"What's with you two today?" I ask.

Martin chuckles. "I'm just giving her a hard time. It keeps her mind off what's really bothering her."

"What do you mean? Did something happen?"

He shrugs. "She's just worried about you. She was upset last weekend when she found out you went to the hospital and didn't tell her."

"I couldn't. I was in the ER, and then I took the pills they gave me and fell asleep."

"Yeah, I know. But your boyfriend called me instead of her, which made her even more upset. Anyway, I find if I poke fun at her a little, it gets her mind off her troubles." He flips the burger. "You sure you're okay to work today? Your boyfriend made it sound like you could barely get out of bed."

"He was exaggerating. I'm a little tired, but otherwise, I feel fine," I say, brushing away beads of sweat from my forehead. I've forgotten how hot the kitchen could get.

"How's it going with you and him?" Martin asks, keeping his eyes on the grill.

"Great! He's really nice. You'll have to meet him sometime."

Martin hesitates, glancing at me. He flips the burger patty. After a long few seconds, he asks, "How are you going to keep this going with you here and him in the city? You're not planning to move there, are you?"

"No," I scoff like he's crazy to even ask that. "There's no way I could afford a place there."

"That's not what I meant. I was asking if you're moving in with him."

Did Evan tell Martin he asked me to move in? Or is it just a coincidence that Martin is asking me this right after Evan made that offer?

"I'm not moving in with him," I say. "We just started dating."

"The way he was talking, he seemed pretty serious about you. A little too serious, if you ask me."

"What do you mean?"

He shrugs. "It's too much, too soon. I've seen it happen with my daughters. They go out with these guys that give them all this attention. Show up with flowers and gifts. And a few weeks later, they end it and break their heart."

"That's not Evan. He doesn't play games like that. He was engaged when he was in his twenties. A lot of guys that age aren't ready to even think about marriage."

"So what happened? Why didn't he marry her?"

"I guess it didn't work out. He didn't go into details."

"How much do you know about him?" Martin asks as he puts a hamburger bun on a plate.

"About Evan? A lot, but I don't know much about his past. He doesn't like talking about it."

"Why not?" Martin takes the burger off the grill and puts it on the bun. "Has he got something to hide?"

"No," I say, although I do wonder why Evan always changes the subject whenever I ask him about his life in California.

"Seems like an excuse to avoid talking about something he doesn't want you to know."

"Have you been talking to Jenna about this? Because that sounds like something she would say. She's not Evan's biggest fan."

"Maybe that should tell you something." He sets the plate under the warming lamp.

"It tells me she's upset I'm spending so much time with Evan instead of her."

"Jenna's known you a lot longer than that boyfriend of yours," Martin says, running the metal spatula over the grill to wipe off some of the excess grease.

"Meaning what?"

He looks at me, raising his bushy gray brows. "Meaning you might want to consider what she's saying. I'm not saying she's right, but I wouldn't be so quick to ignore her opinion, either."

I cross my arms, angry Martin's taking Jenna's side. Why aren't they supporting me? They're supposed to be my friends. They should want me to be happy.

"So now you're siding with Jenna? You think Evan's not good enough for me? You've never even met him."

"You're right. I haven't. But I talked to him on the phone, and I didn't get a good feeling from him." Martin puts a basket of fries on the plate with the burger, then slides it under the warmer.

"Why? What did he say?"

"It wasn't what he said but how he said it." Martin pours pancake batter onto the grill. "He seemed to think he knew what was best for you. Like when I asked him to put you on the phone, he wouldn't do it. He said you needed to rest."

"When was this?"

"Sunday. When he called to tell me you weren't coming in to work this week."

"What time on Sunday?"

"I don't know. A little after ten? It wasn't too long before you called me."

I was awake by ten, getting ready to take my shower. I could've talked to Martin. Why did Evan tell him I couldn't?

Evan didn't mention talking to Martin on Sunday. He said he called him Saturday, and that's when he told him I wouldn't be working this week. But now Martin is saying Evan didn't tell him that until Sunday. Martin wouldn't lie about that, which means Evan did. But why? Was he testing me to see how I'd react to him telling me I couldn't go to work all week? Or did he just decide that's what he wanted, so he said it as though he'd already told Martin?

"You're sure it was Sunday?" I ask. "When you talked to Evan?"

"Yeah. Why?"

I shrug. "I thought he talked to you on Saturday."

"He did, and then he called me Sunday to tell me you wouldn't be at work this week."

I glance at the break room. My brain feels overwhelmed trying to make sense of all the inconsistencies. "I should put my stuff away and get to work."

"Hey," Martin says. "Don't be letting some guy get in the middle of your friendship with Jenna. She's just looking out for you, so give her a break, okay?"

I nod, but I'm still annoyed he's taking Jenna's side. If she doesn't like him, fine, but she doesn't need to turn Martin against him, too.

My shift begins, and the diner gets really busy, to the point I can barely keep up. The busboy called in sick, so Jenna and I have to clear dishes and clean tables in addition to serving. And if that wasn't bad enough, I had to wait on a group of six obnoxious guys who made a mess and didn't bother to leave a tip.

By the time I go on break at three, my feet are aching, and my back hurts. It's one of those days when I really don't like my job. I hear Evan's voice in my head, telling me to quit and move in with him. Given how I'm feeling right now, it's tempting, but I know it's not a good idea. I need to get to know him better before I give up the life I have here for one with him.

Then again, my life here isn't anything great, and I know Jenna would rather live alone. Her apartment is really small, and the bedroom I'm using was meant to be for her relatives when they come visit. She has a big family, and they're always coming to see her, but now, because of me, they have to get a hotel.

I keep telling her I'll get my own place, but I can't because I don't have enough money. She assures me there's no rush and says she likes having me there, but I'm sure she's just saying that to be nice.

If I moved in with Evan, Jenna could finally have her apartment back. I'd have to get a new job, but I'm sure there are plenty of waitress jobs in the city. I bet they pay a lot more, too.

Wait, what am I saying? I'm not moving in with Evan.

But maybe I should at least consider it.

CHAPTER 14

"What was going on out there today?" Jenna says, joining me in the break room. "It's never that busy."

"I know. I'm exhausted." I practically fall to the couch.

"Me too." She collapses beside me.

"Who's watching the diner?" I ask.

"Martin. There's only a few customers. He can handle it."

"Sounds like you got Martin on your side about Evan."

I wasn't going to bring this up now, but it's been bothering me all day, and I feel like I just need to say it.

Jenna looks at me. "What are you talking about?"

"Martin said I should listen to you about Evan. Were you saying bad things about him while I was gone?"

"What?" she says, scrunching her face up. "I didn't talk about him at all."

Jenna's always been a horrible liar. That scrunched-up look is her biggest tell.

"Jenna, don't lie to me. You had to have said something. Martin didn't have a problem with Evan before. Now he does."

"Why? What did he say?"

"That things are moving too fast with us. He thinks Evan's trying to win me over with flowers and gifts and then he'll dump me and break my heart."

Jenna shrugs. "Maybe he's right. Even if he's not, wouldn't you agree things are moving really fast with you two?"

"Maybe, but that doesn't mean it's bad. Sometimes you meet someone and just know they're the one you want to be with."

Her brows rise. "Are you saying Evan's that person?"

"I'm saying I felt something for him the day we met."

"Yeah, attraction. He's a good-looking guy. A lot of girls would feel that way."

"It was more than attraction," I insist, but the truth is, Jenna is right. It was attraction I felt when I met Evan, not some deep connection, but I'm trying to make the point that it doesn't take months to figure out if you really like someone.

"Then why did you only want to be friends with him at first?"

"Because I wasn't sure I could see myself with someone like him. But now what we're together, I realized our differences are actually good. We can learn a lot from each other."

"And what has he learned from you?" she says sarcastically.

"He's learning to not be so serious all the time."

"Like how? What's he done?"

I can't think of any examples right now. Whether that's because I'm tired from work, or because I hate being put on the spot like this, I can't say. Honestly, Evan's still really serious, even when I try to get him to loosen up. But he's really smart and most smart people tend to be serious. They're always in their head. It's hard for them to relax and let go.

"I got him to laugh more," I say, which is true, even though it's only happened a few times.

"Grace, listen to what you're saying." Jenna adjusts how she's sitting, turning toward me more. "You're with a guy that's so uptight, you have to teach him to laugh. Is that really what you want?"

"I wouldn't be with him if it bothered me that he was serious," I say, not looking her way. "And besides, he has other good qualities."

"Like what?"

"I'm not arguing with you about this. Look, I get that you don't like Evan, and I obviously can't change your mind, so let's just not talk about him."

My phone rings, and I see Evan's name on the screen. Jenna sees it, too.

"Aren't you going to answer it?" she asks.

"I'll call him later." I send the call to voicemail.

Martin pops his head in the door. "I need you to get out there," he says to Jenna. "We got busy again."

She gets up and leaves the break room. My phone rings again. It's Evan.

"Hey," I answer in a flirty tone. "Do you miss me?"

"Why didn't you pick up my call?" he says.

I'm taken aback by his harsh tone. "I just did. Why do you sound angry? Did something happen?"

"Yes, I tried to reach my girlfriend, and she ignored my call."

"Evan, I wasn't ignoring you," I say in a lighthearted tone, hoping he'll calm down. "I was talking to Jenna."

"You couldn't excuse yourself and take my call?" he demands.

"I'm sorry. I wasn't trying to—"

"Do you have any idea how worried I was when you didn't pick up? I thought something had happened to you!"

"Evan, I'm fine. Relax."

"How can I relax when you don't answer my call? I thought you'd fallen or passed out or something even worse."

"I told you I'm fine."

"I know that now, Grace, but I didn't just moments ago. I need you to answer the phone when I call. I need to know you're okay. Can you do that for me?" he asks, a little less agitated.

"Yes, I'll answer the phone." I'm suddenly exhausted all over again.

"Good. Thank you," he says, sounding calmer now. "Are you still at work?"

"Yes, I work until eight." I rub my temple, feeling the onset of a headache.

"I wish you wouldn't do that. You were in the hospital just a few days ago. I don't think you should be working at all, but definitely not a full day. You should go home and rest."

"I don't need to." I force some energy into my voice. "I rested for two days. It feels good to be up and moving around. And tonight, I'm going out with Jenna and meeting this guy she started dating. He's the bartender, so we're getting free drinks."

"Grace, you shouldn't be drinking. You're on medication."

"I only take it when I have a headache."

"You really think it's wise to be going out to a bar after a long day of work?"

That hint of condescension from when he suggested cutting my hair echoes over the line. "I'm looking forward to it," I say. "Jenna and I need a girls' night. I haven't been out with her since before you and I started dating."

Evan doesn't say anything.

"I need to go," I say, noticing the time. "My break's almost over."

"I'd like you to reconsider going out tonight," he says with a sigh, "but if you must go, please text me before you leave and when you get home."

"Why? Nothing's going to happen to me. I'll be with Jenna."

"Would you please just text me so I know you're safe?"

"Yeah, okay, fine. I need to get back to work." I slowly get up.

"Goodbye, Grace. I love you."

The call ends, and I shove my phone in my back pocket. I'm still not used to him saying he loves me. It makes me uncomfortable, like he expects me to say it back even though he told me he didn't.

The remainder of my shift is much calmer than earlier in the day, leaving me with plenty of energy to go out. Despite the tense discussion I had with Jenna in the break room, I'm looking forward to having fun with her tonight.

When we get home, we each go to our rooms to get ready. I'm touching up my makeup when Evan calls.

"Hey, I can't talk long," I say. "I'm leaving in a few minutes."

"What if I joined you?" he asks.

I stop with the lipstick tube inches from my mouth. "Joined me?"

"At the place you're going tonight. I could meet you there. Or I could pick you up and we could go together."

"Evan, tonight is a girls' night. I told Jenna it'd just be her and me."

"Didn't you tell me Jenna is meeting her boyfriend there?"

"Yeah, but he'll be working behind the bar."

"Which means your friend will want to sit at the bar and talk to him, while you sit there bored."

"She won't talk to him all night."

"I'd like to be there with you. It'd be a chance for me to get to know your friend."

I consider it for a moment. It's probably true that Jenna will end up talking to that guy all night. And maybe if she sees how happy I am with Evan, she'll stop giving me so much shit about him. I let out a heavy sigh. Jenna's not going to be happy about this.

"Okay, I guess you could go, but Jenna and I are leaving in a few minutes so I'll meet you there."

I give him the name of the place and end the call.

"You ready?" Jenna asks, knocking on my door.

I hurry over and open it. Jenna's wearing a tight black sweater dress with black boots that go up to her knees.

"Wow, you look hot!" I tell her.

"You think so?" She spins around.

"Your new boyfriend's gonna love it."

She laughs. "He's *not* my boyfriend. But I like him so far. We'll see how long it lasts. Let's go. I told him we'd be there at eight."

She takes off as I follow behind. Maybe if I just casually throw it out there, she'll see this isn't a big deal.

"Evan's meeting us there," I blurt out.

Jenna's about to open the door, but she stops and whips back to me. "Evan's meeting us at the bar?"

"Yeah. I thought it'd be okay since—"

"No, Grace, it's not okay," she fires back, raising her voice. "This was supposed to be a girls' night."

"I know, but you'll be talking to that guy all night, so I thought it'd be okay to invite Evan."

"When did you invite him? And why didn't you tell me?"

I sigh. This is not a good start to the night. "I'm telling you now, and I didn't really invite him. He called and suggested he meet us there. He really wants to get to know you."

"You just said I'd be talking to Craig all night," Jenna says, rolling her eyes. "So how would I have time to get to know Evan?"

"Craig? That's the guy's name?"

"Yes, but forget about that. We're talking about Evan, and the fact that he took over our girls' night and you just went along with it. Did you even try to tell him not to come?"

"Why are you getting so upset about this? It'll be like a double date. If Evan wasn't there, I'd just be sitting at the bar while you talked to Craig."

"He won't have time to talk! The bar is really busy on Tuesday nights. They have drink specials and five-dollar burgers. The place will be crazy."

"Then why are we going tonight instead of some other night?"

"Because you agreed to go," Jenna says, throwing her hands up. "It's the first time in weeks you actually wanted to go out with me. I didn't want to suggest another night and risk you turning me down. But I guess it doesn't matter now since you decided to turn this into date night with your boyfriend."

"Jenna, I'm sorry. I didn't know you'd get this upset. You want me to call him and tell him not to meet us there?"

"It's too late. I'm sure he's already on his way." She yanks open the door. "Let's go."

She doesn't talk to me on the way to the bar. I should've told Evan he couldn't come. I knew Jenna wanted a girls' night, and I did too. We'll just have to plan it for some other night.

I was hoping tonight would be a chance for me to show her how great Evan is, but I doubt that'll happen now that she blames him for ruining our girls' night.

Why did Evan have to invite himself? Can't we have one night apart?

CHAPTER 15

"Hey!" Jenna yells to a guy behind the bar as we sit down on the last two available barstools. "Can we get some drinks over here?"

The guy's average height with jet-black hair and a wide, muscular build. I'm assuming that's Craig.

"Hey," he says, smiling at Jenna as he comes over to us. "I didn't think you'd show up."

Jenna shrugs and tosses her hair over her shoulder. "You promised me free drinks."

"That the only reason you're here?" he says, resting an elbow on the bar top, a grin on his face.

"Maybe." Jenna leans forward. "We'll have to see how tonight goes." Jenna sits back and puts her arm around me. "I want you to meet my friend. This is Grace. Grace, meet Craig."

"Hi!" I have to almost scream over the noise filling the room.

"Good to meet you," he says, reaching across the bar to shake my hand. "You're Jenna's roommate, right?"

"I am. It was only supposed to be temporary, but I've been living with her for a year now."

"She's a great roommate," Jenna says, smiling at me like she's no longer angry with me, or maybe she's just putting on an act for Craig. I'm not going to complain either way. It looks like we can salvage the night after all.

"I'd love to talk, but I gotta get back to work," Craig says, glancing at the line of people waiting for drinks. "What can I get you two?"

We each order a beer, and he takes off to get it.

"What do you think?" Jenna asks, turning toward me.

"He seems nice."

"I meant how he looks. Don't you think he's hot?"

"Yeah. He looks like he works out a lot."

"He does. He's always at the gym."

Jenna drops her chin into her hand, and I can practically see the hearts in her eyes. I'm glad she found someone to date. Maybe it'll pull her attention away from *my* relationship.

"Here you go," Craig says, appearing with our beers. "Let me know if you need anything else."

"When's your break?" Jenna asks.

"In a few minutes, but if we're still this busy I may not be able to take it. I gotta go." He races off.

"See? I told you he wouldn't have time for me." Jenna takes a drink of her beer. "That's why tonight was supposed to be a girls' night."

"I'm sorry, okay? We'll do it some other night. Now can you stop being mad at me so we can have some fun?" I take a deep pull of my beer.

"You think I'll have fun watching you make out with your boyfriend?" She rolls her eyes. "You should just leave as soon as he gets here. He's not going to want to be at a place like this. It's beneath him."

"That's not true." I set my bottle down much harder than necessary. "Evan can hang out just fine at a place like this, just like any other guy here."

"Yeah, right," Jenna says with a laugh. "I bet he shows up wearing a suit."

I let out a sigh. "Would you stop attacking my boyfriend? He's going to be here soon, and I don't want you fighting with him the whole time."

"Fine." Jenna faces me, arms crossed. "I'll agree to leave him alone if you agree to stop letting him tell you what to do."

"He doesn't tell me what to do."

"Really? Then why is he coming here tonight? Why didn't you tell him no?"

"I tried to, but . . ." I pause, trying to figure out how to explain this to her in a way that proves Evan isn't like what she's describing.

"He wouldn't take no for an answer," Jenna says smugly. "So, like I said. He tells you what to do, and you do it."

"No. You're wrong." I turn and face the bar, my anger rising. "I don't want to talk about this anymore."

Jenna looks away and mumbles something. I ignore her and drink my beer, wishing I'd ordered something stronger. I can't take all this tension between us. This was supposed to be a fun night out, and instead, all we're doing is fighting.

"Hey, how's it going?" a deep voice says to my left. An arm brushes against mine.

I look over and see a guy with a tan face and blond hair smiling at me. He looks close to my age or maybe a year or two younger.

"Hi." I smile politely at him, then look back at the football game playing on the TV behind the bar.

"Who are you rooting for?" the guy asks.

"I'm not really watching," I say, keeping my focus on the television.

"Who's your friend?" Jenna asks, nudging me.

"Blake," he answers, reaching across me.

"I'm Jenna," she says, shaking his hand and nodding toward me. "And this is Grace."

"Can I get you two another round?" he asks, pointing to our nearly empty glasses.

"I'm good," I tell him. "I'm—"

"Waiting for her boyfriend to arrive," an even deeper voice says from behind me. I smell Evan's cologne and feel his hands settle heavily on my shoulders. "Hello, sweetheart."

I turn back, and he kisses me — just a quick brush of lips. Still, it surprises me since Evan isn't big on PDA. I lean back and say, "Hey. I didn't think you'd be here this soon."

"Good thing I arrived when I did. Apparently, someone was trying to steal you away from me," Evan says, his eyes locked on Blake.

"Hey." Blake puts his hands up. "I just met her, dude. I didn't know she had a boyfriend."

"And now that you see that she does," Evan says, "I think it's time for you to go elsewhere."

The guy makes a hasty retreat. Evan takes his place, standing next to me since all the barstools are still taken.

"How'd you get here so fast?" I ask. It should've taken him close to an hour with the traffic this time of night.

"I was on my way when we spoke on the phone. I was hoping you'd agree to let me join you."

"She only did because you forced her to," Jenna mutters.

I shoot her a look to be nice, but she's not paying any attention to me. She's glaring at Evan like she wishes he'd spontaneously combust already so we could have our planned girls' night after all. I have a feeling tonight's not going to go well.

"Jenna." Evan smiles at her. "It's good to see you again."

"I can't say the same about you," Jenna replies coldly.

"Jenna!" I scold.

"What? It was supposed to just be you and me tonight." She's still glaring at Evan. "No guys."

"I'm sorry to have interrupted your girls' night, Jenna, truly," Evan says. "But I was very worried about Grace. As you know, she had a serious health scare, and I just didn't want her being alone tonight."

"She's not alone," Jenna scoffs. "She's with me."

"Grace said you were on a date," Evan says. "I was concerned you might leave with this man, and then Grace would have no one to get her home safely and to care for her."

"Evan, I'm fine," I assure him. "Jenna doesn't need to take care of me. And neither do you."

"But I want to." He cups my face. "You're mine to care for. It's a job I take very seriously."

He leans down and kisses me. I try to pull back, but Evan's other hand goes behind my head, holding me in place as he presses his tongue between my lips. I feel extremely awkward doing this with Jenna watching us.

"Maybe you guys should go." Jenna sounds as annoyed as I feel.

When Evan ends the kiss, I quickly back away, embarrassed that he did that. I felt like he was marking his territory.

He turns his gaze to my best friend. "Forgive me, Jenna. I can't seem to help myself when I'm around Grace. She's such an amazing woman."

"And why is that?" Jenna challenges him.

Evan looks at her with confusion. "I'm not sure what you mean."

"Tell me why you think Grace is so amazing."

I turn to Jenna and heave a sigh. "Would you stop? He doesn't need to—"

"I can think of many reasons," Evan says. "One, Grace is an extremely hard worker. I don't know how she does it, especially given her health condition."

"It's just some headaches, Evan. I've had then since long before we met," I say. "And I don't get them all the time."

"What else?" Jenna asks, her eyes locked on my boyfriend.

"She's resilient. Despite the tragedy of losing her family, she's been able to move on without them. She's also very kind. She cares about others." He looks at me, nothing but honest adoration in his eyes now. "And obviously, she's beautiful. So beautiful I have a hard time looking away."

"Enough about me," I say, feeling my face getting hot. "Let's talk about something else."

"Like your boyfriend," Jenna says, still staring at him. "So, Evan. Tell me about yourself."

"What would you like to know?" he asks.

"Tell me about your family. Do you have any brothers or sisters?"

Evan's jaw tightens, and his lips purse. I know how much he hates talking about his family.

"I'm an only child," he says stiffly. "My parents wanted to have more children, but my father died before they could."

The guys at the table behind us start yelling. When I look back, I see they're shouting at the TV. Something must've happened in the football game.

"They're very loud," Evan says, glancing at the guys behind us. "Perhaps we should move to a table."

"We kind of need to stay here," I say, giving him a look to go along with it. "Jenna's boyfriend works behind the bar."

"I see," Evan says. "Which one is he?"

"Over there." I point to Craig as he fills a beer from the tap. "His name is Craig. I'll see if I can get his attention."

"I'll do it," Jenna says. She rises a little from her stool and wildly waves. "Hey! Craig!"

Craig glances her way and yells, "Be there in a minute!"

Jenna turns back to us and resumes her inquisition. "Did your mom ever remarry?"

"No. She devoted herself to being a mother."

Evan answers her questions a lot more smoothly than he's ever answered mine.

"What did she do for work?" Jenna asks.

"She didn't. Luckily, my father had enough money saved that when he died, my mother was able to stay home with me."

One more tidbit he's never told me. I assumed his mother worked when he was growing up. It's odd he never talks about her. It's possible they're estranged, but if they were, I think he would've told me that. Maybe they're just not very close.

"Ready for another round?" Craig asks, appearing in front of us.

"Yeah," Jenna says. "And Grace's boyfriend needs to order."

"I'll have your best scotch," Evan says to Craig.

"That's the best we got." He points to the top shelf. "Is that gonna work?"

Evan laughs. "You're joking, right?"

"Why don't you get a beer?" Jenna says. "Or is that not fancy enough for you?"

"Jenna, stop," I say through gritted teeth.

I'm furious that she's not even giving Evan a chance. It's bad enough dealing with her complaints when it's just the two of us, but insulting Evan to his face is taking it too far.

"I'll have the scotch," Evan says to Craig.

"Coming right up." Craig grabs the bottle from the shelf. As he pours the scotch into the glass, he says to Jenna, "I'm taking my break after this. You want to join me?"

She smiles. "Where are we going?"

"My truck." He sets the scotch down in front of Evan. "Unless you've got a better idea."

"How long have you two been seeing each other?" Evan asks Craig.

"We met last week," he says. "I'm Craig."

"Nice to meet you, Craig. I'm Evan."

Craig points to my glass. "I'll grab you another before I go."

"I think she's had enough," Evan says. "She's taking medication."

"You said you didn't take it tonight," Jenna says to me.

"I didn't," I say. "But I drank that beer really fast. I should probably wait a little bit before having another."

Jenna rolls her eyes. "I can't believe you're listening to him."

"Let's go," Craig says to her. "We don't have much time."

Jenna takes off with Craig.

"I'm sorry she's being this way," I say to Evan as he takes Jenna's former spot. "I don't know what her problem is. She's usually not like this."

"It's obvious she cares a great deal for you. Perhaps she thinks I'm not good enough."

I smile at him. "You're a great guy, and you've done so much for me. Jenna has no excuse for acting like she is tonight."

Evan tucks a lock of hair behind my ear. He sips from his glass and grimaces. With a disappointed sigh, he places the glass on a nearby coaster and slides it away. He then returns his attention to me.

"I wouldn't worry about it," he says. "I'm sure she'll come around eventually."

She won't. He doesn't know her like I do. Jenna's stubborn. When she makes her mind up about something, it's nearly impossible to get her to change it. And when it comes to Evan, she's decided she doesn't like him.

At all.

CHAPTER 16

"How was your date?" I ask Jenna when she returns about fifteen minutes later.

"It wasn't a date," she says. "He's taking me out tomorrow, though."

"You talking about me?" Craig says, setting another beer in front of Jenna.

"Yeah, I was telling her your truck's a mess," Jenna says, smiling at him.

"You didn't complain when we were in it," he says before he winks at her. He points to my empty glass. "Can I get you another?"

"Sure," I say, proving to Jenna that I don't always listen to Evan.

As Craig goes to get my beer, Evan says to Jenna, "You should come to the city sometime. Grace and I could take you out. Show you around."

"I don't need you to show me around," she says. "I've been there. Many times."

Why is she being so rude? Evan's trying so hard to be nice to her, but she won't let him.

"We could all go see a play," I suggest, trying to play peacemaker. "Or go to a museum."

"I don't like museums," Jenna says. "And neither do you. Or you didn't until—"

"Until I realized not all museums are boring," I say, interrupting Jenna before she could make what I'm sure would've been yet another rude remark.

"When are you moving back?" Jenna asks Evan.

"Moving back?" he says, sounding confused.

"To California. Grace said you're out here for a job and that it's only temporary. So, when are you moving back?"

"I don't know if I am. I haven't decided."

Jenna snorts. "Don't you think you should before getting involved with someone who lives here?"

I need to stop this. Right now. I'm not going to let Jenna attack Evan for the rest of the night.

"Could you excuse us?" I say to Evan, getting off the barstool. "Jenna and I need to use the restroom."

"I don't need to—"

"Yeah. You do," I say, grabbing her arm. "Come on."

When we get to the restroom, I turn to face her. "Why are you doing this?"

"I'm just asking questions. I thought that's what you wanted."

"You thought I wanted you to attack my boyfriend?" I ask, stepping closer.

Jenna doesn't move back. She just shrugs like her behavior tonight is completely normal. "I'm not attacking him. I'm trying to get to know him."

"You've been rude to him since he got here," I snap. "You're not even giving him a chance."

"I'm rude because I'm asking him questions?" she asks, raising her brows. "Questions any normal boyfriend would be more than happy to answer since they'd know their girlfriend's best friend is—"

"It's the types of questions. And how you're asking them. It's like you're trying to make him look bad."

"If what he says makes him look bad, that's on him. Not me. *I'm* trying to get to know the guy. That's not going to happen by asking him about things that don't matter. What I've asked him tonight is all stuff you should already know, but you don't, because you're afraid to ask, which should tell you something about your relationship."

"I'm not afraid to ask him stuff," I say, getting defensive. "You don't know what Evan and I talk about."

"Grace, you know almost nothing about this guy. Every time I ask you about him, you just tell me how great he is, or where he took you for dinner, or what he bought you. You tell me nothing about his family or even what he did before he moved here."

"That's not true! I told you he used to live in San Francisco. I told you he developed software that made him a lot of money." I pause and let out a sigh. "You know what. I'm not doing this. I shouldn't have to defend my relationship to you."

"I'm just trying to get you to see he's not as perfect as you think he is."

"I never said Evan was perfect. I know he has faults, but so do I. And I haven't tried to hide those faults from Evan. He knows I'm messy and never on time. He knows I struggle to keep a job. He knows I didn't do well in school. But despite all that, he still loves me."

Jenna's brows rise again, and her face pales. "He *loves* you? He actually said that?"

"Yes." I stand straighter. "He told me the other day, when I was staying with him."

"He actually said those words? That he loves you? After only knowing you for a couple of weeks?"

"It's been more than a couple of weeks, and besides, sometimes people know right away."

"What about you? Do you love him?" she asks.

I pause a moment to think about that. I definitely care about Evan, but do I love him?

"You don't," Jenna says. "Just admit it."

"I'm not sure. I've never been in love before. I think I love him, but I don't feel ready to say it. I need more time."

A woman comes into the restroom and walks up to the mirror. She opens her purse and takes out a tube of lipstick.

"We should go," Jenna says, glancing at the woman.

"You go ahead. I need to use the bathroom." I head into the closest stall.

When I'm done, I head back to the bar and see Jenna talking to Evan. She's standing in front of him, pointing her finger at him and looking like she wants to punch him. How did this happen? I leave them together for two minutes, and they're already fighting.

"If you think I'm giving up," I hear Jenna say, "you don't know who you're dealing with."

"What's going on?" I say, intervening before things become even more heated between them. Actually, Evan looks completely calm. It's Jenna who looks furious, her face red, her eyes narrowed.

"Everything's fine," Evan says, pulling me to his side, his arm tight around my back. "Jenna and I were just talking."

"About what?" I ask.

"About how he's brainwashing you," Jenna scoffs. "Or at least trying to."

"Brainwashing?" I sigh. "Jenna, I swear, if you don't stop, Evan and I are leaving."

"Maybe that's for the best," Evan says, rubbing my arm. "This night doesn't seem to be going well."

"It's not going well because of you," Jenna says. "You weren't supposed to be here. But you couldn't let Grace have one night to herself, could you?"

"We should go," Evan says to me. "She's clearly had too much to drink."

"Grace, how can you not see what he's doing?" Jenna says to me. "Making me out to be the bad guy? Like he's totally innocent? You want to know what he said to me while you were in the bathroom?"

"Jenna, please," Evan says. "Don't do this. You're only hurting Grace. I realize and accept that you don't care for me, but that's not a reason to create stories about me that aren't true."

"Aren't true?" Jenna huffs. "So you're just going to deny what you said?"

"Okay, stop it," I say, feeling a stabbing pain behind my eyes. "Both of you. You're making my head hurt."

"Let's get you home," Evan says, taking my hand.

"I'll take her," Jenna says. She grabs my other hand. "Come on, Grace. Let's go."

I'm overwhelmed and confused, feeling like I'm being forced to choose between my best friend and Evan. I'm about to literally be pulled in two different directions. The stress of it is making my headache worse. The blaring music and guys shouting at the TV certainly aren't helping matters.

"I need to sit down," I say.

Evan helps me onto the barstool. He tilts my face up, worry in his eyes, and asks, "Do you need to go to the hospital?"

"No, I just need to relax a minute."

"You can go," Jenna says to Evan. "I've got this."

"I am not leaving her here," Evan says firmly. "Not when she's in this condition. I'll take her to our apartment and keep an eye on her during the night."

"*Our* apartment?" Jenna says, her tone more frigid than it's been all night. "Grace doesn't live with you. She lives here. With me."

"For now, yes, but that's about to change."

"Wait — what?" Jenna looks at me. "What's he talking about? Are you moving in with him?"

I shake my head. "No. Not right now."

"But she will," Evan says. "We've already discussed it. We just need to pick a date."

Jenna's expression turns from concern into outright panic. "Grace, no! You can't move in with him. It's too soon."

"I can't talk about this." I rub my head, the pain getting worse. "I have to get out of here."

"Of course, sweetheart," Evan says. "Let's go."

"You need to take her home. Her actual home," Jenna says. "That's where her meds are."

Evan nods. "Fine. We'll meet you there."

"Craig!" Jenna yells at him. "I gotta go!"

"Yeah, I'll call you later!" he yells back.

Evan tosses some cash on the bar and helps me down from the barstool. He puts his arm around my waist, taking most of my weight. When we get outside and away from the noise of the bar, I feel a little better.

"I really wish you'd go home with me," Evan says as he drives to my apartment.

"I can't. I have to work the early shift tomorrow." I rest back in my seat, letting my eyes drift shut.

"You can't go to work when you're in this much pain."

"I'll be fine by the morning. I just need to take a pill and go to sleep."

He reaches over and holds my hand. "I'm sorry things turned out this way. I really wasn't trying to upset her."

"What happened? I mean, I wasn't even gone that long."

"I merely told her how much you mean to me — and how I've fallen in love with you — but she didn't want to hear it. She became very upset."

"What'd she say?"

"She demanded I end our relationship. She said I'm not good for you and that I'm simply using you to pass the time until I return to California." He rubs the back of my hand with his thumb. "But Grace, I hope you know that none of that is true. I love you, and I would love to someday have a future with you. I have no desire to go back to California. My life is here now. With you."

His words warm my heart. He really does love me. Why can't Jenna see that?

"So what did you tell her?" I ask. "When Jenna told you to leave me?"

"I told her it wasn't possible. I can't imagine you not being in my life. I don't even remember what my life looked like before I met you." He glances at me, continuing to gently rub my hand. "You're mine, Grace. And I'm yours."

I wish he'd stop saying that. I know he's just trying to express how he feels about me, but saying "mine" sounds creepy. It's like he sees me as a possession instead of a person.

"I'll talk to her," I say. "I think she feels like she's losing me as a friend. I've been spending all my time with you and she's probably feeling left out."

"Perhaps now that she has Craig, she won't be so demanding of your time."

"What did you think of him?" I ask.

"Of Craig?" Evan shrugs. "He seemed okay. Working at that bar isn't much of a career for someone his age. I'm guessing he's in his thirties?"

"I don't know, but I'm sure he makes decent money working there. The bar was packed."

"I suppose, but how long could he do it? A job like that is hard on the body, and it's dangerous. People are always getting into fights at bars. He could be injured and have to stop working before he's even forty."

"I guess, but I don't think Jenna's worried about that. I never was either. All the guys we know have jobs where they could get hurt. My dad was always getting sick from the chemicals at the factory he worked at. And Jenna's dad hurt his back working construction. He's on disability now."

"It's a good thing you're with a man who works at a computer all day," Evan says jokingly. "The only injury I'm at risk for is perhaps a little eye strain from staring at the screen."

I take a moment to think about that, remembering how my mom used to worry about my dad. Working at a chemical plant exposed him to all kinds of toxins. He was always having health problems, but I didn't think anything of it because everyone I knew had a father with a dangerous job. Some of the moms did, too.

Evan's right. The chance of him getting hurt or developing a serious health problem because of his job is very low. He'll probably live a long, healthy life. That's really important to me, especially after losing my family. It makes me like Evan even more. I can see us in the future — getting married, growing old together.

"Grace?" Evan says, giving my hand a squeeze. "We're here. You need help getting out?"

"No, I'm okay." I smile at him, thinking once again how lucky I am to have him.

He smiles back at me. "Why are you looking at me like that?"

"Because I just realized something."

"What is it?"

I take a deep breath as I realize my feelings for Evan are much stronger than I've let myself admit. But I'm admitting it now. In my heart, I have completely fallen for Evan. And now, I can't imagine being with anyone else. He's so good to me and good *for* me.

I take another deep breath and whisper, "I love you."

"Oh, Grace." His face is practically glowing now, even under the dull streetlamp outside the apartment building. "You have no idea how happy that makes me."

I'm happy, too. I can't believe I'm dating such an amazing guy. I never in a million years thought I'd be with someone like Evan. If we ever got married, I know I'd have an amazing life. Evan would do whatever it took to give me the world.

I know Jenna has concerns, but I'm not letting that affect how I feel about him. Evan's a kind, loving man, and I'd be a fool not to consider a future with him. Guys like Evan don't come along every day. And if I don't take him, someone else will.

CHAPTER 17

"Go take your medicine," Evan says as we go into my apartment. "I'll pack up your things."

"Evan, I told you I'm staying here."

"Grace, no." He grips my shoulders. "You're coming with me. I don't want you being alone tonight."

"I'm not alone. Jenna will be here any minute." I pull back but offer a smile. "Go. I'll be fine."

Evan doesn't move, and he doesn't smile back. He purses his lips and furrows his brows.

"Evan, I know you're worried about me, but you don't need to be. I already feel better. Why are you upset?"

"I'm not upset with *you*. I'm upset with *her*." He walks away, then turns back. "Can't you see what she's doing?"

"Who?"

"Jenna! She's jealous. Of you. Of our relationship. She's trying to turn you against me."

His eyes are wide, almost frantic. I don't understand what's happened between us getting out of the car and coming inside the apartment.

"That's not true," I say, walking over to him. "I told you. She's just sad that I'm not spending as much time with her."

"Grace, think about what happened tonight. How upset she got when I showed up at the bar. The way she treated me. And when you were in the restroom? She made it clear she'd do whatever it takes to get rid of me." He grips my shoulders again, tighter this time. "Please, Grace. Come home with me. I don't want you around someone like her. She's trying to poison you against me. She doesn't want us to be together."

I look into his eyes. "You really don't get it, do you?"

"Get what?"

"Jenna can say whatever she wants." I softly smile as I continue to gaze into his eyes. I move closer and wrap my arms around his waist. "It won't change my mind. I want to be with you, Evan. I just need us to slow down a little. Things are moving so fast and—"

I stop when I hear the door open. Jenna walks in. She glances at Evan, then says to me, "Are you leaving?"

"No." I back away from Evan. "I'm staying here tonight. I was just saying goodnight to Evan."

"Yeah, okay." She passes us to her room. The door slams hard enough that I wince.

"I should get to bed," I say to Evan.

He steps closer to me and wraps his hands around my face. "Everyone has a motive, Grace. Jenna's is to take you away from me. For her own selfish reasons. She doesn't want you to be happy. But I do. Because I love you."

I walk him to the door. He kisses me and murmurs a goodnight against my lips. Once he's gone, and I close and lock the door, I hear Jenna come out of her room.

"What happened?" she asks, and when I turn around, she's standing by the couch.

"He went home." I walk over to her. "Why did you do it?"

"Do what?"

119

"Why did you tell him to break up with me?"

She rears back. "What are you talking about? I didn't—"

"He told me. He told me what you said when I was in the bathroom. How you demanded he stop seeing me," I say, as tears fill my eyes. "Jenna, why would you—"

"Grace, he's lying. I never told him to break up with you." Jenna looks horrified.

"Then why would he tell me you did?" I sniffle and hastily brush away the few tears that managed to escape.

"Because he doesn't want us being friends!" She grips my arms the same way Evan did moments ago. "You want to know what really happened? Evan told me to stay out of your relationship, and if I didn't, I'd regret it. He threatened me, Grace. Is that really the type of guy you want to be with?"

I yank away and step back. "Evan wouldn't do that. He wouldn't make threats. That's not who he is."

"Are you even listening to yourself?" Jenna throws her hands up. "I'm telling you what he said, and you won't even consider it's possible! Why the hell would I make this up?"

"I think you'd say whatever you have to in order to convince me to break up with him."

"No. I wouldn't." Jenna shakes her head. "You know I wouldn't do that."

"I used to believe that, but now? I think you'd say anything to turn me against Evan."

I'm finally happy with my life. I finally have a loving partner. Why won't she let me have this?

"That is not what's happening. It's Evan who's trying to turn you against me because he knows I can see right through the act he puts on."

"He's not putting on an act. You only think that because you've never met a guy like him."

"Grace, you cannot be this blind. The guy is manipulating you." She lets out a disbelieving laugh. "And you're falling for it!"

"Jenna, I know you don't want me dating Evan, but this isn't your life. It's mine." I sigh, and my shoulders drop. "If I want to be with him, you need to accept that. That's what friends do. They support each other. If you're really my friend, you'll stop interfering in my personal life and just be happy for me."

"I'm not—"

I brush past her. "I don't want to talk about this anymore. I'm going to bed."

* * *

The next morning, my headache is gone, but I'm still stressed about Jenna and the fight we had. I don't want to lose her as a friend, but I'm worried that's what will happen if she refuses to support my relationship.

"Martin," I say, going up to him as he cleans the grill. The morning rush is over, and I'm supposed to be on break, but I need to talk to him.

"What's up?" he asks, scraping the grease from the grill.

"I need some advice. About Jenna. I'm sure you've noticed we aren't getting along."

She hasn't spoken to me all morning. I got here at six, and when she arrived at eight, she didn't greet me or even look my way. She's acting like I don't exist.

"Yeah, I noticed," he says, continuing to scrape the grill. "But I didn't think anything of it. My daughters fight all the time, but eventually they make up and everything goes back to normal."

"I don't think that's going to happen with Jenna and me. We had a really big fight. About Evan. My relationship with him."

I check over my shoulder to make sure Jenna's still out waiting on customers. The last thing I need is her stumbling in on this conversation.

"What's her problem with him?"

"She says he's controlling and trying to manipulate me."

He shrugs. "Maybe she's right."

"Are you saying you believe her? You think Evan's controlling?"

"I'm saying Jenna knows you better than anyone," Martin says. "If she thinks this guy isn't right for you, you might consider that what she's saying has some truth to it."

"She doesn't know him well enough to know if he's right for me. She says stuff about him without any proof that it's true." I check over my shoulder once more. "Last night at the bar, when I was in the restroom, she told Evan to break up with me. He said she demanded he end our relationship."

"That doesn't sound like Jenna," Martin says, walking over to the coffeemaker and refilling his cup.

"I thought the same thing." I pause, my gaze shifting down to the floor. "She swore she didn't say it, but Evan wouldn't just make that up."

"You sure about that?" When I look up, Martin is eyeing me over the rim of his coffee mug. "You've known this guy for what? A few weeks?"

"Yeah, but Jenna's been wanting me to break up with him from the beginning. Since I haven't, she told Evan to do it. She's determined to end our relationship."

"She doesn't get to decide that. It's up to you to figure out if this guy's worth all the trouble he's causing."

"He is." I smile as I think of Evan. "I could see us getting married someday."

"Married?" Martin looks at me with concern, almost letting the mug slip from his hands. "You just met the guy. You shouldn't even be thinking about marriage."

"Why not? I'm not getting any younger, and Evan's a great catch. He's smart. Successful. And way more mature than the other guys I've dated."

Martin shakes his head. "I think you need to slow down and get to know this guy a whole lot better before you think about walking down the aisle."

"I didn't say we were getting married next week."

"You meet his family yet?"

"No. He only has his mother, and she lives in California. Evan doesn't talk about her."

"Why is that?" Martin asks, his brows drawing together. "They don't get along?"

"That's what I'm guessing. He hasn't said that, but it doesn't sound like they talk much."

Martin huffs. "A man should be good to his mother. If he's not, it's a sign he won't be good to you, either."

"I don't think that's true. Maybe she wasn't a good mom, and he doesn't like being around her."

"You need to meet this woman, or at least find out why he doesn't have a relationship with her. That'll tell you a lot about who he is as a man."

I've tried getting Evan to talk about his mother, but he never has much to say. I don't see that as a concern. A lot of people don't have close relationships with their parents. And Evan stays busy with his work. It doesn't surprise me that he doesn't call his mother all the time. I'd actually be concerned if he did. I've dated some mama's boys, and it didn't turn out well.

"You gonna take your break?" Martin asks. "You only got a few minutes left."

"Yeah, I'm going."

When I get to the break room, I check my phone and see a message from Evan asking me to call him. I'm sure he's working, but I call him anyway.

123

"Grace," he answers after several rings. "I've been worried about you. How are you feeling?"

"Good. My headache is gone." I plop down on the ratty couch, wincing when a spring pokes into my back.

"Are you at work?"

"Yeah. I'm on break, but I only have a couple minutes left."

"Did you talk with Jenna?" he asks.

Something about the way he asks unnerves me. I can't quite put my finger on it, so I just say, "Last night. She hasn't spoken to me since."

"I'm sorry to hear that. I was hoping you two could work things out."

"Really?" I keep my eye on the door in case Jenna walks in. "Last night you made it sound like you didn't want us being friends at all."

"That's what I wanted to speak with you about. I need to apologize for my behavior last night. I was angry after that conversation I had with Jenna at the bar. I said some things I shouldn't have. I never meant to imply that you can no longer be friends with her. I know how much you value her friendship."

"I do, but I can't be friends with her if she keeps saying bad things about you."

"What are you referring to?"

"She said you were lying. That she never told you to break up with me. She turned it around and made you the bad guy."

"How? What exactly did she say?"

"That you told her to stay out of our relationship, and then she said you threatened her, which is crazy because I know you'd never do that."

"Of course not. I can assure you I did no such thing."

"It's just — Jenna isn't the kind of person to lie like this."

"That shows you how determined she is to keep us apart," he says gently.

"Which is really sad. She should want me to be happy, and she knows you make me happy." I pause, fighting back tears. "I never imagined us drifting apart like this."

"It's not uncommon for people to become angry when they see someone doing better for themselves. It doesn't mean Jenna doesn't care about you. It means she sees a deficiency in herself. Watching you aspire to something better in life may just be a reminder that her own life is lacking."

"I think that's exactly what she's feeling." I sniffle, then take a few deep breaths.

"It's sad, but it doesn't mean you should feel guilty for what's going well in your life."

"You're right. I've been feeling guilty that things have going well for me, but I shouldn't. Why is it wrong for me to have a better life?"

"It's not. You should have the best life possible, and Jenna should want that for you."

"Except I don't think she does."

"Give it time. She might come around, and if she doesn't, then it's her loss. You're a kind and wonderful woman, Grace. If Jenna can't see that, she doesn't deserve you as a friend."

Hearing him say all that, I feel like Evan's acting like a better friend to me than Jenna. He could've told me to end my friendship with her, to not even try to repair it, but instead, he told me to give her time and that he hoped things would work out with her.

I don't know what's going to happen with Jenna and me. Maybe we'll go back to being friends, or maybe this fight will be the end for us. But one thing I know for sure is that Evan isn't going anywhere. I really think he could be my husband someday.

CHAPTER 18

"Are you ever going to talk to me again?" I ask Jenna as she comes into the break room. I just finished my shift and was going to head home, but then Jenna showed up and I felt like I had to say something.

"What's there to talk about?" she asks, plopping down on the couch and scrolling through her phone.

"Jenna, come on. I hate fighting like this."

"I'm not fighting." Her eyes stay on her phone. "I just have nothing to say."

I sit down beside her. "Don't end our friendship because of what happened last night."

"You're the one ending it by taking your boyfriend's side over mine."

"That's not fair. You can't make me choose. I want you both in my life, but I don't know how that'll happen if you constantly put him down and say he's not right for me."

Jenna shrugs. "Do what you want. I'm done trying to protect you. If you want to believe his bullshit, fine. But don't come running back to me when you learn the truth."

"What truth?" I turn to her. "Seriously, Jenna, what do you think he's hiding? You think he's secretly married? Has a bunch of kids he forgot to tell me about?"

She sets her phone down and looks at me. "I don't know, but the guy is way too secretive to not be hiding something. You don't find it odd that every time you ask him about his past, he changes the subject?"

"I know about his past. We've talked about it."

"Oh, really?" She folds her arms over her chest. "And what has he told you? And don't tell me about his jobs. I want to know about his personal life."

"I already told you what I know." I fiddle with the strap of my purse.

"Which was basically nothing," she scoffs. "What about his family? Do they know about you?"

"He only has his mom, and I don't know if he's told her about me. But why does it matter? I'm not dating his mom."

Jenna picks up her phone and texts someone.

"What are you doing?" I ask.

"Making plans for tonight." She continues to text. "Craig's picking me up at six."

"We're done talking?"

"I guess. Nothing I say seems to matter."

"Jenna, I don't want Evan to come between us. I want things to go back to how they were before," I say, grasping her forearm.

She pulls away roughly and swipes through her phone. "That's not going to happen if you're going to keep taking his side."

I sigh. "That's not fair. He's my boyfriend. Of course I'm going to—"

She tosses her phone down and glares at me. "You really think I told him to break up with you? You honestly think I would do that?"

I pause, feeling conflicted. I'd like to think Jenna wouldn't do something like that, but knowing how much she wants Evan to go away, I think it's definitely possible.

"I guess I have my answer." Jenna huffs and gets to her feet. "You should move out."

"Wait." I stand as well, facing her. "You're kicking me out of the apartment?"

"I didn't say that. I'm saying I think you should go live with your boyfriend. It's what he wants, and clearly you'd be happier with him than with me."

"Why would I move out? I have a job here."

"So quit. What do you need a job for when you have a guy like Evan to pay all your bills? Take you out to fancy restaurants? Buy you fancy clothes?"

"You're jealous. That's what this is about, isn't it? You don't like that Evan buys me things and takes me to nice restaurants when you're stuck here, dating guys like Craig."

"What's wrong with Craig?" she says, raising her voice.

"Nothing. I shouldn't have said that. I just meant that—"

"Forget it," she snaps, putting her hand up in front of me. "I don't want hear it. Just go. Be with Evan."

"Hey!" Martin says, appearing at the door to the break room. "What's with all the shouting in here?"

"We're done," Jenna says, glaring at me. "I'll get back to work."

She storms out of the room.

Martin remains at the door. "What happened with you two?"

"She doesn't want me living with her anymore." My cheeks feel hot, my heart's racing, and I can't stop my hands from trembling.

"She kicked you out?" he asks, sounding surprised.

"Long story." I manage a shaky exhale. "I know it's a lot to ask, but could I take a few weeks off?"

"A few weeks? Grace, I'm already short-staffed. I can't go that long without a third waitress."

"Then I guess I have to quit."

"If this is about you needing somewhere to stay, I'm sure we could find you a place. Let me ask around and see if—"

"No. I'm just going to stay with Evan. I can try to make it back here for work until you find another waitress."

"I don't want you driving all the way here from the city. I'll see if the new girl can fill in until I find someone." He pauses, looking at me with concern. "You sure this is what you want?"

I nod and force a smile on my face. "I'm already at Evan's place so much that I practically live with him. I might as well make it official."

"Something doesn't feel right about this. Why don't you give it some more thought?"

"I don't need to. I've made up my mind."

Martin frowns. "I'm gonna miss you, kid. You better come back and see us."

"I will," I say, still with a forced smile, but my eyes are burning from holding back tears.

"I need to get back to work, but you stay in touch. Let me know you're okay," he says, quirking up an eyebrow.

I nod, afraid if I speak, I might cry. Martin leaves while I remain in the break room, feeling sick to my stomach. Am I really doing this? Am I really quitting my job and moving in with Evan? I don't have much of a choice. Jenna doesn't want me in her apartment anymore. She doesn't even want to be friends with me. So, it's either stay with Evan or resign myself to living out of my car for the foreseeable future.

I get out my phone and call Evan.

"Hey," he says in a cheerful tone. "This is a nice surprise. I wasn't expecting you to call. Is everything okay?"

"Um, yeah. I need to ask you something."

"Go ahead."

"Are you still okay with me moving in with you?"

The phone is silent, then Evan says, "Of course. Why do you ask?"

"Because I need to move in. Tonight."

CHAPTER 19

"I can move things around if you need more space," Evan offers as I stand in his huge walk-in closet.

After I called him, he left work and met me at my apartment. We packed everything up, loaded it into his car and mine, and drove to the city. Evan was smiling the whole time, thrilled that I was moving in. I pretended to be happy about it, but as we packed up the boxes, I felt anxious and sick to my stomach. As much as I like Evan, it's too soon to be living with him. But I don't have a choice. I can't afford to get my own place, and I can't stay with Jenna anymore, not when things are so tense between us.

"I have plenty of room," I say, turning to Evan. "I don't have much for clothes."

"Not currently," he says, putting his arms around me, his smile expanding. "But you will. I'm going to take you shopping. Get you a whole new wardrobe. Would you like that?"

"I really don't need anything new."

"Of course you do. You're living in the city now, Grace. You need to dress like you belong here." He says it in a lighthearted way, not like he's putting me down, and yet I feel like that's what he's doing. Maybe that's just me feeling out of place here. Everything at Evan's apartment is so upscale and expensive. I'm always worried I'll break something. Evan's told me it's fine if I do — that he'll just replace the item — but I think he'd be mad if something actually happened. Last week, I picked up a glass globe he had on a bookshelf, and he snatched it from me and put it back. He said it was very delicate and shouldn't be touched.

"Grace, what's wrong?" Evan asks. He lifts my face enough for our eyes to meet. "Are you not happy to be here?"

"I am. It's just a little sudden. I didn't expect to be moving in today." I look back to the closet filled nearly to the brim with Evan's belongings and at the tiny space left over where my own clothes hang. "I can't believe Jenna kicked me out."

"I'm sorry about that," Evan says, rubbing my arm. "Unfortunately, it doesn't surprise me. I genuinely believe Jenna is jealous of you and the life you have with me. Seeing you every day, living with you, knowing how much happier you've been lately? It might have been too constant a reminder that you have something she will likely never have for herself."

"But Jenna's not like that, or she didn't used to be. I don't know what happened. Why she's suddenly acting like this."

Tears burn my eyes yet again. How did things go so wrong so fast?

"Let's not talk about it." Evan brings me in for a hug. "I hate seeing you so upset. Why don't I take you out? You haven't eaten since this morning. We'll go have a nice relaxing dinner, then we'll come back here and you can get some sleep."

I pull back and look at him. "What if this doesn't work out? What if we break up? I'll have nowhere to go."

"That's not going to happen." Evan slowly runs the back of his hand over my cheek. "You're mine, Grace. And I have no plans to ever let you go."

My chest tightens hearing him say that. I know he's only trying to assure me about our relationship, but instead, it makes me feel trapped here, like Evan wouldn't let me leave even if I wanted to.

I'm being ridiculous. Evan isn't going to hold me hostage. Why am I even thinking that way? Is it because I'm used to being independent? Doing everything on my own? A month ago, I was complaining about that, wishing I had someone in my life to help me. Now I do, and I'm finding fault with him.

What is wrong with me? Am I unable to be happy? Am I so used to struggling that it feels uncomfortable when I'm not?

"Would you like to clean up before we leave?" Evan asks.

I take that to mean I should. I'm wearing jeans and a sweatshirt, my hair's in a messy bun, and I still smell like the diner.

"Yeah, I'll go take a shower," I say.

"Would you care if I join you?" he asks, his voice low and sexy.

How could he think I'd want to be intimate at a time like this? I just lost my best friend. And my job. And my apartment. Making love is the last thing I want to do right now.

"I'd rather shower alone," I say. "Sorry, I'm not in the mood."

"I understand." He gives me a kiss. "Go ahead and get ready. I'll make us a reservation for eight."

It's just before seven. I don't need an hour to get ready. I'd rather go earlier, but Evan has already decided to make the reservation. I don't want to be out late tonight, but I guess it doesn't matter. It's not like I have to get up for work in the morning.

What am I going to do tomorrow? And the next day? And the day after that? I can't just sit around Evan's apartment. I'll lose my mind.

"I need to get a job," I say during dinner. Evan took me to a steakhouse, which isn't the type of restaurant he'd normally choose. He rarely eats red meat, but he knows I love it. He's trying to cheer me up, but it's not working. I'm still really depressed about what happened today.

"You're not getting a job," Evan says, setting his knife and fork down. "I'll pay for whatever you need."

"I don't want you paying for everything. I want to make my own money. And I need something to do. I can't sit around all day."

"You're ill, Grace," he says, taking my hand in his. "You need to rest. Work will only make your condition worse."

"I'm not ill. I get headaches. That's different."

"Maybe so, but your headaches are brought on by stress. Having a job will cause you unnecessary stress."

"It depends on the job."

"We'll discuss this later," he says, rubbing my hand. "There's no rush to decide. For now, it would be good for you to take a few weeks off. You can get to know the city. Go to some museums. Perhaps attend some art exhibits."

I hesitate. "I don't actually like museums, Evan. And I'm not all that into art."

"You don't like it because you haven't experienced it." He smiles, but it looks forced. "It's unfamiliar to you. Once you immerse yourself in the arts, you'll soon find you're enjoying yourself. And it's an excellent way to meet people. You might even consider volunteering."

"I need to do something that pays. I want to make my own money, Evan. It's important to me."

"I understand," he says, but it sounds like he's just agreeing to end the conversation. He lets go of my hand and leans back in his chair. "I love having you here. It's so nice to be able to take you home instead of having to take you all the way back to New Jersey."

Hearing him say that just makes me think of Jenna all over again. She hasn't texted me all day. She would've gotten home from work around five. I thought she'd see my empty room and regret telling me to leave, but if that were true, she would've called. Reaching down to my purse, I take out my phone and check to see if I have any messages.

"What are you doing?" Evan asks.

"Checking my phone," I say, sliding it back into my purse.

"You shouldn't do that at dinner. It's disrespectful."

I wish he wouldn't scold me like that. It's not like I've been looking at my phone all through dinner. It's been in my purse until just now. Even then, all I did was glance at it.

"I was seeing if Jenna called. I thought she might when she got home and saw my stuff was gone."

"Why would she call you about that, Grace? She knew you were moving out. She's the one who ordered you to do it."

I shrug. "I wasn't sure she meant it. I thought maybe she did it just because she was angry."

"What are you saying? That you regret moving in with me?" Evan's jaw tightens.

"No, not at all," I say, but I do kind of regret it. I was hoping Evan and I would date longer before we moved in together. "I just don't like how it happened. I didn't want it to be because Jenna and I were fighting."

"Didn't you say your arrangement was never meant to be permanent? That her offer to let you stay there was only temporary?"

"Yes, but she never pushed me to leave, either," I say. I don't want to think Evan's being purposely blind to my feelings, but he's starting to really make me angry. "She would've let me stay if we hadn't gotten into a fight."

"Maybe, but then what?" Evan crosses his arms. "What if something else happened that caused her to evict you? For example, if she became serious with that bartender and asked him to move in?"

"She wouldn't kick me out because of that."

"My point is that it wasn't a good situation. You weren't on the lease, and you had nothing in writing about your arrangement. I know you consider Jenna a friend, but friends can turn on you, which is precisely what Jenna did. If you didn't have me in your life, you might've ended up homeless."

I pause, then say, "You could do the same thing."

His brows draw together. "What do you mean?"

"You could tell me to leave as easily as Jenna did. If we get into a fight, or you decide you don't want me living with you, you could tell me to go."

"I would never do that." Evan reaches across the table to hold my hand, stroking the back of it with his thumb. "I love you, Grace. You're part of my life."

"Yes, but that doesn't mean—"

"Evan?" a woman says, interrupting me. I look up and see a beautiful blonde woman dressed in a dark suit standing next to our table. She looks close to Evan's age or maybe a year or two younger. "I thought that was you. What a surprise."

"It certainly is," Evan says, pushing his chair back. He stands and gives her a brief hug. "What brings you to New York?"

"I have a new job and the corporate office is here. I'm doing training this week," she says, glancing my way.

"Congratulations on the job," he says, but he doesn't seem sincere.

He seems like he wants her to go away. He's talking fast, and the muscles in his neck look tense enough to snap. Actually, his whole face looks tense.

What's going on with him? Who is this woman? An old girlfriend?

"So, what are you doing in the city?" the woman asks Evan.

"I moved here. A couple months ago. For a consulting job, nothing permanent."

"Meaning you'll be going back to California?"

"I haven't decided. I'm in no rush to return. It's been nice being here. Trying something new."

"I'm sure your mother misses you," the woman says, smiling a little. "She must be completely lost without you."

What is she talking about? Why would Evan's mom be lost without him? It sounds like he never talks to her, and he hasn't gone home to visit her. I assumed they didn't have much of a relationship.

"Not at all," Evan rushes to say. "She keeps busy with all her activities. Anyway, I should get back to dinner and let you be on your way."

"Aren't you going to introduce me?" the woman says, glancing at me again.

"Oh, yes, this is Grace," Evan says. "Grace, this is Ashley, an acquaintance of mine from California."

"Acquaintance?" Ashley says with a laugh. "And here I thought we were friends. After all, I was almost in your—"

"Yes, forgive me," Evan says. "I meant to say friend. It's just I haven't seen you for so long."

"Maybe we could catch up," Ashley says. "I'm here for a couple days. We could meet for a drink. Are you free tomorrow night?"

"I'm afraid not," Evan says. "I have a rather busy week."

"It's because of me," I blurt out, feeling the need to tell this woman who I am. Why didn't Evan say I'm his girlfriend? Is he embarrassed by me? "I just moved in with Evan, and he's helping me get settled."

Ashley looks at me, then back at Evan. "You're living with her? So this must be serious."

"It was lovely seeing you, Ashley, but as you can see, Grace and I are in the middle of dinner. Perhaps I could call you sometime and we could catch up."

"Yes, I think we should," she says in a curt tone. "I must say, I'm rather surprised you've moved on so quickly. I thought it'd be at least a year before you—"

"Ashley, please," Evan interrupts. "My meal is getting cold."

She pauses, then gives him a tight smile. "Call me soon. I look forward to catching up." She looks over at me. "It was nice meeting you, Grace."

"You too," I say, still wondering what Evan's history is with this woman.

As she leaves the restaurant, my mind goes back to what she said about Evan moving on quickly — moving on from *what*? What was she talking about? And why did Evan interrupt her before she could finish whatever she was about to say?

CHAPTER 20

"Would you like dessert?" Evan asks.

"No, I'm good," I say, setting my napkin on the table. "How do you know that woman?"

"She's an old friend."

"When you say *friend*, do you mean girlfriend?"

He chuckles. "No. Absolutely not. She's not my type."

Not his type? Ashley's gorgeous. From the look of the suit she was wearing, she's probably rich, too, with a high-level job. She seems way more like his type than I do.

"She acted like you two had a history." I take a sip from the wine Evan ordered.

"I wouldn't call it that," Evan says, picking up his own wine-glass now. "She was friends with someone I knew, but I never cared much for her. She was always butting in where she shouldn't."

"Like how? What did she do?"

"I don't want to get into it."

I sit back in my chair, my eyes on Evan. "Evan, come on. Don't brush me off like that. Tell me how you know Ashley."

"I already did. There's nothing else to say."

"Why did she seem surprised that you were with me? And that we were living together?"

"I have no idea. It's getting late. We should go," he says, taking out his wallet. He looks around the restaurant. "The server should've checked on us by now."

I'm not leaving until I get the answers I want. "Why are you being so secretive?"

"Grace, let it go. Ashley is simply someone I used to know."

"She's more than that. I could tell. So what's the story?"

Evan lets out an irritated sigh and sets his wallet down. "If you must know, Ashley was friends with a woman I dated."

"Recently?"

"No. It was some time ago."

"Was it serious? Your relationship with this woman?"

"It could've been. Unfortunately, things didn't go as we'd hoped, and it ended."

"If it wasn't recent, why did Ashley say she was surprised you moved on so quickly?"

"I assume she expected me to spend more time grieving the end of the relationship. But I spent more than enough time doing that. I needed to move on, and I did." He smiles at me. "I found someone much better suited for me. A beautiful woman who I love dearly and am completely devoted to."

He's trying to change the subject and focus on me — and us — instead of talking about this woman he used to date. But I'm not done asking questions. There was something odd about that conversation with Ashley. There's something Evan isn't telling me. Something he doesn't want me to know.

"Do you ever talk to her?" I ask. "That woman you used to date?"

Evan leans back, definitely annoyed with me now. "We're done discussing my exes. It's extremely disrespectful to you."

"I don't think it's disrespectful. It doesn't bother me to hear you talk about your exes. What bothers me is that you're refusing to talk about them. Why are you being so secretive about—"

"I'm not being secretive," he says in a hushed, angry tone. He leans forward with narrow eyes and lowers his voice. "I'm being respectful of our relationship. Perhaps you think it's perfectly fine to talk about past lovers, but I find it very distasteful, and I would like you to stop with these incessant questions."

He waves at a server going by, stopping her.

"Is there a problem?" she asks.

"Yes, we've been waiting forever to get our check. Could you please go get our server?"

She nods. "I'll send him right over." She takes off to get him.

"Why are you in such a hurry to leave?" I ask.

"Because I will not argue with you in public."

"We aren't arguing. We're having a discussion," I say as calmly as possible. No use in both of us getting angry.

The server comes over to our table. "Can I get you anything else?"

"The check, please," Evan says, tersely.

He sets it on the table. "I'll take it whenever you're ready. No rush."

As the server leaves, Evan sets cash on top of the bill. "Let's go."

I get up from the table, shocked that Evan is acting like this. We were having a nice dinner, and then that woman showed up, and Evan became a totally different person. There's definitely more to that story than he's telling me.

On the ride home, Evan doesn't say a word to me. He takes my hand, though, and doesn't let go for the entire ride. Maybe I blew things out of proportion at dinner. I still want to continue our conversation, but a night of solid sleep will help me approach it a little more rationally.

"You should get to bed," Evan says when we're back at the apartment. "You've had a long day."

"What about you?" I ask as he goes over to the bar and pours himself a drink. "Aren't you coming to bed?"

"I have some things to do in my office."

"Can't it wait until tomorrow? Whatever you have to do?"

"No." Evan takes a swig of his drink. "I left work to come get you. Now I'm behind and need to finish what I didn't get done."

"Oh," I say, feeling bad he missed work because of me. "Sorry. You should've said something. I could've found somewhere else to stay."

"Grace, no. I didn't mean to imply—" He walks over, looks down, then back up at me. "Forgive me for being harsh with you. I'm just tired. It's been a long day for both of us." He gives me a kiss. "I'll join you as soon as I can."

"Okay. Goodnight."

I give him a slight smile before going down the short hallway leading to the bedroom. As I enter the opulent room, sadness comes over me as I realize I'm not just here for a night or even a week but for good. I should be happy about that. I'm with my boyfriend, living in a beautiful apartment. But I miss my old room and my old apartment. More than that, I miss Jenna.

When I get into bed, I can't fall asleep. I keep thinking about that woman at the restaurant and her strange encounter with Evan. I grab my phone from the nightstand, open a browser window, and do a search for Evan.

I've done this many times before and found almost nothing about him, so I don't know why I think anything would've changed. It hasn't. There's still nothing online about his exes. I can't even find a photo of them together.

Evan can't stand social media, so he doesn't have any accounts. He's very protective of his privacy and has told me many times not to post any personal information online. He said it's dangerous to have that stuff out there and that I'm basically handing over my information to scammers and criminals.

I told him I wasn't worried about it and that I was still going to post stuff online, but he made me promise not to post anything about him or us, including any photos. At the time, I didn't think much of it, knowing how much he values his privacy. But now I'm wondering if he insisted on it because he's worried someone will see us, like an ex-girlfriend.

Or maybe a current girlfriend.

What if that's it? What if Evan has a girlfriend and is hiding her from me? She could live in California and have no idea I exist, just like I didn't know she exists. Maybe that's why Evan looked so panicked when he saw Ashley at the restaurant. Because she knows he has a girlfriend back home. Is that why Evan didn't introduce me as his girlfriend? Because he didn't want her to find out he was cheating?

I blow out a breath. This is ridiculous. I'm coming up with crazy stories that I'm sure aren't even close to the truth. If Evan would just be more open about his past, I wouldn't be questioning him like this. I'd trust that he's being honest with me. But when he keeps refusing to talk about stuff or changes the subject when I ask him questions, it makes me think he's hiding something.

This can't continue. Evan and I are living together now. We're committed to each other. He can't keep things from me, especially about his past. He should be willing to tell me anything.

The only reason he wouldn't is if there's something he doesn't want me to know.

CHAPTER 21

"Good morning, beautiful," Evan says.

I open my eyes and see him sitting beside me on the bed, already dressed for the day.

"What time is it?"

"Nine o'clock." He runs his hand along the side of my face. "How do you feel?"

"Good. I slept really well."

"I noticed," he says. "You didn't hear me come in last night."

"I must've been tired," I say, sitting up and stretching my arms over my head.

Evan grins and gives me a peck on the lips. "Now that you're rested, I'm taking you out for the day."

"Out where?"

"Shopping. You need some new clothes. I don't want you wearing items that have tears or stains. You need to throw those things out."

"Evan, I don't need anything. All I'm doing is sitting around the apartment all day. And I don't really feel like going out. I'm tired. Yesterday was a rough day for me."

He holds my hands. "Grace, moving here is a fresh start. You have a whole new life ahead of you. New clothes will reflect that new life. And we won't just be sitting around. We'll be going out. You need to experience all the city has to offer."

"Or we could stay in." I flash him a sexy smile. "Just the two of us."

"We could, and we will, but I also need to get you out. You've led a very sheltered life. It'll be good for you to experience new things."

What new things is he talking about? And why do I have to experience them now, when I'm already struggling with the new experience of living here? I'm not great with change. It stresses me out. I've told Evan that, but he insists change is a good kind of stress, the kind that makes you grow and learn.

"Go shower and get dressed," he says, getting up. "I've got a full day planned."

"What about your job? Aren't you working today?"

"I took the day off, although I do need to respond to some emails, but other than that, my focus will be completely on you." He leans down for another kiss. "I'll be in my office. Come get me when you're ready."

This is so strange. Why is he taking me shopping? Why today? Couldn't we wait and do it this weekend? I know my clothes aren't great, but I have a few nice things. And Evan's already bought me some dresses to wear when we go out. That's more than enough to get me through the week.

After I shower, I put on my favorite pair of jeans and a loose-knit sweater, then return to the bathroom to finish doing my makeup. I unlock my phone to play some music and see a text from Jenna from last night. My heart races with excitement but also dread, wondering if the text is good or bad. I open it and am disappointed when I see that all it says is, *Hey*. That's all she sent. One word. But I guess it's better than nothing.

I'm tempted to text her, but then I decide it might be better to call her. My heart beats faster as I wait for her to pick up. I hate that I'm nervous to talk to her. Just a day ago, she was my best friend, and now I don't know what I'm going to say to her.

"Grace," she answers. It's followed by an awkward pause. "Are you okay?"

My throat tightens. I miss her so much. "I'm fine. Are you at work?"

"Yeah, but I'm on my break." Another awkward pause. "Did you get my text?"

"I just saw it." I can't tell if we're just going to do the "small talk" thing or if Jenna misses me as much as I miss her.

"I got worried when you didn't respond. I wasn't sure if you were still mad at me or if something had happened to you."

"Nothing happened. I just didn't see your text. And I'm not mad at you. . . I miss you, Jenna."

"I miss you, too. I'm sorry for getting so angry yesterday. I shouldn't have told you to move out. It's not what I wanted. Any chance you'd consider moving back?"

"I can't. I just moved here. I don't want to move again. And I quit my job," I say quietly.

"You could get it back. Martin hasn't hired anyone. He hasn't even started looking."

"It's tempting, but I need to give this a chance. I didn't expect to be living with Evan this soon, but now that I'm here, I feel like we need to try living together and see if we can make it work."

"How's it going so far?"

"Good, but it hasn't even been a day. I need to give it more time."

"What are you going to do for a job? I was thinking you could work at one of those fancy bars near Wall Street." Jenna laughs. "Drunk rich guys probably leave huge tips."

Her laugh makes me smile. "I'll look online and see what's available. I'd do it today, but Evan has plans for us."

"Doesn't he have to work?"

"He took the day off, which is really sweet. He knows I'm feeling a little lost being here with no job and no friends. I'm sure he took the day off to cheer me up."

"What are you guys going to do?"

"He's taking me shopping to get some new clothes."

She's quiet for so long that I check to make sure the call is still connected. "Jenna? You still there?"

"What's wrong with the clothes you have?" Her voice is a bit tenser than it was moments ago.

"They're old and worn out. And Evan says my clothes aren't what people here wear."

"Grace, you can wear whatever you want. You don't have to listen to him."

I sigh. "Jenna, please don't do this. Evan's not the bad guy here."

"I'm not making him the bad guy. I just think you should wear what you want."

"And I will. I didn't say Evan gets to decide what I buy. We'll be picking things out together."

"Or you could shop by yourself and—" She stops herself. "Never mind. I'm going to keep quiet."

"Thank you," I say, relieved she didn't turn this into another fight. "So how was your date with Craig?"

"It was good. We were supposed to go to dinner, but I wasn't feeling up to it because of . . . well, you moving out. I was going to cancel on him, but then he showed up at my door with sacks of groceries and made me dinner."

"Aww, that's so sweet." I'm happy for her. Craig seems good for her.

"I know, right? No guy's ever made me dinner. It was a really good night." I hear a door open. "Oh, I gotta go. My break's almost over."

"It was good talking to you, Jenna."

"You too. I'm glad you're doing okay. And hey, the offer is always there if you decide to move back."

"Thanks, but I really want to give this a chance."

There's a knock on the door. "Grace?"

"I'll talk to you later, Jenna." I end the call, then say to Evan, "I'm almost ready. I just need to do my makeup."

He opens the door, his eyes dropping immediately to my phone. "Who were you talking to?"

"Jenna. I managed to catch her on her break." I slip my phone into my back pocket and face the mirror.

"I thought you were no longer talking to her," Evan says, his brows drawing together.

"That's because we were fighting. Now we're not."

Evan comes into the bathroom and stands directly behind me, a lot closer than I think he should. "I really wish you hadn't done that."

I swallow and eye his reflection in the mirror. "Done what?"

"Talked to her. She just kicked you out of her apartment."

"It's better I talked to her now than later. We just needed to clear the air so we could get back to normal."

"And what's normal? Her trying to turn you against me?"

"That's not what she was doing." I turn to face Evan. "She was trying to look out for me. She just went about it the wrong way."

"Nothing's going to change, Grace. She's still jealous of you, and because of that, she'll continue to make me the villain in her efforts to get you to leave me."

"Didn't you just tell me yesterday that I should give her another chance?"

"That was before she evicted you. A friend wouldn't do that. Jenna is clearly not someone you can count on. You need to get some distance from her, which you have now that you're living here, but I think you need to stop talking to her as well."

"Are you crazy?" I say, thinking he can't possibly mean that. "I'm not going to stop talking to her. She's like family to me."

"But now you have me for family," he says, taking my hand. "You don't need her."

"Actually, I do," I say, pulling my hand away. "And I don't like you telling me I can't talk to her."

He must hear the anger in my voice because his shoulders drop, and he slowly nods. "You're right. I'm sorry, Grace. I just don't like seeing you hurt like you were yesterday. I felt your pain as if it were my own."

My heart melts hearing him say that. I keep doubting his love for me, telling myself it's too soon for him to feel this way, but I know his love is real. He wouldn't say something like that if it wasn't.

"I'll let you finish getting ready." He leaves the bathroom and then turns back. "I made some coffee. Would you like me to bring you some?"

"I'd love that." I give him a small grin. "Thank you."

He returns moments later with the coffee, made with just the right amount of cream. Most guys wouldn't even pay attention to how I take my coffee, but Evan noticed and made it exactly how I like it. It's a small thing, but it's more proof of how much Evan loves me and wants me to be happy.

I was worried our relationship would change when I moved in with him, but so far, things are going well. I just hope it stays that way.

CHAPTER 22

"How do you like it here?" Evan asks, gazing at me across the table. "Are you enjoying living in the city?"

"It's great," I say, even as my shoulders slump. "But I'm exhausted. I'm not used to all the crowds. And all the walking."

Evan smiles. "It takes some getting used to. I felt the same way my first week here. In California, everyone drives. It took time to adjust to all the walking. And a more comfortable pair of shoes."

"Was that an actual joke, Evan Sinclair?" I tease; he's always so serious.

"I suppose it was," he says like he didn't realize it was funny. "Speaking of shoes, we'll have to shop for those next."

"We already did. You got me those walking shoes."

"I meant shoes appropriate for wearing out, not fitness shoes."

"The walking shoes go with jeans, which is mostly what I wear."

"I'd like you to dress up more now that you're here. Dressing well is good for building confidence. Try it, and you'll see what I mean."

I decide not to argue with him. Evan is always saying things like that, as if he needs to teach me things. I just ignore him. I'll dress however I want.

We spent the entire day going to different stores and came home with way more clothes than I'll ever need. I'll have to get rid of some of my old clothes to make room for the new. But most of them needed to go. Even the ones that weren't torn or stained either didn't fit right, or the fabric was faded and pilled. I could've kept wearing them, but it does feel nice to have clothes that are both new and fit me properly.

For the most part, Evan let me buy what I wanted, but it was all from upscale stores and designer brands. Even a basic pair of jeans was way nicer than I'd normally buy. Evan insisted I get some fancier clothes as well. He picked out this long black evening gown that's gorgeous, but I can't imagine ever wearing it. Other than prom, I don't know why anyone would wear a gown like that. Evan picked out several other dresses for me as well, some casual and some more formal. He says I'll need them for the various events he plans to take me to or when we go out for a really nice dinner.

Tonight is one of those occasions. Evan insisted we go out and celebrate my first day here. Before we left the apartment, he picked out one of my new dresses — a silky red dress with a slit up the side — and told me to put it on. Then he surprised me with a diamond necklace. As he clasped it around my neck, I told him it was so sparkly it looked real. He laughed and said that it was and that he'd never buy me fake diamonds. I love the necklace, but now that I know the diamonds are real, I'm worried I'll lose it. I keep checking my neck to make sure it's there.

The restaurant we're at is another fancy, expensive place, which seems to be the only kind of place Evan likes to go. Maybe now that I live with him, I'll convince him to go to some normal restaurants, ones where I can actually pronounce the items on the menu.

"What's on your mind?" Evan asks. "You seem lost in your thoughts."

"This restaurant. I like it, but it's so fancy. I was wondering if we could try some places that are more for normal people."

He smiles a little. "Are you saying I'm not normal?"

"No, I mean places that have normal things on the menu. Like ribs. Or pork chops. Or just a basic hamburger."

"Those places tend to be very loud and overly crowded. I prefer a more intimate setting, especially tonight."

"What's so special about tonight?" I ask.

"I wanted you to have the perfect ending to your first day here."

The perfect ending for me would've been a cheeseburger and fries rather than whatever I just had. I'm not even sure what I ate. I read the description of it, but none of the words made sense. Some of them weren't even in English.

The server comes up to our table and says to Evan, "Are you ready for dessert?"

Evan doesn't look his way. "In a moment."

"Very well," he says, giving Evan a slight smile before leaving.

"We're having dessert?" I lay my fork across my plate. "I don't think I have room for it."

"You can just have a few bites, although you might like it enough to have more than that."

"Why? What is it?"

"You'll see in a minute," Evan says with a sly grin. "First, I need to ask you something."

"Go ahead." I take a drink of water.

"Could you put that down?" Evan asks.

I eye him over the rim, then slowly place the glass beside my plate. Why is he suddenly so concerned about my water glass?

He takes hold of my left hand. "When I said tonight was special, I wasn't just saying that because it's your first day here."

"Then what did you mean?"

"It's special because it's the start of our life together." His eyes lock on mine as he reaches into his suit jacket's inner pocket. "I never expected this to happen, Grace. I never expected to fall for someone this quickly. But the fact that I have tells me that this is right. That you're the one I'm meant to be with. Forever."

Wait, what is happening? What's he talking about? He's not going to . . . No. No way. He wouldn't. It's too soon.

"Grace," he says, sliding back his chair.

My heart's pounding so hard I can feel it in my ears. He's not really doing this, is he? He can't be.

"I love you more than anything," Evan says, coming beside me and getting down on one knee. In his palm is a tiny box from a very famous jewelry store. "And I would be honored if you would agree to be my wife." He opens the tiny box, and I see a large diamond engagement ring. "Grace, will you marry me?"

I'm speechless. Completely shocked. We met a month ago, and now he's proposing? I've heard of people getting engaged this fast, but it's rare, and I bet a lot of them don't stay together. How could they? A month isn't long enough to know someone well enough to *marry* them.

"Grace," he says softly. "Say something."

"I, um . . ." I glance around the restaurant. People are staring at us. I look back at Evan, at the desperate look in his eyes as he anxiously awaits my answer. The word escapes before I can stop it. "Yes."

Relief washes over him, and he gets up from the floor. He takes my hand once more and slides on the ring.

"It's perfect," he murmurs, gazing at the ring on my finger. He kisses me, then whispers in my ear, "You're mine, Grace. Forever."

There are those words again. *You're mine.*

CHAPTER 23

"Good morning, my beautiful bride-to-be," Evan says.

I open my eyes and see Evan's face hovering over mine. He's beaming, looking happier than I've ever seen him. He's already dressed in a white collared button-down shirt and dark-brown slacks with a black leather belt.

"Good morning," I mutter.

My stomach knots as I remember what happened last night. Evan proposed, and I said yes. Why did I say that? What was I thinking?

"How did you sleep?" he asks.

"Fine." I force out a smile. "How about you?"

"I slept better than I have in years." He gives me a kiss. "I had a dream in which we were already married. We had a big, beautiful house and you were . . ."

His voice trails off.

"I was what?"

He glances at my stomach, his smile growing bigger. "You were expecting our first child."

First child? We just got engaged. We've never discussed having children, and he's already having dreams about it?

"I need to get up," I mumble, shoving the covers off. "I'm not feeling well."

"Is it your head? Wait here. I'll get one of your pills."

"Evan, no, it's not my head."

"Then what is it?" He glances at my stomach again. "Do you think you might be—"

"No!" I exclaim, terrified at the thought. I'm not ready to be a mother. I'm not even sure I'm ready to be a wife. "I'm just feeling overwhelmed. So much has happened this week. I quit my job. Moved in with you. And now we're engaged? It's too much all at once."

"I agree, it's a lot," Evan says, taking my hand. "Is there anything I can do to make things easier for you?"

I look at him and notice his happy expression has turned to one of concern, almost sadness. But I have to say this. I can't hold it back. It's not fair to him, and it's not fair to me, either.

"Evan, I care about you. I really do. But what happened last night, us getting engaged . . . I shouldn't have said yes." I look down, not wanting to see the hurt on his face. "I'm sorry, but I can't agree to marry you. Not yet."

"I don't understand. Are you saying you don't want to be with me?" Evan's hand tightens around mine like he's not going to let me go that easily.

"No, it's not that." My eyes rise to his. "I'm just not ready to take such a big step. We just moved in together."

"Grace, we don't have to get married right away. It's only an engagement. A promise to be together. A commitment to making this work. Why wouldn't you want that?"

Technically, he's right. An engagement isn't marriage. I'm not legally bound to him in any way. Being engaged may not even lead to a wedding.

"Okay," I tell him, gazing at the ring on my hand. It's absolutely gorgeous. He did an excellent job picking it out. I can't imagine what it must've cost.

"'Okay'? What does that mean? That you're accepting my proposal?"

"Yes," I say, getting an idea. "Under one condition."

"What is it?"

"I want to meet your mother."

Evan jerks back. "My mother?" he says harshly. "What does my mother have to do with this?"

"She's your only family, and if we get married, she'll be my family, too," I say with a shrug. "I want to meet her or the engagement is off."

"Grace, that's ridiculous." Evan scoffs. "Meeting my mother is not going to change how you feel about our engagement. Either you want to be with me, or you don't."

"I don't think it's unreasonable to want to know more about you before I agree to marry you. If my parents were still alive, I'd want you to meet them. And they'd want to meet you." I pause. "Does your mother even know I exist?"

Evan gets up. "I'm going to go make us some coffee."

He takes off, not answering my question. I can only assume that means his mother doesn't know about me. Does he not think she'd approve of me? Maybe his past girlfriends were all women with college degrees and successful careers. Now he's with someone who barely made it through high school and who, until just recently, worked at a diner. Is that why he hasn't told his mother about me?

"You didn't answer my question," I say, joining Evan in the kitchen.

"What would you like to eat?" he asks, pushing the button to start the coffeemaker.

"Evan, I want an answer." I step in front of him. "Did you tell your mother about me?"

He rubs his hand over his jaw. "No."

"Why? Because you don't think she'd—"

"Because I'm a grown man," Evan says through clenched teeth. "I don't need to run my decisions by my mother."

"I'm not saying you do. I'm just wondering why you wouldn't tell her about me."

"My mother and I aren't that close." He walks to the fridge and takes out a carton of eggs.

"Does that mean you don't talk to her?"

"Of course I talk to her. But I don't tell her every detail of my life," he snaps, closing the fridge. He sets the eggs down on the counter next to the stove. "How many would you like?"

"I'm not hungry." I walk over to him, lean back against the counter, and cross my arms. "Why haven't you told her about me?"

"Because it doesn't concern her. She's not the one marrying you, Grace. I am."

"But she's your mother. You don't think your mother should meet the woman you want to marry?"

"No. I don't." He cracks an egg and drops it in the skillet, then cracks another one. "I'd like you to end this line of questioning. I'm feeling very attacked right now."

"You feel attacked because I'm asking about your mother?" I ask, frustrated. "Evan, these are normal questions. If you think I'm attacking you by asking them, then I don't see how this can work."

"What do you mean?" he asks, turning to face me.

"If we're going to get married, I should be able to ask you anything. If you feel attacked when all I did was ask about your mother, this won't work. I can't be with someone who isn't willing to talk to me, especially about their own family."

Evan sucks air through his nose, then blows it forcefully from his mouth. "Fine. We'll talk about my mother. What do you want to know?"

"I want to know why you haven't told her about me."

"Because my mother feels the need to give me advice, which I don't want to hear. So I've chosen not to tell her about my personal life." He takes a spatula from the drawer and moves the eggs around the skillet.

"Your mom gives you advice about who you're dating? Is that what you mean?"

He takes a plate from the cupboard. "Yes. She thinks she knows what's best for me. She forgets I'm a grown man who is quite capable of choosing a partner."

"What if it gets serious? Like the girl you were engaged to. Did your mom ever meet her?" I go over to the coffeemaker to pour us some coffee.

"Yes. They were actually quite close. My mother was helping her plan the wedding."

"I don't get it. You made it sound like your mom doesn't like the women you date."

"I never said she doesn't like them. Actually, thinking back, there have only been one or two she didn't like."

"And you don't think she'd like me? That's why you haven't told her about me?"

He moves the skillet off the burner. "I don't know if she'd like you, but it doesn't matter. I'm not looking for my mother's approval."

"Then why not just tell her about me? Why keep me a secret?" I add cream to our coffee, hoping that by keeping my attention focused elsewhere, Evan won't feel as attacked as he claims.

"I'll tell her when the time is right." He slides the eggs onto the plate. "Are you sure you don't want me to make you some?"

"No, I'll just have coffee." I watch as Evan gets a fork from the drawer. "When's the right time? When are you going to tell her?"

"I haven't decided."

I turn and face him. "Evan, we're engaged. I think it's time to tell your mother about me."

He sets his plate on the table and walks over to me, his eyes narrowed.

"I said I will tell her when the time is right. I am not discussing this any further." He pauses, his jaw tightening. "I need to spend some time in my office. I won't be able to take today off, but I'll work from home so I'm around if you need me."

He takes off, leaving his uneaten plate of eggs on the table. I'm going to stay away from him. I don't like how he acted just now, and I definitely don't like that he thinks telling his mother about us is only his decision to make. If Evan and I do ultimately get married, this woman is going to be my family. I have the right to meet her, and Evan should want me to. He shouldn't be hiding me from her like I'm some dark, shameful secret.

An hour later, I'm showered and dressed and wondering what to do with my day. I take out my phone to search for jobs and see the giant ring on my finger. I'm suddenly filled with anger, because of Evan and his insistence that he keep me a secret from his mother until he feels it's the right time. I'm not okay with that. I need to meet this woman. She's Evan's mother. She raised him, and she did it mostly on her own since his father died when he was very young.

I bet I could learn a lot from his mother, things Evan won't tell me. He's so secretive about his past, and I'm tired of it. If I'm going to go through with marrying this man, I need to know more about him. And if he won't tell me, I'll have his mother do it.

I storm down the hall to Evan's office and knock on the door. "Evan, can I come in?"

"What do you need?"

I open the door and walk up to his desk. "I want to meet her. I want to meet your mother."

"Grace, we discussed this. I told you—"

"If you don't let me meet her, then I don't want this." I slip the ring off my finger and set it on his desk. "The engagement is off."

Evan exhales a breath before glaring up at me from his high-backed leather desk chair. "Grace, you're being unreasonable. I told you I'd tell her when the time is right. Once I've done so, I'd be happy to let you meet her."

"Yeah, well, that's not good enough. I'm not waiting months, or however long you're thinking, to meet your mother. I want to meet her as soon as possible."

"Why?" He bolts up from his chair, and I instinctively step back. "Why are you so obsessed with meeting my mother?"

"Because she's your *mother*!" I shout, tossing my hands in the air. "I get that you don't understand why this is important to me, but it is, and you need to accept that. If you don't, then maybe you should be with someone else."

"Grace, no." He races over to me. "Don't even say that."

His eyes are filled with that same panic that always appears when I mention us potentially breaking up. "You know how much I love you. There isn't anyone else I'd rather be with than you."

"Then call your mother. Right now. Tell her I want to meet her next week."

"Next week isn't possible. My mother is a very busy woman. She's very active in her community. She volunteers for several organizations."

"I'm sure she'd make time to meet me." I point to his phone on the desk. "Call her. Ask her when she could come here."

"I'll call her later. It's early there. She may not be up yet."

I'm not backing down on this. If his mother's as busy as he says she is, she's probably been up for a while already.

"You're making excuses, Evan. I'm serious. I want you to call her."

"Fine," he snaps. "Go wait in the living room. Close the door on your way out."

"No. I want to be here when you call her." I fold my arms. "If I'm not, you might not do it, or you'll say you did and make up some story about her not being able to come here."

"Are you saying you don't trust me?" Evan asks.

"When it comes to your mother? No. I don't. I don't think you'll call her."

"You're acting like a spoiled child," he sneers.

"I'm acting like a woman who's tired of her boyfriend hiding her from his mother," I say, maintaining a level head. I don't dare say that Evan is the one acting like a spoiled child right now.

"I'm not hiding you. And I'm not your boyfriend. I'm your fiancé."

"Not if you refuse to do this. If you won't let me meet your mother, our engagement is off."

He glances at the ring on his desk, then back at me. He shakes his head. "You're going to regret this."

"Regret what? Making you do this, or meeting your mother?"

He doesn't answer, and I feel a chill ripple down my spine. His comment obviously means something. Is it something about his mother? Or about him?

He goes around his desk and picks up his phone. He makes the call and puts the phone to his ear.

"Hello, Mother. How have you been?" He turns away from me as he listens. "That sounds wonderful. I'm glad it went well. How was the fundraiser last night? Did they reach their goal?" He pauses, then laughs a little. "Yes, that's very odd. He might be getting senile."

Evan seems to know what's going on in his mother's life, which makes me think he calls his mother on a regular basis. Why didn't he tell me that? Is it because he didn't want me to ask about her?

"Mother, I was calling to share some news," Evan says. "I've met a woman, and she'd very much like to meet you. I explained that you're very busy, and it may not be possible for you to come here."

He listens, then says, "Yes, she recently moved in with me. I know it seems sudden, but if you met Grace, you'd see why I've fallen for her so quickly."

As he pauses to listen, his hand tightens around the phone, and his other hand forms a tight fist.

"It doesn't need to be that soon." He clears his throat. "But if you're able to, then yes, of course, I'd love to see you." He nods. "Very well, Mother. Send me your travel details when you get them. Goodbye."

Evan turns to face me. "There." He slams his phone on the desk. "Are you happy? It's done. She'll be here this weekend."

"This weekend? As in tomorrow? That's soon."

"It's what you wanted, isn't it?" he says in a harsh tone. "To meet my mother as soon as possible?"

"Um, yeah," I mumble. Silence descends, heavy and crackling with tension. I finally ask, "Does she need us to do anything? Like book her a hotel or pick her up at the airport?"

"I'll be retrieving her from the airport. As for her travel arrangements, she has someone who will do it for her. And she won't be staying at a hotel. She'll be staying here. With us."

"But we don't have room. The second bedroom is your office."

"She'll be taking our room." He sits down at his desk and wakes up his computer.

"Then where are we going to sleep?"

"The couch converts to a bed," he says, typing on the keyboard. "We'll be sleeping there."

In the living room? We'll have no privacy.

"Why don't we just get your mom a hotel?" I ask.

"My mother insists on staying here. She won't accept anything else." He looks up from his computer and smirks at me. "I told you you'd regret this. Perhaps now you'll listen to me."

What does he mean? Why would I regret meeting his mom? From their brief conversation, it sounds like he gets along with her. I'm sure she's a very nice woman. After all, she raised a nice son. How bad could she be?

CHAPTER 24

Evan left over an hour ago to get his mother at the airport. I thought he'd be home by now. It's possible he got stuck in traffic, or maybe there was a problem at the airport. Maybe the airline lost his mom's luggage. I wish he'd text me and tell me what's going on so I'd know when to expect him.

He insisted on picking his mother up without me. I decided not to argue with him about it. He's been tense and moody ever since his mom agreed to come here. I didn't want to make things worse by demanding I go to the airport with him.

I'm actually glad I didn't go. Meeting his mom for the first time in a loud, crowded airport would only add to my stress. I'm already on edge about meeting her. I don't know what to expect. Evan said her name is Vivian, which is oddly similar to Evan. I wonder if that was intentional.

In my head, I'm picturing Vivian as a short, tiny woman with white hair, but I could be totally off. I almost looked her up online but then decided not to. Sometimes, seeing someone before meeting them forms an impression in your mind that isn't true. I didn't want to make any unfair judgments about her before meeting her.

Despite Evan's cryptic warning about regretting this, I think I'll like having Vivian here. I get along well with older people. The ones I waited on at the diner loved me. They'd come there just to see me. If Vivian is anything like them, we'll get along just fine.

"Grace?" I hear Evan say. "We're home."

I'm in the bedroom and quickly check myself one last time in the mirror. "I'm coming!"

Hurrying down the hall, I slow down as I approach the living room. I'm really nervous, and my heart's beating fast. I take a few deep breaths to calm myself, but I'm still a bundle of nerves.

"There she is," Evan says, smiling at me. "Mother, meet Grace, my fiancé."

Vivian is not at all what I pictured. She's tall and thin with straight blond hair that rests against her shoulders. She has bright blue eyes and nearly perfect skin with very few wrinkles. Her hair looks like she just left the salon, her makeup is flawless, and I can't spot a single wrinkle on her dress. I don't know her age, but she can't be more than sixty, maybe not even that. I thought she'd be in her seventies, but Evan is only thirty-four, so it makes sense she'd be younger than that, especially if she had him in her twenties.

"Hello, Grace," she says, walking over to me. She extends her hand. "It's a pleasure to meet you."

"You too." I shake her hand. "Welcome to New York. Have you been here before?"

She laughs a little. "Yes, many times. I used to take Evan here when he was a little boy. He enjoyed all the museums."

That explains why Evan is always suggesting we go to museums. Apparently, he's loved them since he was a kid. I used to think going to museums was a punishment. So did all the other kids in my class. I bet Evan was one of those nerdy kids who always followed the rules. I'll have to ask his mom about that.

"Mother, would you like to go clean up?" Evan asks. "I've put out fresh towels for you."

Clean up? Why would she need to clean up?

"Evan, where are your manners?" Vivian says. "You haven't even given me a tour."

"I apologize, Mother." He walks up beside her, and she wraps her arm around his. "As you can see, it's an open floor plan. Over there is the kitchen and we're obviously in the living room."

Vivian eyes the space, her lips pursed in a way that screams disapproval.

"I wish you'd let me help you find a place," she says. "This is far too small, especially now that you have Grace living here."

Too small? Is she kidding? For a Manhattan apartment, this place is huge.

"It's fine for now," Evan says, leading his mother across the room. "Let me show you the rest."

I remain where I'm at, assuming Evan will show her the bedroom and office and come right back. But when he returns, Vivian isn't with him.

"Where's your mom?" I ask.

"In the bedroom. She's going to clean up, then she'd like us to take her out."

"Out where?"

"She hasn't decided. I made some suggestions, but she wants to include you in the decision."

"That's nice of her." I step closer to Evan and lower my voice. "How old is your mom? She looks really young."

He smiles. "You should tell her that. She'd be very pleased."

"Is she in her fifties?"

"She turned sixty last summer, but don't tell her I told you that. She hates people knowing her age. Let's go sit down." He takes my hand and leads me to the couch.

"So, what did she say?" I ask, keeping my voice down. "When you told her we're engaged?"

"She was surprised but pleased that I found someone."

"What did you tell her about me?"

"Not much. I wanted you to tell her. She'd like to spend tomorrow with you. Go to lunch. Maybe do some shopping."

"Just the two of us? You wouldn't be going?"

"She wants to go with just you." He looks away, and I notice his jaw tightening. "I'd rather you not be alone with her, but she insists on having you all to herself."

"Why don't you want me to be alone with her?"

He pauses. "Mother has a rather vivid imagination. She sometimes says things that aren't true."

"Intentionally? You're saying she lies?"

"It's not really a lie, at least not in her mind."

"Wait, are you are saying she's confused? Like she has dementia? Or is it something else?"

"I don't know. I've told her my concerns, but she refuses to see a doctor. She believes she's perfectly fine."

"She seemed okay to me."

"You were only with her for a few minutes. You have to be around her more to notice these things."

"What things? What does she do?"

"It's not what she does, but what she says. She'll make up some outlandish story that isn't at all true."

"Like what?"

"I don't want to get into it." He turns to me. "But if she says something that seems off to you, please tell me."

"Does this happen a lot?"

"No. That's why I haven't pushed her to see a doctor. I've wondered if it isn't a medical issue and that perhaps she's playing some kind of joke on me. She's a bit of a prankster, which is something I've never liked about her."

"I can't imagine Vivian being a prankster, at least not like what you're implying. She seems really serious, like you."

"Prankster isn't the right word. I don't know how to describe it. I'd just caution you to not believe everything she says."

Approaching footsteps echo in the hall, and I look over to see Vivian coming into the living room. She's changed into a black pantsuit and a silky white blouse. She looks very chic and sophisticated. She's really pretty. I'm surprised she never remarried. She could easily snag a guy looking like that.

She holds up a necklace glittering with a single, clear diamond pendant. "Grace, dear, would you mind helping me with this?"

"Sure," I say, getting up.

I follow her back to the bedroom and stand behind her. She lays the pendant just below the hollow of her throat, then gives me the two ends.

"This is gorgeous," I say, latching the clasp.

"I love sparkly things. Don't you? You must, given that ring." She turns to me, her eyes dropping to my left hand. "Could I see it?"

I lift my hand and show it to her. "Evan picked it out. I like it, but I'm almost afraid to wear it. I'm afraid something will happen to it."

"Evan knows to insure it." She smiles at me. "I taught him that. Not that I needed to, of course. He's always been very responsible."

"What was he like growing up?" I ask, eager to know what young Evan was like.

"He was a very bright boy. At the top of his class." She walks over to the mirror and checks herself out. "He loved to travel. Every summer we'd travel the world."

"Really? Wasn't that expensive?"

She laughs. "Money wasn't an issue. I paid more for Evan's schooling than our summer trips."

"You mean his college?" I glance toward the door to make sure Evan isn't listening in.

"No, his private school." She turns to me. "Has Evan not told you about his childhood?"

"Not really. He never talks about it. I didn't know he went to private school."

"It was a private boys' academy," she says, walking over to me. "One of the best in the world. He didn't tell you?"

I shake my head. "He never mentioned it."

I'd assumed Evan went to public school like I did. He made it sound like he had a normal childhood, but going to a private academy and traveling the world every summer is the opposite of a normal childhood.

"Evan was very fortunate. He grew up never wanting a thing. Anything he asked for he was given, and yet he never acted spoiled." She smiles a little. "He was such a good boy. A mother's dream for a son."

We're quiet for a moment. Her eyes meet up with mine. "Do you and Evan plan to have children?"

"Oh, um, we haven't talked about it," I say, surprised by the question.

"You're getting married but haven't talked about having children?"

"No, but we will. We have plenty of time. We're not getting married anytime soon."

"Is that so?" Vivian tilts her head to the side. "Evan hasn't suggested a date?"

"No. Why? Did he say something to you? About when he wants to get married?"

"I'd prefer not to get in the middle of this," she says with a slight smile. "I'm sure he'll talk to you about it."

Guess I know now where Evan gets his habit of dodging questions.

"Tell me. What did he say?"

She shrugs. "That he loves you and doesn't want to wait too long before he marries you."

"Did he give you a timeline?"

"Grace, this really is something you should discuss with him. Speaking of Evan, he's probably wondering what's taking us so long. Let's go join your fiancé and plan out the rest of our day."

It sounds strange to hear her call Evan my fiancé, but it's probably because she's the first person who has. She's the only person who knows we're engaged. I haven't told Jenna because I already know she won't approve. And honestly, I want more time to decide if I really want to marry Evan. I think I do, but there's still so much I don't know about him.

Why didn't he tell me he grew up with money? Or that he went to some fancy private school? Did he think I wouldn't date him if I knew all that? That I'd think we're too different and decide it would never work with us?

I'm really glad I insisted Vivian come for a visit. I have a feeling I'm going to learn a lot more about Evan while she's here.

CHAPTER 25

"Thank you for agreeing to this," Evan says as we lie on the fold-out couch in the living room. "I know it's not ideal."

"It's fine." I turn to face him. "It's been a long day. I'll probably fall asleep right away and forget we're even out here."

When we left the apartment this afternoon, we took Vivian to an art gallery, went out for drinks at an upscale bar, and then went to dinner at a French restaurant that served multiple courses. The dinner went on for hours, and we didn't get home until after ten.

"My mother had a wonderful time today." Evan brushes his hand over the side of my face. "I'm glad you talked me into this. You were right. You two needed to meet before the wedding plans begin."

"About that. Your mom said you wanted to get married soon. What does that mean, exactly?"

"That's something we need to discuss, but I was thinking December. I've always loved New York during the holidays. My trips here with Mother were some of my favorite memories."

"December of next year?" I ask, thinking that seems soon. Too soon.

"No, this year." Evan's eyes rove over my face, a slight grin appearing.

He's kidding. He has to be. Then again, Evan isn't much of a kidder. I still struggle to get him to laugh.

"Come on." I sit up. "Be serious."

"I'm completely serious. I'd like to get married in December."

"Evan, that's only two months away! I'm not getting married in two months."

"Grace, calm down," he says, pulling me back beside him. "I know it's soon, but why wait? We love each other, so why wait to start our life together?"

"Because we're still getting to know each other. I literally just met your mother today. And I found out you went to a private academy and took trips around the world with her every summer when you were growing up."

This is the first opportunity I've had to bring this up.

"What does my childhood have to do with us getting married?" Evan asks.

"It's another thing I didn't know about you. I've asked you repeatedly about your childhood, and you never once said you grew up with money."

He sighs. "Because I didn't want you thinking I'm someone I'm not. Yes, my family has money, but that doesn't mean I'm some spoiled trust fund kid. I've worked since getting out of college, and I plan to continue working, just like any other person would."

"But you don't have to, right? You could do nothing and still have plenty of money."

"Yes, but that's not the path I've chosen. I enjoy working. And because I have money, I can decide when I work and how many hours I put in, which is something I think would appeal to you as my future wife. I can take time off to be with you and our children whenever I'd like."

Every time he says things like *wife* or *children*, I tense up. Does that mean I don't want to marry him? Or am I just nervous because it's all happening so fast, and I don't feel ready to be a wife?

"What else did my mother tell you?" Evan asks.

"That was it. We didn't talk long. But we will tomorrow if we spend the whole day together. So if there's something you want to tell me, you should do it now before your mother does."

He doesn't say anything, but when I get a glimpse of his face in the dimly lit room, I notice a scowl on his face.

"What's wrong?"

His scowl immediately flips to a smile. "Nothing. I was trying to think of what to tell you, but I can't come up with anything. I'm sure my mother will have plenty of embarrassing stories to share from my childhood, or perhaps my teen years."

I smile. "I'm looking forward to that."

"I'm sure you are," he says, sounding annoyed, but he's still got that grin on his face. He runs his hand down the side of my body and kisses me, a deep lingering kiss that implies he wants more.

"Evan, no," I say, pulling back. "Your mom could come out here and catch us."

"We're not teenagers, Grace. And I'm quite certain my mother knows we have sex."

"That doesn't mean I want her catching us."

"She won't." His lips press against the side of my neck as his hand moves over my body. "My mother's a very sound sleeper, and she's exhausted from a long day of travel. Not to mention all the hours we dragged her around New York."

"We can't," I whisper, my eyes falling shut as I become aroused by his touch.

My desire wins out, and we make love right there in the middle of the living room. At one point, I swear I hear the bedroom door open, but it was probably just the springs squeaking in the foldout bed.

* * *

In the morning, I wake to find I'm alone. I sit up and look around. "Evan?"

"He's in the shower," Vivian says.

I look back and see Vivian in the kitchen, dressed for the day, her hair and makeup done.

"What time is it?" I ask, tossing the blanket to the side. I'm glad I remembered to put clothes on last night after Evan and I made love. If it were just us here, I wouldn't have bothered.

"It's nine-thirty," Vivian says. "Do you always sleep this late?"

"No, I'm usually up earlier." I get out of bed and stand behind the couch, leaning against it and folding my arms over my chest, trying to cover myself since I'm wearing a thin T-shirt with nothing underneath. It's really awkward having Evan's mother here. Why wouldn't she want to stay in a hotel? This city has plenty of really nice ones, and it's not like Vivian can't afford it.

"Evan said you recently quit your job," Vivian says, pouring herself some coffee.

"I didn't want to, but it was too far a drive from here. The diner's in New Jersey."

"Diner?" She faces me, her coffee cup primly held between her palms. "That's where you worked?"

"Yes, as a waitress. Didn't Evan tell you?"

"He failed to mention it." She takes a sip of her coffee. "So, Evan just happened to stop by? At this diner you worked at?"

"Yeah. He said he wanted to get out of the city, so he went for a drive. He came into the diner, and I happened to be his waitress."

I realize as I'm saying it that I'm surprised this topic didn't come up yesterday. In all the hours we spent with Vivian, she never asked how Evan and I met or what I did for a living. I assumed Evan had already told her, but apparently not.

"He was really sweet," I say. "He asked me to sit with him on my break because he wanted someone to talk to."

"Of course he did," she mutters.

"What was that?" I ask, not sure I heard her right.

She smiles at me. "Evan has a habit of striking up conversations with strangers."

"Really? I've never noticed that."

"Only certain strangers. He's very particular." She winks at me, then takes another small sip of her coffee.

My gaze drops to the floor as my mind goes back to what Jenna said. *Seriously, Grace, do you really think a guy like him would end up with someone like us?*

"I noticed your food selection is rather limited," Vivian says. "I'll need to order some groceries. What service do you use?"

"I don't. I just go to the store."

"In New York?" She laughs. "How do you carry everything home?"

"Oh, I don't know. I guess I haven't had to buy groceries yet. I've only lived here a few days."

"I'll ask Evan. I'm sure he has a delivery service he uses." She walks around the counter and comes over to me, still holding her coffee mug. "How long do you need to get ready? I was hoping we could start our day soon."

"I don't need much time. Maybe a half hour?"

"To shower, dress, and do your hair?" Her brows rise. "I'm impressed. I need at least an hour."

"I'll go see if Evan's done in the shower."

"He's not. I was just in there and he hadn't even turned the water on."

She was in the bathroom? With her son? Maybe she meant she was in the bedroom, but still, she should've left once Evan went in there.

"It sounds like you two had a romantic evening," Vivian says with a slight smile.

"I'm not sure what you mean," I say, hoping it's not what I think she means. "We were both really tired. We went right to bed."

"Grace, dear, you don't need to lie about it. I heard what was going on. I went to get a glass of water and saw you."

"Wait, you were in the kitchen when we were—"

"No. I realized what was going on and went back to my room."

"Sorry about that," I say with a sigh. "I told Evan we shouldn't be doing that when you're here."

"Why shouldn't you? You're both consenting adults, and you're going to be married soon."

She's right, but I still feel bad that she caught us. And she never got her glass of water.

"I think I'll go check on Evan," I say. "See what's taking him so long."

"Yes, go ahead."

I find Evan in the closet, getting dressed.

"Your mom just told me she caught us," I say, going up to him as he buttons his shirt. "I told you she would!"

He leans down and kisses me. "Caught us what?"

"Doing it!" I whisper. "Last night."

"And why is this a problem?"

"Because she's your mother!" I say in a hushed tone. "You're not even a little bit embarrassed by that?"

"Why should I be embarrassed? It's not as though she stuck around and watched." Evan stops buttoning his shirt. "She didn't, did she?"

"*No!* But I'm still embarrassed she caught us." I point my finger at him. "We're not doing that again until she's gone."

"That's not possible." He slides his arms around me and tugs me against him. "I can't go that long without being with you."

"She's leaving tomorrow. I think you can go a day without it."

Evan laughs. "Tomorrow? She's not leaving tomorrow."

"She's not? I thought she was only here for the weekend."

"Grace, she wouldn't fly all that way to be here for a day and a half."

"Then when is she leaving?"

"I don't know. She hasn't decided." He gives me a kiss. "Go get ready. Mother can't wait for your girls' day."

He goes around me and out to the bedroom. I follow behind him.

"What do you mean she hasn't decided? What does her plane ticket say?" I ask.

"She got a one-way ticket. When she decides to go home, she'll buy another one. I'm going to go show her the project I'm doing for work. We'll be in my office."

Evan leaves the bedroom, and I walk over and shut the door. Why didn't I know his mother was staying past Monday? I thought for sure Evan told me she was only coming for the weekend, but maybe I just assumed that's how long she'd be here. I don't mind having Vivian here, but a few days is more than enough. Evan and I need our bedroom back. We need time alone as a couple, without his mother hanging around.

As I head to the bathroom, my eye catches on something on the nightstand. It's a pitcher filled with water, and beside it is a glass. I remember Evan putting it there before his mother went to bed last night.

Vivian told me she got up in the night to get a glass of water. But she didn't need it. She had plenty of water right next to her bed. So why was she up during the night? If she wasn't getting water, then what was she doing?

CHAPTER 26

By ten o'clock, I'm ready for my day with Vivian. I decided to wear my new pair of dark jeans and a beige blouse. I'd normally throw on a T-shirt and hoodie, but I didn't think Vivian would approve of that. She seems like someone who doesn't even own a T-shirt. I imagine her sitting at her house wearing a suit all day, even if no one ever sees her.

As I leave the bathroom, my phone rings. Jenna's name is on the screen. I've been avoiding her all week, texting her that I'm busy trying to get a job and will call her later. I'm tempted to send the call to voicemail, but then decide to talk to her so she doesn't keep calling when I'm out with Vivian.

"Hey, Jenna," I say.

"You finally answered."

"Yeah, sorry, I've been busy."

"Did you get a job?"

"Not yet." I sit down on the bed. "I'm trying to decide if I want to work in a restaurant again or do something else."

"Like what?"

"I don't know, but I'll figure it out."

"What else is new? How's living with your boyfriend? You guys getting along?"

Evan's no longer my boyfriend. He's my fiancé. I really want to tell her that, but I know Jenna. She won't take it well.

"Yeah, we're, um . . . getting along great."

"Why does it sound like you're lying?" she asks.

"I'm not lying. It's just, Evan's mom is here, so Evan and I haven't had much of a chance to be together, just the two of us."

"His mom is there? At Evan's apartment?"

"She got here yesterday from California. She wanted to stay with us instead of at a hotel."

"I thought it was only a one-bedroom."

"It's two, but one of the rooms is Evan's office." I get to my feet again. "Anyway, we're going to have a girls' day today. We're leaving soon, so I can't talk long."

"Why does she want to spend the day with you? Isn't she there to see her son?"

"Well, yeah, but she also wants to get to know me."

"Why? You're just dating him. It's not like you two are getting married."

I keep quiet, debating over whether to tell her the truth.

"Grace?" Jenna says in a hesitant tone. "Why do I get the feeling you're not telling me something?"

"How's Martin? Did he hire anyone yet?"

"Why are you changing the subject?" she says in a suspicious tone. "Evan didn't propose, did he?"

My heart's beating fast, and there's a heavy feeling in my chest. I know she's not going to like this, but I need to tell her.

"Um, yeah. He proposed."

"Are you *serious*?" she yells into the phone. "You didn't tell him yes, did you? Please tell me you didn't agree to this."

"I did. Evan and I are engaged."

"Grace, you barely know the guy!" Her voice turns shrill, and I flinch against the grating on my eardrums. "Why would you agree to marry him?"

"I know him better than you think." Maybe not by much, but I do have a lot more information now than I did before Vivian arrived. "We love each other, so why wouldn't we get married?"

"You just moved in with him! What's the rush to get married? Are you pregnant?"

"No, Jenna, I'm not pregnant, and we're not rushing to get married. We haven't even set a date."

"Good." She breathes out a sigh of relief. "You need to wait at least a year. You can learn a lot about a person in a year. When did this happen?"

"Last week." I clutch the phone tighter to my ear. "I'm sorry I didn't tell you, but I was worried about how you'd react."

"Well, I can't say I'm happy about it, but I mean, if it's what you want, I guess I have to accept it."

I'm really glad she said that. I thought for sure she'd try to talk me out of it.

"Does this mean you're moving to California?" she asks.

"I don't know. We haven't talked about it."

"Wow. I can't believe you're engaged. A month ago, you didn't even want to go on a date."

"I should go," I say, sensing she's about to get into all the reasons why Evan and I won't work out. "Vivian's waiting for me."

"Okay, but you need to come see us. Martin and I miss you."

My throat tightens. I miss her, too, more than she knows.

"I'm not sure when I could get there," I say. "But I'll try. I'll talk to you later."

"Yeah, alright."

I end the call and realize that she never congratulated me on my engagement. But at least she didn't say I'm making a huge mistake and not to go through with it. Telling her actually went a lot better than I thought it would.

"Vivian?" I say, leaving the bedroom. She's not in the living room. She's not in the kitchen, either. She must still be talking to Evan.

I make my way down the hall to his office. The door's closed, so I lift my hand to knock, only to stop when I hear Evan talking. He's muffled through the thick oak door, so I rest my ear against it. The voices get a little clearer, so I can make out just enough of the conversation.

"You are not going to tell her," Evan says in a harsh tone. "Do you understand me? Not one word, Mother."

"She deserves to know," Vivian replies calmly. "The woman is going to be your wife."

"Which is why the focus should be on the *future*, not the past."

"And you think it'll be better if she finds this out after you're married?"

Find out what? What are they talking about?

"She's not going to find out," Evan says. "Not now, not after we're married. Why would I tell her? It doesn't matter."

"What if she finds out some other way? What if she finds something online?"

"She won't. We had everything removed, or anything that was linked to me."

"New content is posted every day. It's possible she could stumble across something."

"Then I'll deal with it then." A pause. Then Evan says, "Why are you insisting she know this? It has nothing to do with her."

"It's never good to start a marriage with secrets, Evan. You know that."

"It isn't a secret. But it also isn't something she needs to know. It has no relevance to our relationship. No bearing on it whatsoever."

"I disagree, but fine. I'll do as you ask and not mention it."

"Thank you, Mother."

"Of course, dear. I didn't mean to upset you. I only want what's best for you. I'm going to go check on your bride and see if she's ready to go."

I hear Vivian's heels clicking on the wood floor and quickly back away from the door. My palms are sweaty, and I fight to slow my breathing.

"I'm pleased that you like her, Mother," Evan says. "It means a great deal to me."

The clicking of Vivian's heels stops. "Grace will make a wonderful wife. I'm happy you found her."

"Yes, I was very fortunate. I hope you two have a wonderful day."

The door opens, and I feign a look of surprise. "Vivian. I was just looking for you.'"

Her eyes move over me. "What an adorable outfit."

"Thank you," I say, although I don't think she meant it as a compliment. "I wasn't sure what we were doing, so I didn't know what to wear."

"You look beautiful," Evan says, smiling at me. "Come say goodbye."

I slip past his mother and over to Evan. He brings me into his arms and drops a kiss on my forehead. "Have a good time. I'll see you tonight."

"Let's go, Grace," Vivian says. "We have a busy day ahead of us."

As we leave, my mind replays the conversation I just overheard. What secret is Evan keeping from me? He told his mom it wasn't relevant to us, but even so, he shouldn't be keeping secrets from the woman he's going to marry.

What could it be? Is it something about his childhood? Or maybe it's about a past relationship. Was he married? Or what if he has a child? No, he'd tell me that. And that's something that would definitely be relevant to our relationship. So then, what's the secret? What doesn't he want me to know?

"You're very quiet today," Vivian says as we sit down for brunch. She insisted we stop somewhere to eat since she didn't have breakfast. She left Evan a list of grocery items to order so she'd have food for the week. I assume that means when the week is over, she'll leave. At least, that's what I'm hoping.

"Sorry, I think I'm just tired," I say.

"No need to apologize." She sits up straighter and adjusts the napkin on her lap. "I only mentioned it because I was concerned your silence was about me."

"What do you mean?" I ask, trying to mirror both her posture and her act with the napkin.

"I know it's an inconvenience having me here, and I'm sure you'd like Evan all to yourself. You two are in that early part of a relationship where everything's new and exciting and you can't keep your hands off each other." She laughs a little. "And then I show up and ruin all the fun."

"Vivian, no. You're not ruining anything. I wanted you to come. It was my idea," I say in a hurry. I might want her gone from our apartment, but I'm glad she's here.

"It was?" she says with surprise. "I thought it was Evan's idea. He couldn't wait for me to meet you."

Couldn't wait? Evan didn't want his mother to even know about me. But I guess she doesn't know that.

"We both wanted you to visit," I say. "And having you here is not an inconvenience. It's just . . . our apartment isn't really set up for guests. Are you sure you wouldn't rather stay at a hotel?"

Please say yes. I don't want to spend all week sleeping in the living room.

Evan and I need privacy, and we won't have any with Vivian there. I feel like she's watching us and listening in on our conversations. Maybe I'm being paranoid. I'm sure she's not spying on us.

But then, what was she doing last night? She wasn't getting a glass of water. So why did she leave her room? And why did she want me to know that she did?

CHAPTER 27

"I don't care for hotels," Vivian says with a shudder. "I don't trust that the housekeeping staff does a thorough enough cleaning job. Just thinking of all the germs and . . . other substances left behind from previous guests makes me sick to my stomach." Vivian takes a drink of her mimosa, then sets it down. "I'm much more comfortable staying with my son, and it gives you and I time to bond, which is really the reason I'm here. I want to spend time with you, Grace. It's so nice you're not working now. It gives us this time to get to know each other."

"That's true, but I really do need to look for a job this week."

"Nonsense," she says, waving off my statement. "Evan has more than enough resources to care for you. You'll never have to work again."

"But I want to. I like making my own money."

Even with all their wealth, neither Vivian nor her son seem to understand the concept of financial independence. I don't want to rely on Evan for every little thing, especially not his money.

"By working at a diner?" Vivian's brows rise. "What kind of life is that? Did you really enjoy being on your feet all day? Wiping tables? Coming home smelling like grease?"

"It wasn't all bad. I met a lot of nice people." I smile. "Like Evan."

"Have you spoken to him about this?"

"About what?"

"Getting a job."

"Yes. He knows I want to find something here in the city."

"Grace, dear," she says, leaning toward me. "I feel I should tell you that my son is very traditional. He doesn't believe a wife should work. He wants her at home. Caring for the children. Volunteering at their school. Tending to the house."

What is she talking about? Evan's not like that. He's never once told me he expects me to stay home after we get married. He said I don't need to get a job, but he didn't forbid me from having one. Even if he tried, that would be a discussion to be had between us, not us and his mother.

"I don't know why you think that," I say. "Evan has no problem with me working."

"You've talked to him about this?" she asks.

"Yes, and I've made it clear I want to work."

I change topics and ask her about California. I've only been to three states, all bordering New Jersey. I'd love to visit the West Coast and all the other places I haven't been. That's one of the things I'm most looking forward to once Evan and I get married. He's promised to take me all over the world.

"Are you ready to go?" Vivian asks at the end of our brunch.

"Yeah, just let me check my phone." I look and see I don't have any messages. I thought Evan would text me to ask how things are going. I wonder what he's been doing all day.

"Oh, how sweet," Vivian says, looking at her phone. "Evan asked if we're having a nice time."

Evan texted his mother, but not me? Vivian texts him back.

"What are you telling him?" I ask.

She stops texting and looks up at me with a small grin. "That we enjoyed a wonderful brunch and will be leaving soon to do some shopping."

More shopping? I've shopped more in the past few days than I have in the past few years. Of course, not having money was the reason for that, but even if I had money, I don't think I'd shop every day.

Vivian picks the stores we go to, and at each one, she tries stuff on. I don't mind since it gives me a chance to sit and rest. Vivian's wearing me out. She walks so fast that I can barely keep up. And she talks a lot and keeps asking me questions, meaning I have to pay attention.

"Thank you for being so patient," she says, coming out of the umpteenth dressing room. "I'm all set. We can go now. The clerk will charge everything to Evan's account and have it delivered to the apartment."

Evan is paying for his mom's clothes? I find that strange, but maybe he's just being nice. Evan's been very generous with me, so I shouldn't be surprised he's that way with his mother, too.

"It's been a long day," Vivian says as we leave the store. "Let's go have a cocktail."

It's after five. We've been going for almost seven hours. I was hoping we could end our "girls' day" and go home.

"Why don't we stop at the apartment and get Evan?" I say. "He's probably bored being there all day by himself."

"Evan's never bored," she says, walking quickly down the street. "He's always been good at entertaining himself. He's probably lost himself in a book and hasn't even noticed how long we've been gone."

"But don't you want to spend time with him? He'll be working tomorrow and the rest of the week."

"I'll see plenty of Evan this week. I want to spend time with you, my future daughter-in-law. Oh! This is it." She points to the hotel on our right. "They make the best cocktails. You must try one!"

We go into the hotel, and Vivian leads me straight to the bar area. It's very elegant, with marble floors, velvet-lined booths, and crystal chandeliers.

"Evan adores this place," Vivian says as we sit in one of the small circular booths. "We've been here many times."

"Welcome, ladies," a server greets us, handing us each a menu.

I didn't even see him approach. Naturally, the drinks don't have prices attached, which means they're probably thirty dollars each, maybe more. It used to take me hours of hard work to make that much money, but Vivian acts like it's nothing. Evan does, too.

"Isn't this fun?" Vivian says after we order our drinks. "Just us girls, having a cocktail after a day of shopping and wandering the streets of New York."

"Yeah, it's been a good day," I admit.

I was dreading spending an entire day with Vivian, but it wasn't nearly as bad as I imagined. I wouldn't say it was fun, but it gave me a chance to get to know her, which was the point.

"I thought your trips to New York were all when Evan was a child," I say.

"No, we've come here many times over the years."

Why was Evan going on all these trips with his mother? Most grown men wouldn't choose to travel with their mom. I'm not saying there's anything wrong with it. I just find it a little odd, especially since it sounds like it wasn't just one or two trips but several.

"I must tell you, Grace," Vivian says, bringing my attention back to her. "I think you're a wonderful young woman. I think you'll make Evan very happy."

"Thanks," I say, surprised by the compliment.

I've been worried she'd think I wasn't good enough for Evan, that he should be with someone more educated and sophisticated, like that woman who came up to Evan at dinner last week. I haven't thought of her in a while, but now I wonder if I can get Vivian's insight.

The server delivers our drinks to the table. "Enjoy, ladies."

As he leaves, Vivian picks up her cocktail and takes a sip. "Just as good as I remember. Try yours, Grace."

I take a sip of my drink. I only picked it because it had a funny name. None of the drinks were anything I recognized. The server said they're all unique creations from the in-house mixologist.

"It's really good," I say, setting my drink down. "Hey, do you know a woman named Ashley?"

"You'll have to be more specific. I know several women with that name."

"She's someone Evan used to know. She's tall with long blond hair. Blue eyes. Evan said she was friends with one of his exes."

"Oh." Vivian looks surprised. "Yes, I know Ashley quite well, or I did. How do you know about her?"

"She was here in New York last week. Evan and I were having dinner, and she came up to us at the restaurant."

"Is that so?" Vivian picks up her drink and swirls it around her glass. "I'm surprised Evan didn't tell me."

"He acted like he didn't know her that well."

"He did, but she's part of his past that he's trying to forget." She sips her drink, her eyes now focused on the bar area.

"Do you mean his ex-girlfriend? Was it a bad breakup?"

"Dana wasn't his—" Vivian clears her throat. "Perhaps we should talk about something else."

"Dana? That's her name?" I lean back in the booth. Yet another piece of the Evan puzzle. "Evan didn't tell me her name. He wouldn't tell me anything about her. But Ashley made it sound like he took the breakup pretty hard. How long did he date her?"

"For several months." Vivian puts her drink down, lets out a heavy sigh, and then finally shifts her eyes to me. "And she wasn't his girlfriend. Dana was his fiancé."

My stomach drops, and I feel like there's a heavy weight on my chest. Evan didn't tell me she was his fiancé. Why would he keep that a secret?

"He was engaged to this woman?" I ask. "I thought he was engaged when he was in his twenties."

"That was to someone else. A young woman named Lori. She was a very sweet girl," Vivian says in a wistful tone.

"Wait, so . . . Evan's been engaged twice?"

"Yes. He didn't tell you?"

"He told me it was only once." I rest my hands on the table, on both sides of my drink. "When was the other engagement?"

"A little over a year ago. I can't remember the exact date he proposed, but it was sometime in the summer."

"I don't understand. Why wouldn't Evan tell me this? It's not like I'd worry he'd get back together with her."

"No. He wouldn't go back to Dana," Vivian says. "It isn't possible."

"Why? Is she married?"

Vivian's eyes lock on mine. "She's dead."

CHAPTER 28

"His fiancé *died*?" I say, shocked that Evan didn't tell me this. "When they were still together?"

"Yes, unfortunately." Vivian sighs. "It was terribly sad. Evan was so excited to marry her. The two of them were nearly finished with the wedding plans when it happened."

"When what happened? How did she . . ." I don't want to say it. I still can't believe it. Evan's fiancé died? And he didn't think I should know this?

"It was an accident," Vivian says. "A tragic accident that never should've happened." She pauses. "I don't feel right telling you this. You should ask Evan to tell you the story."

"But he won't. He didn't even tell me she died."

"It's because he finds it so difficult to talk about her. I thought he'd moved on, but perhaps not."

"Vivian, please. Tell me what happened. I want to know. Was it a car accident?"

She shakes her head. "It was an accidental drowning. In the bathtub at Evan's house."

"She drowned in the bathtub?" I say.

That's a horrible way to die. Not that there's a good way to die, but I've always thought drowning would be one of the worst ways to go.

"She'd been drinking," Vivian says. "And she'd taken some pills to help her sleep. The combination made her so drowsy, she fell asleep and slipped under the water."

"But when she realized she couldn't breathe, wouldn't that wake her up?" I don't know why I'm asking this. The woman is dead. She clearly didn't wake up when she slipped under the water.

"She wasn't conscious enough to wake up. The pills she took were quite strong, and they were not to be taken with alcohol."

My heart aches as I think about this young woman. A life and a future lost in one fell swoop.

"Where was Evan when this happened?" I ask.

"He was out taking a walk. He and Dana had been fighting that night. He hated losing his temper with her, so he went on a walk to calm down. He assumed he'd come back, they'd talk things out, and all would go back to normal." Vivian uses a napkin to blot the moisture from her eyes. "But instead, he returned to find her lifeless body in the tub."

"That's horrible," I mutter, imagining the scene in my head.

Maybe it's wrong of me to be mad at Evan for not telling me this. It's such a tragic story. I'm sure it's difficult for him to talk about, and telling me the story is almost like having to relive it.

"I'm sorry he didn't tell you," Vivian says. "He doesn't like discussing it."

"When did she die?"

"It was last October, so it hasn't even been a year. I'm sure the anniversary will be difficult for him." She smiles a little. "But at least he has you now. I'm glad he won't be alone."

Evan's fiancé died less than a year ago, and now he's engaged to me? Why does that seem wrong? Is it, or am I overreacting? I've heard that men move on to a new relationship quicker than women do, but that's when a man gets divorced. I'm not sure if the same is true for a man who lost his fiancé to an accidental drowning.

I shudder as I think about that. About Evan coming home and seeing this woman's body in the tub.

"Grace, are you okay?" Vivian asks. "I didn't mean to upset you."

"It's fine. I wanted to know. It's just the image of that is . . . really disturbing," I say, shaking my head. "I can't imagine how horrible that must've been for Evan, to come home and find her like that."

"It was very difficult for him, but I was proud of how he handled it."

"Why? What did he do?"

"He got her out of the tub and immediately called for help. The emergency operator walked him through the steps to resuscitate her, and he followed them exactly." Vivian takes a sip of her drink. "He wasn't able to save her, but he made a valiant attempt. Most people would be in too much shock to take action like that, but Evan was very strong. I honestly didn't think he had it in him."

"When did you find out she was gone?"

"He called me when the paramedics arrived. My house is an hour away, but I'd been in the area that day to see a girlfriend of mine. In fact, I was with her when Evan called. Of course, I immediately went to him and stayed with him for several months."

Months? That's a long time to live with your mother, but I guess when something like that happens, you want your family with you.

"Ashley and I planned the funeral," Vivian continues. "Evan couldn't do it, which is completely understandable. He was supposed to be planning a wedding, not a funeral."

"What about her family? Why didn't they plan the funeral?"

"Dana didn't have any family, or if she did, we couldn't locate them."

"So that's why you know Ashley so well," I say, putting the pieces together. Those things Ashley said to Evan that night are finally making sense. How it hasn't even been a year, and that she was almost in his wedding. She didn't say 'wedding,' but I assume that's what she meant now that I know what happened.

"How did Ashley know Dana?" I ask. "Did they go to college together?"

"No," Vivian says with a short laugh. "Dana didn't attend college. She worked for Ashley's family. She was the maid. She worked for them for years, and in that time, Ashley became friends with her. I never understood why. Like Evan, Ashley comes from a very wealthy family and attended private school with other wealthy children. She had nothing in common with someone like Dana. But you know what they say . . . opposites attract."

That must be how Vivian makes sense of why Evan is with me. Why else would he want to be with a diner waitress who grew up poor instead of someone who's more like himself?

Vivian looks to her left, and I see the server heading our way. A single wave of Vivian's hand, though, and he scurries away.

"So Ashley was going to be in the wedding?" I say.

"She was the maid of honor. She had Dana's bachelorette party planned for that week. The week she passed." Vivian looks down at the table. "Ashley was devastated when she heard the news. It was a very difficult time for all of us."

"Did Evan see Ashley after the funeral?"

"No, he didn't want to. Seeing her reminded him of Dana, so he ended all contact with her, which was really quite sad. I think she could've helped him with his grief. Ashley and I met for lunch a few times after Dana's death, but I didn't tell Evan. I thought it might upset him." Vivian puts her hand over mine. "Please don't tell him I told you any of this. If he finds out I said something, he'd be furious with me."

This family and its insistence on keeping secrets from each other isn't right. If I'm going to be part of this family, that's going to have to change, whether Vivian *or* her son likes it or not.

"Vivian, I can't pretend I don't know this. Evan and I are gonna have to talk about this."

"Then could you at least make it sound like you asked me about it? I don't want him thinking I did it intentionally."

"Well, I did ask you, so yes."

"He'll still be upset that I told you, but as his future wife, this is something you needed to know. I tried to tell Evan that, but he disagreed." She picks up her empty glass. "Shall we get another?"

"Yeah, I could have another."

Vivian calls the server over and orders us another round. I was going to suggest we leave, but then decided to stay and see if Vivian will tell me more about Evan's past. I'm surprised she shared so much about Dana. Then again, it might be because of the alcohol. These drinks are really strong, which makes sense, given what they cost. The cheap drinks I'd get when I went out with Jenna had almost no alcohol. I could have two and not even feel a buzz.

"What do you know about the other woman Evan was engaged to?" I ask once our new drinks arrive.

"Her name was Lori." Vivian takes a sip of her drink and then sets it down. "She was one of those people who would do anything to help someone, sometimes to her detriment."

"What do you mean?"

"She was easily conned. She could only see the good in people, so she'd believe whatever they told her. She loaned money to a woman who claimed to be homeless but really wasn't. Lori ended up broke and living out of her car. That's when she met Evan. They'd been dating for several weeks before he realized she had nowhere to live. He asked her to move in with him, and a week later, they were engaged."

That sounds eerily similar to my history with Evan. I dated him for a few weeks, then moved in with him because I had nowhere else to go. And then he proposed.

"If Evan met her when she was living out of her car," I say, "why did it take weeks for him to find out she didn't have a place to live?"

"She hid the fact that she had nowhere to go. She didn't want Evan finding out. She was embarrassed that she'd been conned."

"Couldn't her family help her out?"

"She didn't have any. Her parents and only brother died in a fire. I believe it was caused by a gas leak at their house. Luckily, Lori wasn't home at the time."

This woman had no family. I don't either. It's another similarity between her and me. And didn't Vivian say Dana also didn't have any family?

"Lori's parents had very little money, so she was basically left with nothing," Vivian says. "She got a job at a gas station and stayed with a friend until she saved enough to get her own apartment. But then that horrible woman conned her out of what little money she had."

"So how did Evan meet her?"

"The gas station she worked at was close to Evan's apartment. He'd see her there and strike up a conversation. I don't know how long it was before he asked her out, but I know he fell for her very quickly. After their second date, he called and told me he'd found the woman he was going to marry." She smirks. "I didn't believe him, of course. I thought he was simply infatuated with this girl."

"You must've been shocked when he told you he was engaged to her."

"I wouldn't say I was shocked. Evan's always been very impulsive. I told him he wasn't ready to get married, but he wouldn't listen to me." She sips her drink. "You know how it is when you're young like that. You make decisions with your heart, not your head."

"But it sounds like he figured out it wasn't going to work. Was he the one who called off the engagement?"

"Called it off?" Vivian puts her drink down harshly. Some of the liquid splashes onto the table. "Is that what he told you? That he ended the engagement?"

"He just said things didn't work out. He didn't say who ended it."

"I see." She looks away, her eyes darting around the bar.

She's quiet for so long that I'm concerned she's checked out completely. I reach across the table for her hand. "Vivian?"

She looks back at me and clears her throat. "You really should be speaking to Evan about this."

"I tried. He wouldn't tell me anything."

"Then perhaps he was right," she says, so quiet I almost don't hear her. "It's best if we leave the past in the past."

"What are you not telling me?" I ask.

There has to be a logical reason why Vivian's being so tight-lipped about this. Did Evan and this woman end up getting married, and Evan doesn't want me to know? Did he get the woman pregnant? Does Evan have a child out there he hasn't told me about?

"Is Evan a father?" I blurt out. "Did he have a child with this woman?"

"Of course not." Vivian scoffs. "Do you really think Evan would hide something like that from you?"

He might, given all the other things he's hidden, like the fact that he was engaged to not just one, but two women. And one of them died!

"Then what is it?" I sit back and cross my arms. "Why are you and Evan being so secretive about this woman?"

Vivian leans toward me across the table. "When something happens once, people think nothing of it. But if it happens more than once, people come up with all sorts of ridiculous reasons why. They can't accept that it's simply a coincidence. That it's possible that tragedy could strike twice."

"Tragedy?" I say, a knot forming in my stomach. "Are you saying something happened to Lori?"

She sits back. "What if it did? Would that change how you see my son? Would you no longer love him?"

"No. I mean . . . I guess it depends on what it is."

"Then you're no better than anyone else," she huffs. "Judging him for something he had nothing to do with."

"I'm not judging him. I don't even know what we're talking about."

Vivian looks across the table at me. She leans forward again. "Evan didn't call off the engagement. He wanted to marry Lori. He loved her."

"So what happened?" I ask, my heart beating faster.

"Lori died. Two weeks before the wedding."

CHAPTER 29

My mind's spinning as I try to process what Vivian just told me. Evan's had two fiancés? And both died? How is that possible? What are the odds? Is it just a coincidence, like Vivian said? Tragedy striking twice? Or is it something else? Something I don't even want to think about?

"It was an accident," Vivian explains. "Lori used to go hiking in the mountains around San Francisco. She loved being out in nature. Evan's never been a big fan of the outdoors, so Lori would go without him. He worried about her hiking alone and would ask her to text him while she was out, just so he'd know she was okay."

I'm already imagining it in my head — how Lori died — even without Vivian continuing. Yet, I don't interrupt her.

"The day she died," Vivian says, "Evan had gone several hours without hearing from her. He went searching for her and that's when he . . ." She pauses, spinning her glass and keeping her eyes down. "When he found her body. He called the police, of course, and they searched the area. It seems Lori had accidentally fallen off the side of the mountain. The ground was wet, and the police found Lori's shoe marks where they believe she fell. The front of her shoes faced inward and the backs were near the drop-off, leading police to believe she was about to take a photo of herself and didn't realize how close she was to the edge."

"That's so sad," I mutter, visualizing this poor woman innocently trying to take a selfie, probably to send to Evan, and accidentally backing off the edge of the cliff. "Evan must've been devastated."

"He was heartbroken. Days would go by where he wouldn't even get out of bed. He moved home and lived with me for several months. He was unable to work or do much of anything." Her voice cracks. "It was a very difficult time, for both of us. I hated him seeing him that way."

"How was he able to move on?"

"I encouraged him to get back into programming, knowing how much he loved computers. He did, but he became consumed with it. It's all he wanted to do. He moved out, got his own place, and wrote code all day. He created some apps and sold them for an impressive amount of money. Even with all he'd earned, however, he continued to lose himself in his work. That is, until he met Dana."

"Then he was single for a long time."

Vivian nods. "He went on some dates in between Lori's death and meeting Dana, but they didn't go anywhere. They were all women who were just as consumed with their careers as Evan was, so it didn't surprise me that he didn't end up with any of them. When he met Dana, it was clear my son has a type. She was very similar to Lori." Vivian gives me a slight smile. "And you're similar to both of them. I see why Evan was so drawn to you."

"How am I similar?"

"Think about it, Grace. When Evan found you, you were a waitress at a diner, struggling to pay your bills. You had a disagreement with your roommate and had nowhere to live. Evan swept in and saved you. Gave you a new life. Just as he did with the other two women he loved."

And now those women are dead.

I let out a slow breath and try to remind myself that Evan had nothing to do with that. Their deaths were accidental. So why do I suddenly feel like I can't breathe? Why is my stomach knotting up? Why is there a chill going through me?

"You look just like her," Vivian says, gazing at me. "But that's not surprising. Lori was Evan's first love. I can see why he was drawn to a woman who looks similar to her."

"How similar? What did she look like?"

Vivian gets out her phone. She swipes through what I assume is her photo gallery, then turns the screen toward me. "Obviously, she's younger than you, but you can see the similarities."

I feel sick as I stare at the image of Evan's first fiancé. With her straight dark hair, thin frame, and a face very similar to mine, she could be my sister.

Is that why Evan couldn't stop staring at me when he first met me? Because I look so much like Lori? Is that why he asked me out? Did he see me as some kind of substitute for his dead fiancé?

"Grace, you're going to spill your drink," Vivian says, taking it from me.

Looking at the table, I notice some of it already spilled.

"Your hand is shaking," Vivian says. "Are you okay?"

"Not really. This is a lot to take in."

"It is, which is why I wish Evan would've told you this himself. He'd be able to comfort you in a way that I can't."

"He won't comfort me. He won't even talk about it."

"He will now that everything's out in the open. It was a mistake for him to keep this from you. As horrible as it was for him to go through all that, it's part of who he is. It shaped him into the man he is now. That's why I was so insistent that he tell you. I told him that sharing this with you would only bring you two closer."

"But he still didn't want to tell me."

"Because he thought you'd leave him if you found out, which is ridiculous. Those women's deaths had nothing to do with Evan." She shrugs. "I suppose if you're someone who's highly superstitious, you might think Evan is cursed in some way, but I'm sure you don't believe in such things."

I shake my head. "I don't believe in that kind of stuff."

"Good." She smiles. "Now, let's talk about something else, like what we're going to do tomorrow. I was thinking a morning walk in Central Park would be nice. I've always loved New York in the fall. The weather's supposed to be beautiful and . . ."

Vivian continues to ramble on, but I'm not listening. I can't, not after she just dropped that bomb on me about Evan's former fiancés.

There are so many questions running through my head right now. Like why would Lori take a selfie at the edge of a cliff? It sounds like she knew the terrain well. Vivian said she hiked there all the time. So wouldn't she know better than to stand close to the edge while taking a photo?

As for Dana, why would she mix alcohol with sleeping pills? Everyone knows that's a dangerous combination. And then she gets in the bathtub? Without even considering she could fall asleep? And if she'd been fighting with Evan, why would she take sleeping pills? Wouldn't she want to be awake when he got home so they could talk things out?

"Can I get you ladies another round?" the server asks, pulling me from my thoughts.

"No," I tell him. "We'll take the check."

"Are you in a hurry?" Vivian asks as the server leaves.

"I'm not feeling well," I mutter.

"Oh, Grace, I hope I didn't upset you. I was only trying to be honest."

"I'm glad you told me. But I need to get home. Evan and I need to talk about this."

"I understand. Let me take care of the bill." She gets out her credit card and waves it at the server. He comes over and takes it.

"I'll let Evan know we're heading back," I say, taking out my phone.

The server returns with Vivian's credit card. "Have a wonderful evening."

"Thank you," Vivian says.

I will not be having a wonderful evening. I'm dreading going home and having to confront Evan about this. We'll just end up fighting, which will be made worse by his mother being there. And I don't see myself sleeping much tonight, either, not with all this rolling around my head.

"We're all set," Vivian says.

Her cheerful tone grates my nerves. She's acting as if we can just go on as normal. Maybe she can, but I feel like my whole world just collapsed. I was planning a future with Evan. And now I feel like I don't even know him.

How could he think it was okay to keep this from me? This isn't some insignificant detail from his past. These are two major events that changed the course of his life and deeply affected him as a person. You don't lose one woman you loved and just move on from it, as if it never happened. Let alone two.

What if he's still mourning Dana? What if he's using me to get over her? What if he sees me as her replacement? A stand-in for the woman he really loved? Or maybe he considers me a replacement for Lori, his first love. The woman who looks eerily similar to me.

When we get back to the apartment, Vivian stops me before I open the door. "Maybe I should go," she says.

"Go where?" I ask in a daze.

"You and Evan need to discuss this privately. I'll find a place to have dinner. I don't want to be in the way."

I nod. "I'd appreciate that."

She goes down the hall and gets on the elevator. I remain at the door, feeling nervous and sick to my stomach. I don't know what to say to Evan. Part of me wants to scream at him for not telling me this, but the other part feels bad for him. Losing one love would be hard, but losing two? I can't imagine how painful that must've been for him.

Taking a deep breath, I put my key in the lock and twist until I hear the latch clear. When I enter, Evan is on the couch, reading a book. Only when I shut the door behind me does he look my way.

"Grace!" His face lights up. "How was your day?"

"It was fine," I say, not moving from my spot in front of the door.

Evan looks past me. "Where's Mother?"

"She went to have dinner."

"Without us?"

"She wanted to give us some time alone."

"That was nice of her," he says, getting up from the couch. He comes over to me, pulls me into his arms, and kisses me. "Let's not waste any time."

"Evan, no," I say, pushing him away. "That's not why she left."

"Then what is it? Why'd she leave?" he asks, his brows furrowed, lips turned down.

"She told me some things." I look him in the eye. "About you. And the two women you almost married."

He curses under his breath, and his face starts turning red, the color slowly moving down his neck.

"She wasn't supposed to tell you," he says in a voice much deeper than his usual voice. It frightens me. It doesn't even sound like him.

"I needed to know," I say, my heart pounding. "We're getting married, Evan. You shouldn't have kept this from me."

"Why the hell would I tell you?" he shouts, startling me. "It's over! Do you really think I want to relive that time of my life?"

"I'm not asking you to relive it. I'm asking you to be honest with me."

"Apparently, I don't need to now that my mother's told you everything!" Evan's hands are fisted, and he looks like he's about to explode with anger.

"Why are you yelling at me? I didn't do anything wrong. You're the one who kept all these secrets from me!"

"What secrets?" he growls, his eyes narrowing. "What did she tell you?"

"That they died," I say, my voice shaking. It's because of Evan. He's scaring me. Instead of comforting me or apologizing to me, he's attacking me — making me feel like I'm not safe. "She said they died in tragic accidents. And that you were engaged to both of them. It wasn't just Lori."

His face tenses when I say her name. He looks at me for a long moment, then storms off, leaving the room and going down the hall.

Where did he go? He can't take off like that.

Now I'm the one getting angry. Evan's acting like a child. If we're getting married, we should be able to talk about things without him storming off like that.

When I don't find him in the bedroom, I immediately head to his office. I don't let the closed door stop me. I open it and see Evan standing by the window, his back to me. He's staring down at the floor, mumbling to himself.

"Evan, you can't do this," I say, coming into the room. "You can't walk away from me like that."

"Grace, please," he says in a much softer voice than before. "Please leave me alone right now."

I slowly move toward him, only stopping when I'm a few feet behind him. "We need to talk about this."

"We don't. You already know."

"I know what happened. But I don't know what it means. How it affected you. How it affects *us*."

"It has nothing to do with us. Unless . . ." He shakes his head.

"Unless *what*? What were you going to say?"

"Unless it means you're leaving me." He turns around. His eyes are red, and a tear slides down his cheek. "Are you, Grace? Are you leaving me because of this?"

CHAPTER 30

My heart breaks hearing Evan say that and seeing the tears in his eyes.

"Evan, no." I grip his arm. "I'm not leaving you. I'm trying to understand why you didn't tell me about this."

"I couldn't." Evan wipes his eyes and takes a breath. "I was afraid if you knew, you'd blame me."

"Why would I blame you? It was an accident."

"Yes, but there were people who said it wasn't. And I understand why. It's always the husband — or the fiancé, in my case. That's what everyone assumes." Evan's eyes meet up with mine. "But I promise you, Grace, I had nothing to do with their deaths. I would never harm the woman I love."

"I know you wouldn't." I rub his arm. I didn't come in here to comfort him, but part of me can't stand to see the anguish in his eyes. "I'm sorry those people accused you of that. Your mother said you weren't even there when it happened, so it doesn't make sense for people to accuse you."

"And yet they did. My mother hired the best lawyers money could buy to prove my innocence."

"Why did you need lawyers? You were never charged with anything." I pause. "Were you?"

"I wasn't charged, but there was an investigation. Both times. As you can imagine, the second time was far worse. The police were certain I was involved because of what happened to the first woman."

First woman? Why doesn't he use her name? He was engaged to her. He loved her. It seems odd to refer to her as the 'first woman.'

"What did they do?" I ask. "For the investigation?"

"Questioned my friends. Coworkers. My mother. They talked to anyone I had a connection with, trying to build a case against me."

"A case for what? You weren't there when either of them died."

"No, but I was in the vicinity."

"Not with Lori. Your mom said she went hiking alone that day."

He shakes his head. "When I didn't hear from her, I went looking for her. I searched all the trails I thought she might have taken. When I finally found her, she was gone. The police didn't believe me. They said I followed her there and . . ." He swallows. "Pushed her."

"But they didn't charge you, right?" I say.

"They couldn't. There was no proof to their accusations, and no motive. I had no reason to harm her."

"What about Dana? Your mom said you were on a walk when it happened."

"Yes, which the police didn't believe. They knew we'd been fighting and took that as a motive, as if it isn't normal for couples to fight," he huffs. "The police wanted proof that I'd gone on a walk. They interviewed my neighbors, but none of them could corroborate my story, which isn't surprising. It was a cold, damp day. People were inside their homes, not out wandering the streets. I was furious the police would even think that I would harm her. It made no sense. I'd planned to have a life with her. I couldn't wait to marry her." Evan sighs. "I shouldn't have said that. I'm sorry, Grace."

"Don't be. You didn't even know me back then." I pause. I feel bad asking him this, but if I don't, I won't be able to stop thinking about it. "I need to ask you something, and I need you to be totally honest."

"What is it?"

"Am I a replacement for Dana? Someone to—"

"No!" Evan shouts. "Grace, how could you even think that? You know I'd never use you that way."

"Yeah, but she hasn't even been gone a year, and now you're engaged to me."

"Because I love you." He grips my shoulders. "It has nothing to do with her."

"But don't you think it's really soon for us to be engaged when you were engaged to Dana at this time last year?"

When I say that out loud, it sounds even creepier than it did in my head. Last September, Evan was engaged to someone else. He was living with someone else, like he's now living with me.

"It isn't something I planned," he says. "I had no intention of falling in love this soon. I didn't even plan to date. I thought I'd move here for a few months, complete the job, and leave. But then I met you, and I just happened to fall in love. I wasn't going to let you go because of some made-up rule saying it was too soon."

I get what he's saying. You can't control when you'll meet the person you'll fall in love with, but I still wish more time had passed after Dana's death.

"What about Lori?" I ask. "Did you pick me because I look like her?"

"Of course not. Why would you—"

"Your mother showed me a photo. She looks like me. Not exactly, but similar."

"That is not the reason I chose you," he says through gritted teeth. "I'm insulted you would even think that about me."

"Evan, you have to admit I look like her."

"And why is that a problem? I like a woman with a certain look. Everyone has a type, and you happen to be mine."

Is that all it is? Is Evan simply drawn to women who look like me? Or did he purposely choose me because I looked like his former fiancé?

The day we met, Evan looked at me like he knew me. Was it because I reminded him of Lori?

"It's after six," Evan says. He straightens and motions to the office door. "Why don't you go order something for dinner?"

"Evan, I'm not done talking about this."

"We can talk more later." He rubs his jaw and looks down at the floor. "It's very difficult for me to go back to that time in my life, Grace. I can only do it in small doses."

It sounds like an excuse, but maybe he's telling the truth. Not having been through something like that, it's hard to judge how he's feeling.

"What do you want for dinner?" I ask.

I'll let the conversation go for now. But this isn't the end. There's more I want to know.

"You choose," he says. "Get whatever you'd like."

"I'm not hungry."

"I am. I got busy and forgot to eat lunch. Why don't you order something for both of us? You can always eat it later." He sits down at his desk and starts up his computer. "I'll be out in a minute."

"You're working?" I ask.

"I just need to check something. It won't take long," Evan mutters.

After that tense conversation, I don't know how he can focus on work or whatever he's doing. I also don't know how he could have an appetite. I made him talk about what I'm sure were the two worst times of his life. It brought him to tears. And then, just like that, he sends me off to order dinner?

I'm being too judgmental. Everyone handles grief differently, and it's not like this happened yesterday. He's had time to work through it.

I leave him alone and go to the kitchen. I open the drawer where we keep the takeout menus. Looking through them, nothing sounds good. Evan should pick. He's the one who's hungry.

With the menus in hand, I go back to Evan's office. I stop in the doorway. He's writing something on a pad of paper and has a smirk on his face, or maybe it's a smile. It's hard to tell with his head down. He taps the pen on his desk and chuckles to himself.

Why is he laughing? He almost never laughs, and of all the times to laugh, this certainly isn't one of them. Minutes ago, we were talking about his dead fiancés. How could he go from being sad to laughing?

"Evan?" I say.

His head jerks up, and the smile drops from his face. "Did you order the food?"

"No, I couldn't decide what to get." I walk up to his desk, and he quickly flips the pad of paper over. "What were you writing?"

"Nothing. I was doodling. It calms my mind when I'm feeling stressed."

He didn't look too stressed when he was laughing. And if he was doodling, why was he so quick to flip the pad of paper over so I couldn't see it?

"Here." I hand him the menus. "Pick something and I'll order it."

"Go with this one," he says, referring to the top menu, not even looking at the rest. "Get me the usual." He shoves the stack at me, then wakes up his computer and types on the keyboard.

This feels really strange. It's almost like our conversation never happened. Like Evan's already moved on. But I haven't. I want to ask more questions. I want Evan to open up to me more.

Maybe he will. Maybe he needs more time. I'll let it go for now and try to talk to him later.

I order the food, then watch TV as I wait for it to arrive. I assume Evan will come out and join me, but a half hour later, he's still in his office. I'm about to go check on him when someone knocks on the door. I assume it's the delivery person, but when I open the door, I find Vivian standing there.

"How did it go?" she says in a hushed tone. "Do you need more time?"

"No, we're done," I say, letting her in and shutting the door. "Evan's in his office. I ordered dinner, but it hasn't arrived yet. Did you eat?"

"Yes, I had a wonderful meal at a restaurant just down the street." She glances toward Evan's office. "He wasn't angry?" she says in a hushed tone.

"He was, but he calmed down."

"Good," she says with a sigh of relief.

"I was worried he might—" She stops herself and shakes her head. "Never mind."

"No, tell me. You worried he might what?"

She takes my arm and leads me over to the kitchen, far enough away that Evan wouldn't hear us unless he walked into the room.

"I don't know if you've realized this, but Evan has a bit of a temper. I was worried how he'd react to you knowing about Lori and Dana. Just hearing their names infuriates him. But seeing how gentle he is with you, and how much he cares for you, I was confident he'd be able to control himself when you confronted him with this. And, of course, the medication he's on helps a great deal. He's better able to control his emotions."

I jerk back. "What medication? Evan isn't taking anything."

"Do you know this for a fact?" she says with concern. "Did he tell you this?"

"No, but I've never seen him take any pills."

"Perhaps he doesn't want you knowing he's on them, although you really should. As his wife, it will be your responsibility to make sure he takes them."

"What are the pills for?"

"They're mood stabilizers," she says, keeping her voice down. "They help regulate his emotions. When Evan was younger, he had difficulty controlling his anger. It got even worse during his teen years when he became involved with girls. He'd fall for them very quickly, putting him in a euphoric high of being in love, and then when the girl wanted to end things, Evan would become extremely angry."

There's another knock on the door, and this time, it's the delivery person. I quickly pay him so I can get back to Vivian. As I portion out the food, Vivian continues to tell me about Evan.

"During these fits of anger, Evan would tear apart the house and break things. That would be followed by a time of deep despair and depression. I took him to a psychiatrist who put him on medication. It helped a great deal. He never acted that way again. But if you're saying he's no longer taking them . . ."

"Maybe he is, but he's never said anything to me about being on medication." I pour sparkling water into two glasses, and Vivian and I move everything over to the table.

Once we have everything in place, Vivian turns to me and holds both my hands. "Grace, I'm becoming very concerned."

"About what?"

"You and Evan. He's not being honest with you. It's not fair to you, especially when you're about to marry him. There shouldn't be secrets between you two."

"I agree, but he won't tell me anything. Even about you. Whenever I used to ask him about you, he'd change the subject."

She nods. "He was just as secretive about you. I asked him if he was seeing anyone, but he wouldn't tell me."

"But why? I don't understand."

She sighs. "He didn't want me meeting you. He knows I wouldn't let him get away with lying to you. I love my son, but I can't deny the fact he has issues. And I don't think it's right for him to hide those issues from the woman who will soon be his wife."

"Why can't he just be honest with me?"

"Because telling you these things means he might lose you," she says with a sad smile. "It's clear how much he loves you. I could tell the moment I saw him with you." She pauses, looking down, then back up at me. "I'm sure you know this isn't what I wanted. I didn't want Evan rushing into another engagement, and I didn't want him marrying someone like you. I didn't think you were good enough for my son."

My eyes widen, and I step back.

She must see the hurt look on my face because she rushes to say, "But all that has changed. Getting to know you, seeing how much you care about Evan, I think you're the perfect girl for him. That's why I'm being so honest with you. I want this marriage to last, but I'm afraid it won't if Evan hides the parts of himself he doesn't want you to see. Finding these things out after you're married might lead to divorce, and I don't think Evan could handle a loss like that, not after the other losses he's suffered."

"I'm glad you told me all this, but I have to admit, knowing Evan's been hiding so much from me makes me nervous about our future."

"I wouldn't worry about it," Vivian says. "Once you're married and he feels like you're truly his, I'm sure he'll be more open with you."

I feel uneasy when she says I'll be *his* once we're married. I'm reminded of the time Evan said, *You're mine, Grace*, like he owns me.

"Mother," Evan says, appearing from the hall. "You're back." He smiles at her as he walks over to us in the kitchen. "How was your day?"

"I had a wonderful time." She glances at me. "Grace and I had such fun shopping and getting to know each other. I took her to that bar you and I used to go to."

"I've been meaning to take you there," Evan says to me. "Did you enjoy it?"

"Yes, the drinks were really good."

"I'll leave you two be," Vivian says. "It's been a long day. I think I'll get to bed early." She gives Evan a kiss on the cheek. "Goodnight, sweetheart."

"Goodnight, Mother."

She turns to me. "Thank you, Grace, for a lovely day."

I smile and give her a quick nod. "Goodnight."

She goes to her room as Evan opens a bottle of wine and pours himself a glass. "Would you like some?"

"No. I have a headache."

He sets the wine down. "I'll go get your pills."

"I don't need them. It's not that bad."

"Not yet, but it might get worse. I'll be right back."

When he returns with the pills, I only take one instead of the two recommended on the bottle. I don't like taking more than I need because they make me really groggy.

Evan eats his entire meal while I just pick at mine. I don't have an appetite after finding out yet another secret about Evan.

Why didn't he tell me he's on medication? Is it because he's not taking it anymore? Maybe he doesn't need it, although I have noticed his mood can change dramatically from one moment to another. It doesn't happen often, but when it does, it concerns me. Like tonight, when I brought up his former fiancé, he exploded with anger after being completely calm moments before. Or when he was tearfully saying how he thought I might leave him, then laughing to himself a few minutes later.

I need to talk to him about this. If the medication helps him, he needs to take it. And if he's already taking it, he needs to tell me that, too. These secrets need to end. If he can't be honest with me, I don't see how I can marry him.

Our engagement will have to end.

CHAPTER 31

"I missed you today," Evan says as we lie on the foldout bed. He kisses my neck as his hand moves down my body.

"Evan, stop," I whisper. "I don't want to do this with your mother here."

"She's asleep." He continues to kiss me. "She went to sleep hours ago."

"But she could wake up and come out here and catch us." I push him away. "I mean it, Evan. I'm not doing this until she's gone."

He lets out a frustrated sigh and falls onto his back, staring up at the ceiling.

"I need to ask you something." I turn on my side, facing him. "Are you taking medication?"

"No." He looks at me. "Why would you ask me that?"

"Your mother said you take pills for, um, your mental health."

"Was she joking?" he says with a laugh.

"No. Why would she joke about that?"

"Because it's comical to even consider. She knows I don't take pills. I don't take them for anything, but certainly not my mental health." He turns to me. "What exactly did she say?"

"That you couldn't control your emotions. She said she took you to see a psychiatrist when you were a teenager and that you were given a mood stabilizer. She said you've taken them ever since."

Evan turns and lays on his back, his arms folded tightly, not looking at me. "She's lying. Grace, I swear to you, I am not on any kind of medication, and I have never once seen a psychiatrist."

"Then why would she tell me that?"

He pauses, then says, "Remember when I told you my mother sometimes makes up stories? Says things that aren't true?"

"Yeah."

"This is one of those times. I don't know if it's intentional or if she says it without realizing it's all in her head and not actually true. How did she sound when she told you?"

"Like it actually happened. She said when you were a teenager, you'd date girls and get angry if they broke up with you. She said you'd lose control and destroy the house and break things."

He shakes his head. "I never did that. Not once."

Every time I learn something about Evan, something that doesn't cast him in a perfect light, he denies it. It's a trait I don't like about him.

"Then why would she say it, Evan?" I ask. "How would she even come up with something like that?"

"She's confusing me with her father. When my mother was growing up, her father couldn't control his temper. When he was angry, he'd tear the house apart. Break things. Scream at her. She described him as being very abusive. But after he died, it's as if she rewrote history. She spoke of him as though he was a wonderful man who could do no wrong. That's when the stories began. She started telling me things that weren't true, not just about her father, but other things." Evan lets out a heavy sigh. "I don't know what to do. She refuses to see a doctor."

"Maybe I could talk to her. Sometimes things like this are better coming from someone who isn't a family member."

"No. Grace, please, don't say anything to her. She wouldn't even know what you're talking about. She honestly believes these things. Telling her they aren't true would only confuse her more."

"Do you think there might something wrong with her brain? I've heard brain tumors can make people confused and not act like themselves."

"I don't think that's it." He gives me a kiss. "Don't worry about it. I'll handle it. Let's get some sleep."

Evan is snoring within minutes, but I'm wide awake, concerned about Vivian. I wonder what's wrong with her. I hope it's nothing serious. I finally drift off to sleep, and when I wake only a few hours later, Evan is no longer beside me.

"Evan?" I say, thinking he might be in the kitchen.

When he doesn't answer, I figure he must've gone to the bathroom. I'm about to go back to sleep when I hear a noise coming from down the hall. I get out of bed and follow the sound to the bedroom. The door is closed, but I can hear Evan talking. His voice is so quiet I can't tell what he's saying.

Why is Evan talking to his mother in the middle of the night? Is he telling her what I said about him being on pills? If so, now isn't the time to confront her about that or tell her his concerns. Maybe he caught her wandering out of her room, like she did the night she caught Evan and I having sex. I thought she was spying on us, but maybe she was just confused.

I'm surprised she's having these issues. In the short time I've known her, her mind seems very sharp. She talks fast and never struggles to find the right words. Even at my age, I sometimes can't come up with a certain word. One time I was trying to tell Jenna I needed a new hairdryer but couldn't think of what it was called. She thought it was hilarious.

I rouse from my thoughts when I hear Evan walking toward the door. I race back to bed and quickly get under the covers. The bedroom door quietly opens and closes, followed by Evan's soft footsteps heading back to the living room.

"Evan?" I say as he gets into bed.

"I'm right here," he whispers, kissing my forehead.

"Why were you talking to your mom?"

"I wasn't. I was using the bathroom."

"I heard you in her room. I heard you talking to her."

"Grace, I was in the bathroom. I was not talking to my mother. You must've been dreaming."

"No, I was awake. And I heard you in her room."

"You're confused. Probably because of those pills you took. They knock you out to the point that you confuse your dreams with reality." He gives me a kiss, then turns his back to me, pulling the covers over his shoulders. "Go back to sleep."

It wasn't a dream. It was real. One pill is not enough to make me confuse a dream with reality. I clearly remember getting up and hearing Evan in Vivian's room.

I'm really starting to question if I want to marry Evan. On the plus side, I'll never have to worry about money again. I'll have a nice house, nice clothes, and a car that works. But is it worth having those things if I'm married to a man who can't be honest with me?

* * *

The next day, Vivian doesn't come out of her room until well after Evan has left for work. I wonder if that's intentional or if she just took more time to get ready this morning.

"Good morning," I say as she joins me in the kitchen. She's already dressed for the day in black pants, a black turtleneck, and black heels. I don't know how she walks around in heels all day. My feet would be killing me.

"Good morning." She smiles at me as she goes to get herself a cup of coffee. "What do you have planned for today?"

"I thought we'd decide together. Is there somewhere you want to go?"

She picks up her cup of coffee and turns to me. "I'm sorry, Grace, but I've already made other plans."

"Oh," I say, confused. Yesterday, she made it sound like she wanted to spend every day with me until she went home. "I must've misunderstood. I thought we were hanging out today."

"We were, but then I realized you shouldn't have to spend every second with me. You have your own life. Your own schedule." She sips her coffee. "I'll be back this afternoon. Maybe we could do something then."

"What are you doing today?" I ask.

"I'm going to the salon." She runs her hand over her hair, which doesn't need a trip to the salon. It looks like she just had it done. "I've also scheduled a facial and a massage."

I could've joined her for all that. It could've been another girls' day, but she either didn't think to invite me or didn't want me going with her. Is this because of Evan? Did he tell her to stay away from me? Is that why he was in her room last night? Did he get mad at her for telling me he was on meds and then decide he doesn't trust her to be around me? I really want to know what Evan said to her, but if I asked him, I'm not sure he'd tell me the truth.

"Oh, and then I'm having lunch with Ashley," Vivian adds.

"Ashley? Evan's friend?"

"She was never really friends with him. It was more like they tolerated each other. But yes, that's her. When you told me she was in town, I called her up and asked if she had time to meet."

That's odd. Why would she meet with Ashley? The friend of Evan's dead fiancé? She should be having lunch with me, Evan's current fiancé.

"I didn't realize you and Ashley still talked."

"We don't, at least not anymore. That's why I invited her to lunch. I thought it'd be fun for us to catch up. Her new job sounds very impressive. I can't wait to hear about it." She sets her coffee cup in the sink.

"Does Evan know you're having lunch with her?"

"Why is it Evan's concern?" she says with a laugh. "I don't need my son's approval to have lunch with someone."

"Yeah, that's not what I meant."

She walks up to me. "Then what did you mean, Grace?"

"Nothing. Never mind."

Vivian tilts her head. "Did Evan say something to you last night? About me? Or what you and I talked about?"

"No," I say, hoping she'll believe me. "Why?"

"You don't seem like yourself today. I hope you and Evan didn't have a fight."

"We didn't. I'm just tired. I didn't sleep well."

"Why is that? Was something keeping you up?"

The way she said it makes me think she knows I overheard her talking to Evan last night. But that's not possible. How would she know?

"I think it was the cocktails," I say. "Those drinks were a lot stronger than I'm used to. I think they affected my sleep."

"I slept quite well. Didn't wake up once," she says, heading to the closet to get her coat.

She's lying, but why? What doesn't she want me to know? Did Evan tell her to keep their late-night conversation a secret?

"I need to get going. Don't want to be late for my beauty treatments." She slips on her coat before heading to the door, offering an almost dismissive wave as she exits. "Enjoy your day!"

When she's gone, I call Evan.

"I'm heading into a meeting," he says when he answers. "Did you need something?"

"Your mom made plans for today without me," I say.

"Is that a problem?" he asks.

"No, I'm just surprised. She said she wanted to spend all this time with me, and now she's off doing her own thing." I plop down on the couch. "Did you say something to her? Like tell her not to spend time with me?"

"Of course not. She probably just realized that spending the entire week with you was too much and decided to do something on her own."

It fits with what Vivian said, so maybe that's it. Maybe it had nothing to do with what Evan said to her last night.

"Did you know she's having lunch with Ashley?" I ask.

He's silent, then says, "No, she didn't mention it. Grace, I need to get to this meeting."

"Yeah, okay, bye."

I end the call and try to figure out what to do today. At the very least, it's time to start looking for jobs. I find a website that lists server jobs for the Manhattan area. As I'm reading through the descriptions, I keep seeing things like 'fast-paced environment' or 'must work well under stress' and worry I won't be able to do it. These are not places that would be okay with me leaving in the middle of a shift because my head hurts. They wouldn't understand. I have pills now, but they take too long to kick in, and they make me drowsy. I couldn't take one and work at a busy restaurant.

In the afternoon, I watch TV, thinking Vivian will be home soon and might want to do something. But she never shows up. At five, she's still not home. I'm about to call Evan when he comes through the door.

"Hey," I say, greeting him with a hug. "Your mom never came home. Do you think she's okay?"

"She's fine. I just talked to her." He walks past me to the kitchen and takes out a bottle of scotch.

"Where is she?" I ask, watching as he pours himself a drink.

"At a hotel. The one where you two had cocktails."

"She's having drinks? By herself?"

"I'm sure she will later." He sips his scotch. "Right now, she's resting in her room."

"Her room?" I go over to him. "She's staying there?"

"I thought it was for the best. It wasn't working out with her here." He takes another drink of his scotch.

"When did you decide this? And why didn't you tell me?"

"I don't need your approval to put my mother up in a hotel," he says, staring at me over the rim of his glass.

"I'm not saying you do. But I thought you'd at least tell me. I was worried about her."

"That's sweet," he says in a condescending tone. "But I can assure you, she's fine. She loves that hotel. She'll be very happy there."

"What about dinner? Are we meeting her somewhere?"

"She's having dinner on her own." Evan sets his glass down and pulls me into his arms. "As for you and me, I got us a reservation at a very nice restaurant I think you'll enjoy. I've been there myself several times."

"Evan, this isn't right. Your mom is here to see you, and now she's in a hotel all by herself."

"My mother is quite capable of doing things on her own. You do realize she's single. She's used to being alone. And here in New York, she has plenty of things to do to keep her busy."

"Yes, but I'm sure she'd rather be with her son."

"And I'd rather be with my future wife." He kisses me. "Now that we have our bedroom back, why don't we go use it?"

"Not now," I say, pulling away from him.

"What's wrong?"

"I feel bad that you kicked her out."

"You didn't want my mother staying here in the first place!" he says, raising his voice. "And now you want her back?"

"No, I'm not saying that. I think it's better if she's at a hotel."

"Then what's the problem?"

"Your mom goes from wanting to spend all her time with me to not seeing me all day? That doesn't make sense. Something must've happened."

"Nothing happened. You're being paranoid. Honestly, Grace, make up your damn mind!" he says, his voice still raised. "You complain about my mother staying too long, taking up all your time, and now you're upset she didn't spend the day with you?"

"Stop yelling at me." I walk away, not wanting to be near him. "I didn't say I was upset. I'm saying it doesn't make sense for your mom to be one way yesterday and totally different today. It's almost like you told her to stay away from me."

"Okay, fine," he says. "I did."

"Did what?"

"I told my mother to stay away from you."

CHAPTER 32

"Evan, why would you do that?" I say. "She's your mother. Your only family. I thought you wanted me to spend time with her."

"I didn't care either way. My mother's opinion of you doesn't matter to me. It never has." Evan shrugs before retrieving his scotch. "You're the one who insisted on meeting her. When you told me she was saying things about me that aren't true, I decided it's best that you don't spend time with her anymore."

"Why is that your decision? What if I want to spend time with her?"

"Why would you want that?" He walks up to me. "You know she thinks you're beneath her."

I don't respond because I do wonder if she thinks that about me.

"Did you notice how she looked at you the first time she saw you?" Evan asks.

"She didn't know me then. Now she does, and she likes me."

"You think she does because she's a good actor. But her first reaction to someone is always how she truly feels."

"Your mom and I got along great yesterday. There's no way she was acting."

"I think I know my mother a little better than you do, Grace. She's fooling you."

I'm not sure I believe him. I don't doubt that Vivian puts on an act when she needs to, but I don't think she's doing that with me. She seemed sincere when she told me she likes me and thinks I'm good for Evan. If she didn't believe that, why would she say it? She could've kept quiet and said nothing about her feelings for me or my relationship with her son.

"I want to be alone," I whisper, walking away.

"Grace, I didn't say this to hurt you," Evan calls out as I go down the hall. "I wanted you to know the truth."

I go into the bedroom and slam the door, angry at Evan and needing a moment to calm down. Vivian's jewelry is on top of the dresser, her phone charger is on the nightstand, and her clothes are still in the closet. Is Evan going to bring these things to her? If not, I feel like I should do it myself.

I don't know what's going on, but I don't like that Evan's treating his mother this way. Even if it's true that she doesn't like me, he should still be nice to his mom and bring her things to the hotel.

Sitting on the bed, I get out my phone and call Vivian. After only two rings, it goes straight to voicemail. A text pops up from Vivian: *I've had a long day. I'm going to bed early. Goodnight.*

It's not even six, and she's going to bed? I don't believe her. I think it's an excuse to not answer my call. What did Evan say to her? Did he forbid her from talking to me?

I text, *Forget whatever Evan told you. I want to see you tomorrow. Maybe we could meet for lunch?*

She doesn't respond. Several minutes pass before another text appears. *I don't think it's a good idea. Evan would be very upset.*

Who cares if he's upset? He can't tell me what to do. If I want to meet his mother for lunch, I will. Why is Vivian even listening to Evan? She seems like a strong-willed woman who doesn't take orders from anyone, including her son, so I'm surprised she's going along with this.

I try calling again. This time, she answers.

"Grace, we shouldn't be talking. Evan made it very clear he—"

"I don't care what he said," I interrupt. "He doesn't get to decide who I can talk to. You came here so we could get to know each other, so that's what we're going to do. Why don't you come over in the morning? You can pick up your things, then we'll figure out what to do for the day."

"Evan is having my things delivered to the hotel." She pauses. "Grace, I would love for us to spend the day together, but I don't want to do it behind Evan's back."

"Then I'll tell him. I'll say it was my idea."

"No, don't do that. You and Evan will end up getting into an argument, and the last thing I want is to be the cause of friction between you two."

"Don't worry about that." I glare at the bedroom door. "I'll deal with Evan."

"I really wish you wouldn't. When Evan doesn't get what he wants, he can become very angry. I wouldn't want something happening." When I don't say anything, she quickly adds, "Not that anything would. Evan would never harm you. I simply meant that I don't want him becoming angry at you because of me."

"I'll deal with Evan." I stand and start pacing. "You get some sleep. I'll call you in the morning. Goodnight, Vivian."

"Goodnight, Grace."

I end the call, even more furious with Evan. Whatever he said to his mother made her afraid to see me, as though he would punish her if she does. I won't stand for it. Vivian is going to be my mother-in-law. I decide whether I want to spend time with her and get to know her, not the man I'm supposed to be marrying.

Storming out of the bedroom, I go to the living room and find Evan seated on the couch, holding his glass of scotch. The TV's on, turned to one of the financial news channels.

"We need to talk." I snatch up the remote and turn the TV off.

"Grace, if this is about my mother . . ."

"It's not just about Vivian," I say, remaining standing. "It's about you telling me I can't see her or talk to her. You don't get to boss me around like that. That's not the way this works."

"I was trying to protect you," he says, getting up. "And protect us. I didn't want my mother's ridiculous stories affecting how you see me."

"I don't need your mother to do that," I say, putting my hands on my hips. "You're doing that all by yourself."

"What is that supposed to mean?" he asks, slowly setting the glass on the table between us.

"Kicking out your mother? Not bringing her things to the hotel? Not letting her have dinner with us? Yelling at me for trying to get to know her? That tells me a lot about who you are as a person. And I don't like it, Evan. I don't like this side of you." I pause, my heart beating faster. "I don't know if this going to work."

His brows draw together. "If *what* is going to work?"

"This. Us. I don't want to be married to someone who acts like this. Someone who treats his own mother this way."

Evan steps around the table and comes over to me. "Grace, what are you saying?"

"I'm saying . . ." I hesitate, not sure I should do this when I'm angry and not thinking straight. And yet, I find myself sliding the ring off my finger.

"No!" Evan says in a panic as I hold out the ring. "Grace, please, I'll do anything! I'll tell Mother she can see you again! I'll—"

"I can't." I set the ring on the table, right next to his glass. "I need to think about this. But right now, I can't agree to marry you when you won't let your own mother have anything to do with me."

"Grace, forget all that." He grips my hand. "You can see her whenever you wish. I'll call her right now. We can go see her together. We'll bring her things to the hotel." He's talking fast, willing to say anything to change my mind. That's why it's meaningless. He isn't saying all this because it's what he wants. He's saying it so I'll put the ring back on and agree to marry him.

"I just talked to her," I say. "She's going to bed. I told her I'd call her tomorrow."

"Great! That's wonderful!" His tone and expression brighten. "You can take my credit card. Have a spa day. Go on a shopping spree. Whatever you want—"

"Evan, you can't fix this with money." I shake my head and move past him to the couch. "Maybe the two of us just aren't right for each other."

"Grace, no! Don't say that." Evan sits beside me. "I love you. You're everything I could ever want."

"Only if I do what you tell me to," I say, realizing Jenna was right. Evan can be very controlling. I turn to him. "If I don't do what you want, you get mad. I can't live that way."

"You won't have to. I promise." He holds both my hands and looks me in the eye. "I've made some mistakes. I admit that. But it's only because I'm so afraid to lose you. I sensed my mother was coming between us and I panicked." He gazes down at my hand, and his voice drops to a whisper. "Please put the ring back on."

"I can't," I say.

"Grace, please," he begs. "Don't do this. Don't end this."

"I didn't say I was ending this. I'm saying I need time. I need you to be okay with that."

He nods, the heartbroken look on his face making me feel so bad I almost agree to put the ring back on. But I know this is for the best. We raced into this, and now I need to take a step back and decide if it's really what I want.

"We'd have a good life, Grace," Evan says, his eyes on mine. "That's one thing I'm certain of. I can see it in my mind." He smiles a little. "We'd have a beautiful house in whatever location you'd like. And we'd have beautiful children, as many as you want, and send them to the very best private schools. I'd take you on vacations all over the world. We'd stay at the best places. Eat at the nicest restaurants. Shop at the finest stores. I know material things aren't as important to you as they are others, but consider this, Grace." He looks to the ring for a moment, then back up at me. "Wouldn't it be nice to never have to worry about money again? To no longer have to struggle?"

He's painting a nice picture of a future that, up until recently, was nothing more than a fantasy for me. But I still can't agree to marry him. Not until I give it more thought.

"I need time," I tell him. "I'm not saying the answer won't be yes, but I'm not saying it won't be no, either."

"I understand." He lets go of my hands and sits back on the couch. "Would you like me to leave? Go stay somewhere else?"

"No. Evan, this is your apartment. I can stay on the couch."

"You'll stay in our room. I'll take the couch."

He's handling this much better than I thought he would. Given how angry he was earlier, I was expecting him to react a similar way to me calling off our engagement.

"I need to go out for a while," he says, getting up.

"Out where?"

"I don't know." He gets his coat and walks to the door. "Goodnight, Grace."

He's gone before I have a chance to tell him goodbye. This is not how I thought tonight would go. I assumed Evan would come home from work, Vivian would be here, and we'd all go out for dinner. But instead, Vivian's been moved to a hotel, Evan's off to do who knows what, and I'm alone and no longer engaged.

So much has changed in just a few days. I've gone from being thrilled to marry Evan to uncertain if he's the right guy for me. Evan would blame his mother for that. He'd say she told me things about him she shouldn't have, but it was all stuff he should've told me himself. We can't have a relationship built on secrets and lies. I'd like to think he's not hiding anything else, but telling his mother to no longer talk to me makes me think there's more he doesn't want me to know.

CHAPTER 33

In the morning, I get up and find Evan has already left for work. I'm surprised he didn't wake me to kiss me goodbye. Maybe he felt he couldn't now that I've broken off our engagement.

Walking over to the table next to the couch, I see my ring is still where I left it. I bring it to the bedroom and put it in the same box Evan pulled out of his suit jacket the night he proposed. It wasn't that long ago, yet it seems like forever. So much has happened since then.

Once the ring is safely tucked away, I call Vivian. Her phone rings several times before going to voicemail. I leave a message asking her to call me back. Moments after I hang up, Evan calls.

"Hey, I just called your mom," I say. "She didn't pick up. Have you talked to her?"

"Yes, she's not feeling well. She's going to stay in this morning and rest."

"I could check on her. Does she need any medicine?" I leave the bedroom and head to the kitchen for coffee.

"I think she just had one too many cocktails at the bar last night. She'll be fine."

I walk over to the coffee machine. "Where did you go last night?"

"I took a walk. Stopped for a drink." He pauses. "What do you have planned for today?"

"I was going to go see your mom, but if she's not feeling well, I'll find something else to do."

"Yes, well, I'll let you get on with your day. I just wanted to let you know about Mother. Goodbye, Grace."

"Bye," I mutter, noticing the distance between us.

There was no warmth in Evan's tone, just detachment, and he didn't end the call by saying he loved me. It's like he's already decided it's over between us.

My phone rings again. I pick it up, thinking — hoping — it's Evan calling back to at least tell me he loves me. But it's not. It's Jenna.

"Hey," I answer. "Are you off today?"

"No, I'm at work. Martin was asking how you were doing. I told him I didn't know so he asked me to call you. So how are you doing?"

"Okay," I say, not wanting to get into the whole broken engagement story.

"You don't sound okay," Jenna says. "What's wrong?"

"Evan and I had an argument, but it's not a big deal. We'll work it out."

"You should come to the diner. Martin said he'd give you a free meal if you show up. And you can pick up your paycheck. Oh, and I've got some mail for you."

"Yeah, okay," I tell her.

It'd be nice to get away for a few hours. Since Vivian's not feeling well, and I still don't know anybody in the city that I could hang out with, going to see my friends sounds like a great idea.

"Really?" Jenna sounds both surprised and excited. "You're really coming?"

"Yeah, I just need to get ready and then I'll head out."

"Awesome! See you soon!"

It's just past eleven o'clock when I arrive at the diner. The lunch rush has begun, and the place is packed. Poor Jenna looks like she can barely keep up. An older man is yelling at her to take his order as she wipes up chocolate milk spilled all over the floor. I'm tempted to step in and help. Where's the other waitress? There should be two people working the lunch shift.

"Hey!" the old man yells at Jenna. "Is anyone gonna take my order?"

By instinct, I race over to him. "I will. What can I get you?"

He looks at me, scrunching up his face. "You don't work here."

"No, but I did a few weeks ago." For all his yelling, it's weird he focuses on that. "If you tell me what you want, I'll get your order in."

"The patty melt with a side of beans and a chocolate shake." He points at me. "If you're some kind of scammer, I'm gonna—"

"I'll go put your order in," I say, walking away.

I don't miss customers like him. I used to get a lot of them. Old guys who complain all the time and bark orders. And then they leave a lousy tip or nothing at all.

"You're here!" Jenna squeals, catching up to me on my way to the kitchen. "Did you take that guy's order?"

"Yeah, but only because he wouldn't shut up. Where's the other waitress?"

"Car trouble. She may not make it in." Jenna rolls her eyes. "She's always missing work."

"Well, look who's here," Martin says, smiling at me from behind the grill. "You finally decided to visit."

"It hasn't been that long," I say, smiling back. "I need a patty melt with a side of beans."

"She stepped in while I cleaned up a spill," Jenna explains as she adds two more order slips to the lineup.

"You can't be doing that, Grace," Martin says. "I could get in trouble."

"Relax. All I did was take an order." I roll my eyes playfully, getting the same in return.

"Did you hear from Kara?" Jenna asks Martin.

"I'm here!" Kara yells, coming out of the break room. "My boyfriend gave me a ride."

"Go on and get out there," Martin tells her, nodding toward the diner.

"How's she working out?" I ask when she's gone.

Martin gives Jenna a look.

"That bad?" I say with a laugh.

"Come on," Jenna says, grabbing my arm. "There's one seat left at the counter."

"Don't forget that patty melt and beans," I call out to Martin as Jenna drags me away. "Cheeseburger and fries for me!"

"Coming right up," he calls back.

My mouth is watering thinking about that burger. I've missed greasy diner food. The places Evan takes me are nice, but the food is too fancy for me. Even the burgers are fancy, topped with gourmet sauces and stinky cheese. I have simple tastes. I just want a basic burger with cheddar.

As I sit at the counter, I watch Jenna and Kara race around the diner, delivering food, wiping up spills, and refilling drinks. That used to be me, and it would be again if I broke up with Evan. I know Martin would give me my job back, but why would I want it? Seeing Jenna running around and hearing people yell at her reminds me of all the things I didn't like about being a waitress.

There's a loud crashing sound behind me, and I turn back to see Jenna on the floor, surrounded by shards of dirty dishes.

"Jenna!" I race over to her. "Are you okay?"

"I will be," she mutters, rubbing her back.

"Where's Jared?" I ask, referring to the busboy. "I'll go get him to clean this up."

"He called in sick," she says, picking up the broken shards.

"Hey, lady!" some guy yells at Jenna, holding up his glass. "I need a refill!"

"I'll get it," I tell her. "Or you get it, and I'll clean this up."

"I'll do it. You don't work here anymore."

"If I don't get a refill," the guy yells, "you ain't getting a tip!"

Jenna groans as she pushes up from the floor. "Be right there!"

She hobbles over to him. She really hurt herself when she fell. Despite her telling me not to, I clean up the mess and take the tray of broken dishes to the kitchen.

"Hey!" Martin yells when he sees me. "You aren't allowed to do that! I told you I could get in big trouble."

"Yeah, alright, I got it." I leave the tray and go back to my seat at the counter. It feels wrong to just sit here. It's obvious Jenna needs serious help, but I can't do anything. I'm not allowed to.

"Sorry I can't talk," Jenna says when she drops off my burger. She looks exhausted, but it'll be at least two hours before things calm down. "You'll stay, right? Until my break?"

"I'll be here," I say, smiling at her.

She takes off again. As I watch her work the lunch rush, I realize this isn't what I want. I could definitely do it if I had to. If I ended things with Evan, I could come back here and fall back into the life I had before, but why would I?

My life was so much harder before I met Evan. Every day was a struggle. I was always worried I wouldn't have enough money to pay my bills. My car would break down, and I couldn't afford to get it fixed. My headaches would get bad, and I couldn't afford to see a doctor or get my meds refilled. I lived in a constant state of stress, going from one crisis to another.

Now, my life is easy. I have no worries. No expenses. I'm with a man who loves me. A man who would give me an amazing life.

I want to marry Evan. I really do. I just wish he'd told me the truth about his past. There's so much he left out, but it's the death of his former fiancés that bothers me the most. I'm still upset I had to find that out from his mother instead of him.

"Let's go," Jenna says when she finally gets her break. "Kara can finish cleaning up."

I look back and see Kara checking her phone. She didn't work nearly as hard as Jenna did today.

Jenna and I go into the break room, and she immediately collapses on the small, faded couch.

"So, what's new?" she says with a tired smile.

I feel bad for her, which is strange because just a week ago, I *was* her. I'd be on that same couch, resting my aching feet after hours of hard work, making next to nothing.

I sigh and sit next to her on the couch. "Things have just been . . . weird."

"What do you mean?"

"It's a lot of stuff, but most recently, Evan's mom."

Jenna leans back and turns toward me. Concern fills her eyes. "Is that why you're here? To get away from her?"

"No. I actually like her, but Evan doesn't want me around her. He claims she's confused and says things that aren't true. But some of those things *are* true, which makes me wonder . . ." I pick at a loose thread on my T-shirt. "I don't know. I guess what I'm saying is that I don't know Evan as well as I thought I did."

"It's hard to really know someone after a few weeks," Jenna says.

"It's been longer than that, and I live with him. I see him every day. I should know him better than this by now."

"What's this about? Did something happen?"

I tell her about Evan's former fiancés and how they both died in tragic accidents. I leave out the other stuff Vivian told me, deciding the fiancé news is enough for now.

"He was engaged twice?" Jenna says, blinking slowly. "And both women died?"

"Yes, but they were both accidents," I say quickly.

"That you know of," she mutters.

"The police did an investigation. Evan wasn't involved."

"Doesn't matter. The guy could be cursed."

I roll my eyes. "He's not cursed."

"You're seriously not worried about this? You're his *third fiancé*. I'd be freaking out!"

"That's why he didn't tell me. He thought I'd react the same way you are and break up with him."

"But you're still with him, right?"

"Yeah. Why?"

"You're not wearing your ring," she says, motioning to my left hand.

I glance down and realize I forgot my ring. I was going to put it on to show Jenna and to hide the fact I was no longer engaged.

"I took it off last night," I tell her.

"Does this mean you're not engaged?"

"I told Evan I needed time to think about it. But what is waiting really going to do?" I shrug and rub my thumb where the ring used to sit. "It won't change anything."

"It might. It'll at least give you more time to get to know him."

"I already know him. And I want to marry him. Just imagine the life I'd have if I did," I say wistfully. "I'd never have to worry about money again."

"Oh, that reminds me." She jumps up and goes over to the locker where she keeps her stuff. She opens it, takes out a stack of envelopes, and brings them to me. "Here's your mail. I think there might be some bills in there."

I flip through the envelopes and see one from a medical clinic and another one from the hospital I went to after the accident.

"You see what I mean?" I hold up one of the bills. "I wouldn't have to stress about how I'm going to pay this if I married Evan."

"Yeah, but would you be happy?" she asks, crossing her arms.

"Evan and I were happy before all this, so I know we can be happy again."

Kara saunters into the room, looks between me and Jenna, then says to Jenna, "Your break's over."

Jenna groans and massages her lower back as she gets up. She's not even thirty and is acting like she has the aches and pains of someone twice her age. I don't want that to be me, but I know it would be if I came back to this life.

I rip open the hospital bill, feeling sick to my stomach when I see the balance. It's been almost two years since the accident, and I've been paying every month. How could I still owe this much money? I open the bill from the clinic I was going to for my headaches last year and see they added a late charge because I didn't make a payment last month. Someone like Evan would just pay the bill in full, but I'm on a payment plan, and last month, I couldn't afford to send in any money.

I don't want to keep living this way. Always struggling. Never getting ahead. I have a chance to escape this life, so why wouldn't I take it?

Evan and I can work this out. I know we can.

I'm not giving up on us. I've made my decision. The engagement is back on.

CHAPTER 34

When Evan arrives home just after five, I'm waiting on the couch for him, excited to tell him my news. I don't know what I was thinking ending our engagement. I love Evan, and I love the life he's given me. Why did I even consider giving it up?

I was letting the secrets of Evan's past affect how I felt about him, but that was wrong. What happened to those women was a tragedy. I understand why he didn't want to talk about it. Not only does it bring back painful memories, but he's worried that telling me would cause me to leave him.

Seeing Jenna's reaction today when I told her about those women showed me why Evan was so concerned about me finding out. He thought I'd react like Jenna did and want to run away from him, fearing he killed them or that he's cursed, which is ridiculous. Their deaths were unfortunate accidents that have nothing to do with me.

"How was your day?" Evan asks as I get up from the couch.

"Good! I went to the diner." I go to give him a hug, but he puts his hand up, stopping me.

"Why did you go to the diner?"

"To see Jenna and Martin and pick up my paycheck."

"Oh," he says, sounding relieved. Did he think I went there to get my old job back? "How did it go?"

"It was nice seeing Jenna and Martin, but I didn't like being back there."

"Why? Did something happen?"

"I realized that's not me anymore. That's not my life." I smile and look into his eyes. "My life is here. With you."

"What are you saying?"

"I thought about it, and I get why you hid your past from me. I shouldn't have held it against you. You've been through so much, Evan. I can't even imagine going through that not just once, but twice. Anyway, I need you to know I'm committed to you, and to us."

A huge smile spreads across his face. He pulls me close, wrapping his arms around me. "I'm so happy you said that. I was worried I'd come home, and you'd be gone. Moved out. And all I'd have left is a note telling me it's over."

"Evan, I'd never do something like that. If I was ending things, I would've talked to you face-to-face," I say, putting my arms around his neck.

He really thought our relationship was over, even after I told him it wasn't and that I just needed time to think. It shows me how fragile he is after the massive losses he's suffered. He assumes he'll never have love — that it'll always be taken away from him.

"I love you so much, Grace," he whispers.

"I love you too." I pull back and give him a sexy smile. "Why don't we go in the bedroom?"

He sighs. "I would, but my mother is coming over. I invited her to dinner. She'll be here any minute."

"Does this mean you're not mad at her anymore?"

"I wasn't mad at her." Evan lets me go and walks over to the kitchen. "I was disappointed she didn't respect my wishes and told you about my past."

I follow and watch as he pulls out the scotch and pours a healthy amount into a glass. "But that's Mother. She always thinks she knows what's best for me."

The doorbell rings.

"That's her," he says before taking a swig of his drink. "Do you mind getting it?"

"Sure." I answer the door and find Vivian dressed in an ivory-colored pantsuit and matching coat. She looks beautiful, as always.

"Grace," she says, looking surprised. "Evan didn't think you'd be able to join us."

I wonder if he told her I called off the engagement. Or did he make up some other excuse for why I wouldn't be having dinner with them?

"I was out just for the day," I tell her. I step aside and wave her in. "Come on in."

She walks into the apartment, stopping next to the couch.

"Hello, Evan," she says in a formal tone. "Thank you for having my things delivered."

That's odd. She'd usually go up to him and kiss his cheek.

"You're welcome, Mother," he says, remaining in the kitchen. He leans back against the counter, his glass held firmly in his hand. "I hope you've found the hotel is suitable for your needs."

"Yes, very." She smiles a little. "It has all the comforts of home."

The two of them are acting very strangely. Something's going on between them, but I have no idea what, and I doubt Evan will tell me. But I've decided I don't need to know everything, especially when it involves him and his mother.

"Grace, you should change for dinner," Evan says. "We need to leave soon, or we'll miss our reservation."

"I was going to wear what I have on," I say, glancing down at my black jeans and white sweater."

Evan laughs a little. "We don't have time for jokes. We need to get going. Please go put on something appropriate."

I wasn't joking. I was really going to wear this, but I guess it's not fancy enough for wherever we're going. I change into one of the many black dresses Evan bought me, put on some heels, and go back out to the living room.

"Much better," Evan says, smiling at me.

He takes us to a ritzy French restaurant. I can't understand anything on the menu, so Evan orders for me. When I ask him what I'm getting, he says I'll have to wait and find out. He says it like he's being playful, but I find it annoying. I want to know what I'm eating.

When my meal arrives, Evan reveals it's sweetbreads. I don't know what that is, but the name is misleading because what's on my plate doesn't look like bread and doesn't smell sweet. After I take a bite, Evan explains it's the pancreas of a calf. Knowing that's what I ate, I almost throw up, but instead, I gulp down my wine and decide I'm no longer hungry.

"Grace, finish your meal," Evan says like I'm a child. He's already finished his, which was chicken with some kind of sauce. Why didn't he order that for me?

"I'm done," I tell him. "I didn't care for it."

"How would you know? You only had a few bites."

"Which was all I needed to know I don't like it."

I give him a look to let it go. I don't want to argue in front of his mother. I glance over at her and see her sliding her sleeve up to check the time. There's a large bruise on her arm, just above her watch.

"What happened?" I ask.

"Mother can be rather clumsy when she drinks," Evan says, looking at Vivian. "Isn't that right, Mother?"

"Yes." She smiles at me. "I had a few too many cocktails and bumped my arm on the bathroom door."

"It looks painful," I say. "Did you put ice on it?"

"She'll be fine," Evan says. "Mother is quite capable of taking care of herself."

Vivian purses her lips and glares at Evan across the table. What is going on with them?

Evan pays the check, and just as we're about to leave, he smiles and says, "I'd like to share some news."

Vivian and I wait for him to continue.

He turns to me and takes my hand. "Please understand I wanted to include you in this, but I wasn't able to. I had to act quickly. We could always back out, but that would mean losing our deposit."

"What are you talking about?" I ask.

"I booked a location for our wedding. It's a beautiful historic hotel. The ballroom is on the top floor with stunning views of the city."

"You already booked it?" I say. My heart drops. "When?"

"Yesterday. I was going to tell you last night but then . . . well, we were sidetracked, and I wasn't able to."

By sidetracked, he means we got into an argument that ended with him leaving.

"When's the date?" Vivian asks Evan.

"The first Saturday in November."

"*This* November?" I ask. My palms go sweaty, and my throat dries up. "Like a few weeks from now?"

Evan smiles. "I know it's soon, but why wait? I have the resources to hire out all the wedding plans. You'll just need to show up."

"Evan, no. I'm not ready to get married," I say. My heart is now racing, and my chest tightens up. "I wanted to wait at least a year."

"A year?" He laughs. "Grace, we're not getting any younger. I don't want to be an old man by the time we have children."

"If the marriage is in November," Vivian says, "this changes my plans. I certainly won't be heading home on Sunday."

"Why wouldn't you?" Evan asks.

"I need to plan a party," she says, like he should already know this.

"What party?" I ask.

"An engagement party." She smiles at me. "You can't be married without first having an engagement party. It wouldn't be proper."

"An engagement party would be wonderful, Mother," Evan says, beaming. "Grace and I would very much appreciate that. I assume the guest list would include all your acquaintances here in New York?"

"Yes, of course, and I'd want to invite your work colleagues along with any friends Grace would like to invite."

"Wait." I hold my hand up. "Can you two stop for a minute? I'm not ready for this."

Evan looks at his mother. "Perhaps we should skip the party. It does feel rather rushed."

"Nonsense," Vivian says. "I can pull together a party in a week if I have to."

"But I don't know if I want one." I look at Evan. "We need to talk about this. Alone."

Vivian stands. "I'll head back to the hotel. You two talk it over and let me know what you decide in the morning."

I watch her as she walks off. My cheeks feel flushed, and I can't tell if I'm feeling panicked or outraged. Probably both.

"November?" I say to Evan. "And you booked the place without telling me?"

"We'll discuss it when we get home," he says, getting up.

When we're back at the apartment, I storm up to Evan. "I can't believe you did this!"

"Did what?" He asks as he cups my face. "Arrange to marry the woman I love as soon as possible? Most women would be thrilled about that."

"Don't try to make me the bad guy here," I snap, shoving his hands off my face. "You shouldn't have done this without talking to me."

"Grace, I wanted to, but I wasn't able to. If I hadn't booked it when I did, it would've gone to someone else."

"Yeah? So? There are plenty of other places to get married. We could've found a place we both liked for a date we *both* agreed on."

He frowns. "I'm sorry, Grace. I got swept up in my excitement to marry you and acted impulsively." He holds my hands. "You're right. I shouldn't have done it. If you'd like me to cancel the booking, I will, but will you please at least let me show you the brochure?"

I sigh. "Okay, fine."

His face lights up. "I'll be right back."

I sit on the couch while Evan goes down to his office. I feel better now that he's agreed to cancel the booking. I thought for sure he'd try to pressure me into doing this. He seemed so insistent at the restaurant like he wasn't going to back down. Maybe seeing my anger when we got home helped him realize his mistake.

He comes back with a folder and hands it to me. "That's the information I was given about the hotel. Go ahead and look through it."

I pull out a glossy brochure showing a ballroom overlooking Manhattan. Inside are photos of the ballroom decorated for weddings that took place there. I have to admit, the photos are absolutely gorgeous. If that's what my wedding could look like, maybe I shouldn't be so quick to dismiss the place.

"What do you think?" Evan asks, sitting beside me.

"It's beautiful, but why can't we have the wedding here next year?"

"They're booked three years out. The only reason I was able to reserve it was because there was a cancellation. Grace, I think it's a sign. It's telling us not to wait."

I shake my head. "It's too soon."

"It only seems that way because you had a later date in mind," he says.

"How did you even know about this?" I hold up the brochure. "Were you looking for a place without telling me?"

"No, I overheard a woman talking when I was waiting in line to get coffee. She happened to be the hotel's wedding coordinator, and she was telling her friend that they had a cancellation, which she said almost never happens. I politely interrupted their conversation and asked if I could see the place. She took me there, and I booked it on the spot. If I hadn't, we would've lost it."

I gaze at the beautiful photos in the brochure, my mind imagining what it would be like to have my wedding there. Maybe I should do it. Evan's right. Why wait? I know I want to marry him, so why wait another year or two to do it?

"What do you think?" Evan asks. "Any chance you'd at least consider it?"

"Actually, I think you might've convinced me."

"Convinced you of what?" he asks hesitantly.

"That we should get married here. It's beautiful. More beautiful than I could've ever imagined."

"What are you saying?"

"I'm in." I set the brochure down and look at Evan. "Let's do it."

CHAPTER 35

"This November?" Jenna yells into the phone. "Are you serious?"

"It's the only time we could book the ballroom," I say. "You should see this place, Jenna. It's gorgeous, like something out of a movie. And I don't have to do anything. Evan's hiring people to do all the planning."

"And you're okay with this? Getting married this soon?"

"Why wait? I know I'm going to marry him, so why not do it now?"

It's been three days since Evan announced he booked a wedding location, and I'm slowly coming to realize this is actually happening. That I'm actually getting married in a few weeks. I've put off searching for jobs for now. After the wedding, Evan wants to take me on a month-long honeymoon trip through Europe. I can't start a job and then take a month off.

"You shouldn't be rushing to get married based on when a ballroom is available," Jenna says.

"That's not why I'm doing it. I mean, yes, that obviously determined the date, but I thought about it some more, and decided I don't need to keep waiting. I love Evan and want to marry him."

The doorbell rings.

"Jenna, I have to go. Vivian's here."

"Okay, talk to you later."

I end the call and drop my phone on the couch.

"Hi, Vivian," I say, answering the door.

"Good morning, Grace." She comes into the apartment holding a binder. "I brought the catering menus for you to review."

The engagement party is next Saturday, a week from tomorrow. It's going to be on the top floor of a fancy hotel in a ballroom that's similar to the one where we're having the wedding. Vivian's invited almost a hundred guests, most of whom are people she knows. I get the feeling this is less about Evan and me and more about Vivian having a party to announce to her high-society friends that her son is getting married. I don't understand that world, but Evan said this is something rich people do. Apparently, they have parties for everything.

"This looks good," I say, pointing to a picture of a taco platter.

Vivian's sitting beside me at the table and leans over to see the photo. She returns her gaze to me. "Grace, that's for children's parties."

"Why can't it be for adults? Everyone loves tacos."

"They aren't appropriate for an engagement party. We need something elegant." She flips through the binder. "Like this."

She points to a photo showing silver platters topped with artfully arranged seafood. I'm not a big fan of seafood, but I know a lot of people love it, including Evan.

"I guess that'd be okay," I say.

"Excellent!" Vivian takes the binder from me. "I think that was all we had left to decide."

Vivian has been coming over every day to discuss the party. Then we go out for lunch or go shopping or just hang out here. Spending all this time with her, I'm starting to feel a lot closer to her. I think she feels the same way about me. I think she's even starting to see me like a daughter.

"Can I ask you something?" I say.

"About the party?"

"No, about the wedding." I hesitate, not sure I should say this, but I want her opinion, although I'm not sure she'll be honest since it involves her son. "Do you think Evan and I are rushing into this?"

"That's up to you and Evan to decide," she says.

"Yes, but if you were me, would you be waiting longer?"

"Only if I had doubts." She pauses, looking at me with concern. "You aren't having doubts, are you?"

"It's just that sometimes I feel like I only know part of Evan. The part that lives here."

"I'm not sure what you mean."

"He had this whole other life in California. I've never met the friends he has there. I've never been to his house or seen where he grew up."

"I'm sure Evan would love to take you there, but I doubt there would be time before the wedding." She taps her fingers on the table. "I probably shouldn't suggest this, but maybe it would help."

"What is it?"

"When I met Ashley for lunch that day, she mentioned wanting to talk to you. I didn't think it was a good idea, given that she was Dana's friend, and Evan is obviously trying to move past that part of his life, but perhaps we wouldn't have to tell him."

"Why does Ashley want to talk to me?"

"I don't know. She didn't say. She's back in California now, but you could call her and ask her whatever questions you have about Evan. You could always ask me, of course, but as his mother, he doesn't tell me much. Ashley spent quite a bit of time with Evan when he was with Dana. She'd be able to share what he was like back then, if that's of interest to you."

I didn't care for Ashley when we met, but I'm curious what she would say about Evan. You can learn a lot by talking to someone's friends.

"Um, yeah, that might be a good idea," I say. "Could I get her number?"

Vivian takes out her phone and texts me the number. "I won't tell Evan. I'll let you decide if he needs to know."

* * *

We spend the rest of the morning together and go out for lunch. Then Vivian heads to her hotel while I return to the apartment. I can't decide if I should call Ashley. It seems strange to call her and ask her about Evan.

After pacing the apartment for an hour, rolling the pros and cons around in my head, I call Ashley's number. She's probably at work and won't pick up, but I'll leave her a message.

"Hello, this is Ashley," she answers after a single ring.

I stop in the middle of the living room. I wasn't prepared for her to answer. I thought for sure the call would go to voicemail.

"Hello?" she says. "Is anyone there?"

"Yes, sorry. This is Grace, Evan Sinclair's fiancé. We met a few weeks ago at a restaurant in New York?"

"Yes, I remember," she says, sounding like she's wondering why I called.

"Vivian gave me your number because I was telling her I've never met any of Evan's friends. Your name came up, so I thought I'd give you a call, but if you're busy—"

"No, I have time." I hear a door close, and then Ashley says, "I wouldn't say Evan and I were friends. I only knew him because of Dana."

"But you could tell me about him, right?"

She laughs a little. "Don't you already know him? You're marrying him."

"Yeah, I know it sounds odd for me to say that, but what I'm asking is what Evan's life was like back in California. What his

251

friends were like. He hasn't told me much. And you know how they say you can learn a lot about someone from their friends."

"Evan didn't really have any friends, at least not that I know of. He spent all his time with Dana, to the point that we stopped having girls' nights. Evan didn't want us hanging out. He wanted all of Dana's time to be spent with him."

"I'm sure she wanted that, too. They were in love. About to get married."

"You're not getting it." Her voice is low, and I sense frustration. "He didn't just *want* her spending time with him. He *demanded* it. I kept telling her he was being controlling, but she didn't see it."

It sounds like Jenna and me. She's told me the same thing about Evan.

"I don't think Evan wanting to spend time with her is controlling," I say.

"It wasn't just that. It was other stuff, like telling her how to dress or making her read the books he gave her. He even made her take classes. He said it was to help her grow and expand her interests, but to me, he was making her into whatever he wanted for a wife."

"If she wasn't what he wanted, why didn't he find someone else?"

"Because she was his type. You know Evan has to save women, right?"

"Save them? What do you mean?"

"He finds girls who don't have much going for them and rescues them. I think it makes him feel powerful."

Her comment reminds me of what Vivian told me about Evan's first fiancé working at a gas station. Dana was a maid, and I worked at a diner, but that doesn't mean Ashley's theory is correct. Evan didn't ask me out because I needed to be rescued. My life wasn't great back then, but I would've been fine if he'd never showed up.

"What else can you tell me?" I ask, wanting to hurry this along. I regret calling her. She clearly has something against Evan. She hasn't said one good thing about him.

"Well, like I said, he didn't really have any friends. He asked some guys he went to school with to be his groomsmen at the wedding. Their mothers are all friends with Evan's mother, so they kind of had to agree to it."

"But Evan wasn't friends with them?"

"No, he doesn't like being social. He'll do it if he has to, but he'd rather be alone, reading a book or writing code. He's extremely smart. I'll give him that. But he's not someone you'd want to invite to a party."

"Maybe he's changed, because the Evan I know isn't anything like that."

"He is. You just don't see it because you're marrying him. You see what you want to see."

I'm getting upset hearing her say these things about Evan. I think it's time to end this conversation.

"Just be careful, okay?" Ashley says.

"Careful about what?"

"Evan." She pauses. "The police said he wasn't involved, but . . . I'm not sure I believe it. That's why Vivian wanted me to talk to you. Just in case it didn't happen the way we thought."

"Wait, *Vivian* wanted us to talk? She said you were the one who wanted to talk to me."

"No, it was her. She knew I had concerns about Evan, and I guess she wanted me to warn you."

"That doesn't make sense. Vivian wouldn't tell you to warn me about her own son."

"She would if it meant saving your life," Ashley says.

My stomach clenches, and a sharp pain shoots through my head.

"What are you saying?" I ask. "That Vivian thinks Evan might hurt me?"

"I'm just telling you to be careful. Evan can't always control his anger. Dana said when they'd argue, he'd sometimes get so angry, he had to leave so he wouldn't do something he'd regret. The night she died, they'd been fighting. Evan told the police he went on a walk to cool down, but I think he did something before he left. I think he put the sleeping pills in her wine, knowing it would knock her out and she'd drown."

"Evan wouldn't do that," I say, the pain in my head getting worse. "He would never hurt anyone. I know he wouldn't."

"Do you?" she asks. "Or is that just what you want to believe?"

"I have to go," I say. I end the call and toss the phone on the couch.

She's wrong. Evan had nothing to do with Dana's death. It was horrible of Ashley to even say that. She only did it because she doesn't like Evan and because she doesn't want to believe her friend was stupid enough to combine sleeping pills and wine while taking a bath. The police ruled it an accident, and that's what it was.

What concerns me is what she said about Vivian. Did she really tell Ashley to warn me about Evan? That can't be right. Ashley is probably just angry that Evan is marrying me so soon after Dana's death, so she's trying to break us up. She wants to convince me Evan is dangerous so that I'll leave him.

"Grace," Evan says, startling me. I turn and see him coming through the door. "I thought you'd be out with my mother."

"I was, but she went back to the hotel. What are you doing home?"

"I left my notes here for the project I'm working on. I decided I'll finish the day here instead of going back to the office."

I stumble over to the couch, my headache causing my vision to blur.

Evan hurries over me. "Grace, what's wrong?"

"My head," I say.

The room is spinning, and the pain in my head is getting worse. It's because of Ashley and the stress she caused me by saying those horrible things about Evan.

"I'll be right back."

He returns quickly with one of my pills and a glass of water, handing them to me as he sits beside me. I gulp down the pill, then hand Evan the glass.

"When did it start?" he asks.

"A few minutes ago." I hug my knees to my chest and close my eyes. "It's really bad."

"Do you know what caused it?"

I shake my head, not wanting to tell him about my call with Ashley.

"Come here." He puts his arm around me, and I rest my head on his shoulder. He places a gentle kiss on my forehead. "I'll take the rest of the day off. Work can wait. It's more important I take care of you. Anything you need, just tell me."

If Ashley was witnessing this, she'd feel like an idiot for thinking Evan would ever hurt someone, especially someone he cares about. I wish I'd never talked to her.

CHAPTER 36

"You look like you're feeling better," Vivian says the next morning. It's Saturday, and she's joining us for breakfast. Evan's making it. He didn't think we should go out. He was worried a noisy restaurant might make my headache return.

"I'm a lot better," I say. "But I had to take twice the pills I normally do."

"She was in rough shape," Evan says, pouring his mother some coffee. "I almost took her to the ER."

"Evan took very good care of me," I say to Vivian as she sits next to me at the table. "You should be very proud."

"I'm always proud of my son," she says, smiling at him.

"Here you go, Mother," Evan hands her a plate with an omelet and a side of fruit. "And for my lovely bride-to-be," he says, giving me the other plate.

"This looks wonderful," Vivian says.

"I'm lucky to be marrying a guy who can cook," I say, smiling at Evan.

He returns to the table with a plate for himself. He's about to sit down when his phone rings. He looks at it. "It's someone from work. I'll go take it in my office."

I watch as he answers the call and walks off.

"This is excellent," Vivian says, eating her omelet. "I didn't know my son was so talented at making eggs."

I pick up my fork and cut off a small portion of my omelet. "Has he ever cooked for you?"

"Many times. But usually not breakfast. He took up cooking as a hobby toward the end of his college career." She smiles. "I think he only did it as a way to get girls."

"Yeah, probably," I say with a laugh.

I really want to talk to her about my call with Ashley, but I don't want Evan walking in on us. I need to hurry and say this before he comes back.

"I talked to Ashley yesterday," I blurt out.

"And?" Vivian looks at me. "What did she have to say?"

"She said you told her to talk to me. That it wasn't her idea."

"Of course it was her idea," Vivian scoffs. "I have no reason for you two to talk."

"That's what I thought, but . . ." I shake my head. "I don't know. She wasn't making sense."

"Why? What are you referring to?"

"She implied Evan was involved in Dana's death. She said he can't control his temper and that I should be careful around him."

Vivian picks up her coffee and takes a sip. Her silence puts me on edge. Why isn't she denying what Ashley said?

"She was lying, right?" I say. "I mean, obviously Evan didn't do anything."

"The police ruled it an accident," Vivian says, not looking at me as she sets her coffee down.

That's all she has to say? Why isn't she defending Evan? Calling Ashley a liar? Getting angry that Ashley would even think to accuse Evan of this?

"Why would Ashley say something like that?" I ask. "It's completely ridiculous. Evan wouldn't hurt anyone."

Vivian glances at her arm where I saw the bruise the other day. Is she trying to tell me Evan did that? No. She can't be. He wouldn't do that. He'd never hurt his mother.

She puts her hand over mine and looks at me. "It's true Evan struggles to control his temper, but all men do. We, as women, simply have to try not to trigger it."

My anger spikes hearing her say that, as if women are to blame for men's bad behavior. We shouldn't have to keep quiet or behave like they want us to in order to keep them from acting out.

"If you're saying I have to walk on eggshells around Evan to keep him from losing his temper, it's not going to happen. I can't live that way."

"You're free to do as you choose," she says, taking her hand off mine. "You just have to accept the consequences."

What consequences? What is she trying to say?

"Sorry about that," Evan says, coming back into the room. "I've told them not to call me on the weekend." He joins us at the table, smiling at me. "Weekends are for spending with my beautiful fiancé."

Vivian dabs the corner of her mouth with a napkin. "Have you two decided where you're going to live once you're married?"

"I'd like to live here," I say. "Not in the city, but somewhere nearby. Maybe New Jersey. That's where I grew up."

"And you've agreed to this?" Vivian asks Evan. "To remain on the East Coast?"

"We haven't decided." He takes a bite of his omelet and follows it with a sip of coffee. "We need to discuss it more. Mother, how are the plans for the engagement party going? Will everything be ready in time?"

"Yes. Everything's done. Grace and I finalized the menu, which was the last thing on my list. Now we can all relax until the big day."

"When are you going home?" he asks.

"I haven't decided." She laughs a little. "Are you in a hurry to get rid of me?"

"Of course not, Mother, but I'm sure you want to get back to your home and all your social activities."

"Not at all. I'm very much enjoying my time here. In fact, I was thinking I might stay until the wedding."

"Mother, that's weeks from now."

"And why is that an issue?"

"It's not," Evan says with a strained smile. "I just think you'd get bored being here for that long."

"There's plenty to do to keep me from being bored." She takes a sip of her coffee. "I could help Grace with the wedding plans."

"I've hired people for that," Evan says. "There's nothing you and Grace need to do."

Vivian sets her coffee down and looks at her son. "Why don't you just say what you mean, Evan?"

"Please, Mother," he says with a sigh. "Don't be dramatic. I'm not implying I don't want you here."

"Wonderful! Then the decision is made. I'm staying."

Evan glares at her, his nostrils flared, his jaw tightening. "It's not necessary, Mother. Grace and I don't need help with the wedding."

"Yes, you've made that quite clear. But I'm still going to stay." She reaches over and grips Evan's arm. "Don't worry, dear. I won't bother you. I know how important it is for you to spend time with your lovely bride." She pushes her chair back. "Thank you for breakfast. I hope you two have a lovely day."

"You're not staying?" I ask. "I thought you wanted to go dress shopping for the engagement party."

"Evan can go with you," she says, getting up. "He has an eye for what looks good on a woman. He's helped me many times."

"You helped your mother shop?" I ask.

"When I lived with her, yes," Evan says, not looking at Vivian.

Why is he acting so rude to his mom? So what if she wants to stay? At least she's at a hotel now instead of with us.

"Bye, Vivian," I say as she's leaving.

Evan says nothing and just continues to eat his breakfast.

"What is wrong with you?" I say to Evan once Vivian is gone. "Are you mad because she's staying?"

"Drop it, Grace," Evan snaps. "I don't want to talk about my mother. She can do as she pleases."

"Then why are you so upset?"

"I'm not." He clears his throat and puts on a fake smile. "What would you like to do today?"

"I need to find a dress for the party."

"I know the perfect place." He gets up and takes our plates to the sink, though I was nowhere near finished with my meal. "I'll clean this up, then we can go."

As I watch him load the dishwasher, my mind goes back to Ashley and what she said about Evan. I know none of it is true, so why can't I let it go? Why is it still bothering me?

"Would you come sit down?" I say. "I need to ask you something."

He wipes his hands on a dishtowel and joins me at the table. "What is it?"

"Did you ever call Ashley?"

"Ashley?"

"That woman who came up to us at the restaurant. You said you were going to call her."

"I said that so she'd leave us alone. I never intended to call her."

"Why? Do you not like her?"

He cocks his head to the side. "Why do you care?"

I shrug. "I just wondered. I realized I've never met any of your friends except Ashley."

"Ashley is not my friend. She's just someone I used to know."

"Why don't you like her?"

"Why are you suddenly asking me about Ashley?"

"I'm just trying to figure out why you wouldn't call her. She acted like she really wanted to talk to you."

"She was simply making conversation. She has no interest in speaking with me, just as I have no interest in speaking with her."

"So you two don't get along."

He sighs. "No. Ashley didn't approve of my relationship with Dana. Therefore, she tried to make me the enemy."

"Why didn't she approve?"

"She felt I was taking up too much of Dana's time. Time Ashley felt should've been spent with her. She's like Jenna that way. The situations are strangely similar."

"What do you mean?"

"Jenna didn't like me spending time with you. She tried to turn you against me."

"She just wasn't sure we were a good match."

"We don't need to get into it. The point is, Ashley didn't want me being with Dana, so she tried to make me into a villain. She did everything possible to try to harm my relationship with Dana, and because of that, I have no interest in ever speaking to Ashley again."

Now that I know his history with her, it makes sense that she would try to blame Evan for Dana's death. But if she still has such a negative opinion of Evan, why is Vivian friends with her? Why would she have lunch with a woman who's telling people Evan killed his fiancé?

There's something else going on here. I feel like Vivian knows something about Evan that she's not telling me.

CHAPTER 37

"You look absolutely stunning," Evan says as he comes into the bedroom. I'm wearing the dress he picked out, which is so much better than what I would've chosen. His mother was right. Her son has a talent for knowing what looks good on a woman.

"You look nice, too," I say, smiling at him in his tuxedo.

It's the night of our engagement party. I'm excited but also a little nervous since I don't know most of the people there. Evan's coworkers were invited, so I'll finally get to meet them. Jenna and Martin will be there, too, so I'll know at least two of the guests.

"Tonight is our official debut as a couple," Evan says, putting his arms around me. "I can't wait to show you off to everyone."

I rest my hands on his shoulders. "We should do something nice for your mother to thank her. Planning this party was a lot of work."

"She loved doing it. She was just telling me yesterday how much she enjoyed putting it together."

"I'd still like to do something for her. Maybe we could book her a spa day."

"Whatever you'd like." His phone chimes with a text notification. "I'm guessing that's her, asking if we've left."

"I'll go grab my coat."

Evan holds onto me. "Not yet." He gives me a kiss, then whispers in my ear, "You're mine, Grace. Forever."

I still get chills when he says that, and not in a good way. I should tell him I don't like it, so he'll stop saying it. Now isn't the time, though. If we don't leave right away, we'll be late.

Outside the building, a limo is waiting. Vivian reserved it for us. I told her we didn't need it, but she insisted we ride in style. When we arrive at the hotel, we take the elevator to the top floor. Evan takes my hand as we enter the ballroom. I gasp when I see it. The tables are adorned with beautiful floral arrangements in shades of white and cream. Tall pillar candles surround them, providing a soft glow in the dimly lit room. Twinkling white fairy lights are suspended from the ceiling, adding a magical feel.

"It's beautiful," I say, gazing at the room.

"As are you," Evan says, leaning down to kiss my cheek.

Vivian races up to us. She's wearing a gorgeous royal blue gown. She told me about it, but this is the first time I'm seeing it.

"The guests of honor have arrived," she says with a broad smile.

"Vivian, this place looks absolutely amazing," I say.

"Thank you. I was thinking it was lacking, but I did the best I could, given the timing."

"It's very nice, Mother," Evan says, leaning down to kiss her cheek. "Thank you for doing this."

"I was happy to." She motions us to follow her. "Let's get you two some champagne."

As we walk through the ballroom, I look around at all the guests. Most seem to be around Vivian's age, and all of them are very well-dressed. The women are dripping in diamonds, including Vivian, who has on a diamond necklace, bracelet, and earrings.

I wonder how much all that jewelry is worth? Probably more than I could make in a lifetime working at the diner. It's hard to believe that used to be my life, and now I'm here, in this elegant ballroom high above New York City, surrounded by wealth. If Evan hadn't come into the diner that day, none of this would have happened. I'd be spending my night watching TV on Jenna's worn-out couch, eating a bag of microwaved popcorn. That was a typical Saturday night.

Now look at me.

It doesn't even seem real.

Champagne in hand, Evan and I make our rounds, talking to people I don't know and shaking their hands while they congratulate us. A band is playing jazz music off to the side. Vivian only let me choose between jazz and classical, so I went with jazz. It seemed less stuffy.

"Grace!" someone yells. When I turn back, I see Jenna and Martin heading my way.

"You made it!" I race over to them and throw my arms around Jenna.

"Of course we made it," she says. "Did you think we wouldn't come? There's free food and drinks!"

I laugh. "That's the only reason you're here?"

"It's one of them," she jokes.

"You look nice, kid," Martin says.

"Thanks." I release Jenna and give him an equally tight hug. "Thanks for being here. I know you don't like coming to the city."

"I can make an exception now and then," he says with a wink. When we part, he looks around. "This is quite the party. What's something like this cost?"

"I don't know. Evan's mom took care of it."

"So now you're one of these rich people," Martin says, glancing at some of the guests. "How's it feel?"

"I feel like the same old Grace." I lower my voice. "Honestly, I don't feel like I belong here."

"Hey, Evan," Jenna says.

"Hello, Jenna." Evan comes up next to me. "I'm glad you could make it."

"This is Martin," I say to Evan. "I don't think you two have met."

"No, we haven't," Martin says, shaking Evan's hand. "It's good to finally meet you."

"You as well. I'm pleased you could be here tonight for Grace." He glances at me. "I know how important it is for her to have you and Jenna here."

"Looks like we're the only two people you know," Jenna says, scanning the room. "Who are all these old people?"

"They're my mother's friends," Evan says. "Despite not living here, she knows a surprisingly large number of people in the area."

Jenna points to my champagne glass. "Where can I get one of those?"

"Come with me," I say, motioning her. "Martin, you want one?"

"If not, we have other options," Evan says to him. "I can show you to the bar."

"I'm going with him," Martin says, pointing at Evan.

The men head to the bar while Jenna grabs a champagne glass from the closest server. I finish what's left of mine and help myself to another.

"What do you think?" I say to Jenna, motioning around the room. "Can you believe this?"

"It's like something on TV." She gulps her champagne. "Remember that soap opera we used to watch with all the rich people? It looks like one of their parties."

"It does," I say.

"I guess you're really doing this, huh?" she asks quietly.

"Doing what?"

"Marrying Evan. I wasn't sure if you were gonna go through with it when I saw you at the diner without your ring."

"That was just cold feet. I'm over that now."

Jenna looks around. "Where's Evan's mom?"

"Over there." I point Vivian out.

"She's a lot younger than I was picturing."

"I thought the same thing when I first met her."

"Are you two still getting along?"

"Yeah, we've actually gotten really close. Sometimes I feel closer to her than to Evan. She's more open to talking about stuff than he is."

Jenna turns to me. "Evan still won't talk to you? Grace, you're *marrying* this guy! This is a major problem. Communication is everything."

I gulp my drink, not wanting to get into another argument about Evan. "Forget I said anything. Let's go find Martin."

"He's over there," Jenna says, nodding behind me.

I look back and see Martin standing by himself, a drink in his hand, looking very uncomfortable. What happened to Evan? I was hoping he'd talk to Martin for a few minutes. Jenna and I make our way over to him.

"Where's Evan?" I ask.

"He left." Martin sips his drink. "Had to take a phone call."

Phone call? Seriously?

"You sure he's the right guy?" Martin asks, interrupting my thoughts.

"Well, yeah, I'm marrying him," I say with a laugh.

He nods, then takes a drink.

"Why'd you ask?" I say.

"I didn't get a good feel from him." Martin shrugs and swirls his drink. It takes a moment before he looks at me. "But hey, maybe it's just me."

Jenna jumps in. "I've felt that way since I met him, but Grace thinks I'm crazy."

"I didn't say you were crazy," I tell her. "I just don't think it's fair to say that when you don't know him."

"She's right. Let's give the guy a chance," Martin says, nudging Jenna. "If Grace likes him, he can't be that bad."

"Thanks, Martin," I say.

The three of us talk until Evan returns and takes me away to meet more of our guests. He's good at making conversation with strangers, which just proves that what Ashley said was a lie. She made Evan sound like a socially awkward loner, but that's not at all what I'm seeing tonight.

"Where are the people you work with?" I ask Evan after nearly an hour of mingling.

"Most of them couldn't make it."

"Then I'll meet the ones that are here. Where are they?"

He looks around. "It looks like they left."

My shoulders drop. "Already? The party just started."

"It's been going on for over an hour. People have things to do, Grace. They don't want to spend all evening here."

"Why didn't you introduce me to them before they left?"

"Why would you want to meet the people I work with?"

"I just do. Why do I need a reason?"

"Stop arguing with me," he says in a hushed tone. "People are staring."

"I'm not arguing. I just really wanted to meet these people, and now they're gone."

"There's nothing I can do about that, so stop making a scene." He smiles at an older woman going past us. "Good evening."

"Good evening," she says. "It's a wonderful party."

"Thank you," he says as she moves along.

The night continues with the food being served and Vivian pausing the band to make a short speech and a toast. By ten o'clock, I'm exhausted and ready to go home. Unfortunately, as the guest of honor, that's not an option. I'll be stuck here until the party ends at midnight.

Jenna and Martin left a few minutes ago. They said they had a good time, but whenever I saw them, they looked bored out of their minds. Nobody talked to them all night except me, and I was usually off with Evan.

Speaking of him, I don't know where he went. He was talking to someone at the bar, but now he's not there. I get up to go look for him and see him coming toward me.

"There you are," I say, smiling at him.

He doesn't smile back. "I need to speak to you. Let's go out in the hall."

"Speak to me about what?"

"Grace, please. Don't argue about this."

We make our way through the ballroom and out to the hall.

"What is it?" I ask. "What's this about?"

He grabs my arm. "Did you talk to Ashley behind my back?"

"Evan, let go of me." I try to pull away. "You're hurting me."

"Answer me," he says in an angry tone. His grip tightens. "Did you talk to her without telling me?"

"Yes, but it was her idea." I finally manage to yank away from him. "She told your mother she wanted to talk to me."

"Why is my mother involved in this?"

"She went to lunch with her, remember? It was when Ashley was in town."

"And what did Ashley have to say to you?" he sneers.

"The same thing you said. That you two didn't get along."

"What else?"

"Why does it matter? It's not like I believed her." I rub my arm, feeling a sting where he had his hand

"She told you her theory," he huffs. "About me being involved in what happened to Dana."

268

"Yes, but I told her you'd never hurt anyone. I didn't believe a word of it."

"You never should've talked to her!" Evan says. "She was trying to turn you against me just like she did with Dana. And you let her!"

"Everything okay out here?" Vivian says, coming out of the ballroom. "I saw you leaving and—"

"We're fine, Mother," Evan snaps. "Go back to the party."

"Grace?" she says, like she's concerned for me.

"Evan and I were just talking," I tell her. "But we're done now."

"Wonderful!" She smiles. "Why don't you come back to the party?"

Evan's eyes pause on me a moment; then he storms past me back into the ballroom.

Vivian walks over to me. "Are you okay? You can be honest, Grace. He's gone."

I take a calming breath. "Yes, I'm fine."

She glances at the ballroom, then back at me. "I need to tell you something. Something I should've said a long time ago. About Evan."

"What about him?" I ask, fearing what she's going to say.

"Not here. I don't want Evan catching us." She looks down the hall. "Over there. Come on."

I follow her. "Where are we going?"

"To the rooftop, if the door isn't locked."

We climb the stairs and find we're able to go out the door. The cold wind smacks me in the face.

"It's freezing out here," I say, rubbing my arms.

"This won't take long," she says, ushering me away from the door. She stops suddenly and turns to face me. "You can't marry Evan."

"Why?" I ask, but I feel like I already know the answer. Evan is dangerous. He really did kill Dana, and probably Lori too. And his mother knows but was afraid to tell me. Maybe she thought he'd changed. Maybe he promised her it'd never happen again.

Vivian hasn't answered me. What is she waiting for?

"Just tell me," I say. "Why don't you want me to marry Evan?"

She sneers at me. "Because he's mine."

"Yours? What are you talking about?"

She steps closer to me, forcing me to step back.

"Evan is mine," she says, breathing heavily, her eyes narrowed. "He's *my* son. He belongs to *me*. And I won't let some cheap tramp take him away!"

My heart is racing, a sharp pain slicing through my skull. "What do mean? What's going on here?"

"I'm taking my son back."

I don't even have a chance to respond before she reaches under the hem of her dress and pulls out a knife, aiming it directly at me.

I gasp. "Vivian, what are you doing?"

"There's nothing like the love between a mother and her son. Evan is my entire world. When his father died, he was all I had." She gets this weird smile on her face. It contorts her features into something out of a nightmare. "He took care of me. Doted on me. He was such a good boy. Until some girl caught his eye."

Her smile drops, and she points the knife at my face. "She tried to take him from me! So did all the others. But I wouldn't let them. And I won't let you!"

She lunges at me, and I stumble back. I glance behind me and see I'm just inches from the edge of the roof. It barely rises past my ankle. There's no railing. Nothing to grasp onto. If I lose my balance fall back, it's over. I'll be dead.

"Vivian, stop," I beg. "You don't have to do this. I'll go away. I won't marry Evan."

"It's too late," she snaps. "He loves you. He's not giving you up. The only way you'll be gone is if I get rid of you. Just like I did Lori and Dana."

I stare at her in disbelief. "You . . . you killed them?"

She laughs a little, sounding like a maniac. I try to keep my eyes on the knife instead of her face.

"I invited myself to hike with Lori that day. She was thrilled. She thought I wanted to get to know her. You can imagine her shock when I pushed her to her death."

Vivian steps closer. When I back away, the edge of the roof scrapes the back of my ankle.

"As for Dana, I went to see Evan that night, but I heard him arguing with her. I decided to wait outside. When Evan left, I knocked on the door and Dana answered, sobbing about Evan running off. I told her to relax and take a nice bath, then I poured her a glass of wine, dissolved the pills in it, and that was that." She laughs again. "I really had her fooled. Dana loved me. In fact, when I met Ashley for lunch, she told me how Dana used to tell her she thought of me as a mother."

My heart's pounding so hard I feel like I can't breathe. I trusted Vivian. Confided in her. Believed she was on my side. But like Evan said, it was all an act.

The woman is completely deranged.

She killed two women. All so she could have Evan to herself. I need to get away from her, but I can't with that knife pointing straight at my heart. And I'm afraid if I try to fight her, one or both of us will end up going over the edge of the roof.

"I didn't want to do this, Grace. I actually liked you. Far more than the others."

"Then don't!" I put my hands up and notice they're shaking. "Don't do it!"

"I tried everything to get you to leave him." She sighs dramatically. "Telling you about his dead fiancés. Dropping hints that he was dangerous. Bruising myself hoping you'd think he did it. Having you talk to Ashley, knowing she'd tell you her theory that

Evan killed Dana. How could you possibly stay with him after all that?"

"Because I love him," I say, tears now spilling down my cheeks. "I didn't want to believe any of that was true."

"If only you had . . . we wouldn't be here. If only you'd paid attention to all the signs I was giving you and done what you should have. You'd be back living your life in New Jersey instead of being here, seconds away from death."

CHAPTER 38

"No! I'm begging you! Don't do this!" I yell. I'm now dangerously close to the edge of the roof. One strong gust of wind could make me lose my balance and send me falling to my death.

I've been pleading with Vivian for what I'm guessing has been several minutes now, trying to buy myself time in the hope that someone will find us. But I doubt that'll happen since nobody knows we're up here.

"I'll . . . I'll leave!" I stutter, desperately trying to come up with the right words to convince her that I won't get in her way — that she can have her son back. "I'll tell Evan I don't love him!"

"It's too late," she snaps, whipping the knife around, almost nicking my face. "Have you not seen how he treats you? How he's always taking your side over mine? He's never giving you up. No matter what you say, he'll always choose you over me."

I hear a noise and look past Vivian to see Evan coming out the door.

"Evan!" I scream.

Vivian glances back, and I take the opportunity to run past her and over to Evan. "She's trying to kill me! She—"

"Mother, what the hell are you doing?" Evan demands, putting himself in front of me.

The pain in my head is excruciating. I feel like my skull is about to explode, but I force myself to stay alert, not sure what Vivian's going to do next.

"She's poisoning you, Evan," Vivian says. "You have to see that! She's no good for you!"

"Put the knife down, Mother," he says, walking closer to her. "You are not going to hurt Grace. I love her. I'm going to marry her."

"No!" Vivian says, shaking her head. "You're mine. You're all I have. You're moving back with me. You'll live in your old room. I'll fix it up however you like."

"I am not going back there," Evan says. He takes a step closer. "I'm a grown man. I'm not going to live with my mother."

"You would if you hadn't been brainwashed by her!" Vivian points at me. "She'll never make you happy, Evan. She'll leave you just like all the others."

"Those women didn't leave me," Evan growls, stepping even closer to Vivian. "You killed them!"

"Because they weren't good for you," Vivian rushes to say. "You couldn't see it, but I could. None of those women would've loved you the way I do. A mother's love is like no other. I'll love you no matter what. Someone like Grace will leave you at the first sign of trouble. That's why you need to let her go."

"I am not leaving Grace," Evan says, his voice deepening, growing louder. "And you are not going to harm her." He points his finger at Vivian's face. "Do you hear me, Mother? You will not harm her. I will not allow it!"

"I'm sorry she's done this to you," Vivian says, frowning at Evan. "But I'm here now, sweetheart. I'm here to save you from her. And from yourself. We'll go home. Back to California." She smiles and lowers the knife to her side. "You'll move back with me, and it'll be just like it was before. Before women like Grace ruined you."

"She didn't ruin me, Mother." He pauses. "*You* did!"

Evan shoves Vivian, and I watch in horror as she falls over the edge of the roof.

I collapse to my knees, gasping for breath, not believing what I just saw. Did he really just do that? Did Evan just kill his own mother?

He turns and walks back to me. "I'm sorry you had to see that."

I'm shaking. Completely stunned. This can't possibly be real, but I know it is. I saw her go over the edge. She's gone. Vivian just fell to her death.

"It had to be done," Evan says. "You heard her. She wouldn't allow me to have a life. She wanted me to live with her forever."

"Evan, you . . . you killed her," I say, my voice trembling. "You killed your own mother."

"Who was seconds away from killing my fiancé," he calmly says. "She promised me it'd be different this time. She went on and on about how much she liked you. But as you can see, it was all a lie. Just like she lied about the others."

"You . . . you knew? You knew she killed them?"

"She wouldn't admit it, but I suspected she was involved. She'd make little comments, hinting at it, but never actually saying what she'd done. I told her if she interfered with my life again, that would be it. I'd end all contact with her. She acted as though she had no idea what I was talking about."

"That's why you didn't want her to know about me," I mutter.

"It's why I moved here," he says. "I didn't trust that she wouldn't do it again if I were to meet someone. I tried to warn you, Grace, but you wouldn't listen."

"Did she say anything to you? About wanting to hurt me?"

"No. She genuinely seemed to like you. She told me I'd finally found the right woman. She said she was happy for me. I truly thought she meant it, but clearly, I was wrong. You're lucky I arrived when I did." He reaches down and grasps my arm, and eases me to my feet. "Let's get back to the party."

"The party?" I say. He must be in shock or denial, or both. "Evan, we have to call the police! We have to tell them—"

"We will do no such thing," he says in a stern tone. "What happened tonight was an accident." He lifts my face up to his. "Do you understand me? It was an *accident*."

I slowly nod, seeing the darkness in his eyes, the slight grin on his face. He's not in shock. He's crazy! He's just as unhinged as his mother. He threw her off the roof. Killed her. And yet he's eerily calm. He doesn't seem to think what he did was in any way wrong. He thinks we can just return to the party as if nothing happened.

"She was trying to take you from me," Evan says, almost like he's talking to himself, justifying why he did it. "I was protecting you, Grace. Can't you see that? Can't you see how much I love you? I chose you over my own mother."

"But it didn't have to be that way. You could've talked to her. You could've—"

"No. You don't understand. When my mother wanted something, she didn't stop until she got it. And what she wanted was for me to be with her, not you. She didn't want me getting married and having my own life." He starts pulling me toward the doorway that will take us back inside. "That's why I moved here. To get away from her. It wasn't for a job. I have more than enough money. I have no need to work."

"You don't have a job?" I say. "But you showed me the software you're developing. You said you had meetings. You got calls from people at work."

"It was all a performance, Grace. I didn't want you thinking I was living off my mother's money."

"You've never had a job? Even in California?"

"I've worked on and off for years, but only when I chose to, and never for anyone else. When I'm bored, I'll develop an app or some software and sell it to whoever will give me the most money."

"So where have you been going during the day?"

"Museums. Art galleries. Historical sites. This city has so much to offer, it's easy to fill my time." He smiles a little. "Now that Mother's gone and not consuming your time, you can join me. We'll spend our days together roaming the city, exploring new places."

"Evan, that's not what I want. I want to—"

"I don't care what you want!" He grabs my shoulders and shakes me. "You're mine, Grace, and you will do as I say!"

Jenna was right. Evan wants to control me. It was his goal from the beginning. That's why he chose me. I was a poor, struggling waitress who would do anything to escape that life. He took advantage of that. He said and did all the right things to convince me he'd give me the life of my dreams.

When was he going to tell me the truth? After the wedding? Was that why he was in such a hurry to get married?

Sirens wail in the distance. Someone on the street must've called the police. There's probably a crowd gathered around Vivian's body.

"Let's go," Evan says, yanking me to the door. "We can't be out here."

Keeping hold of me, he goes down the stairs, stopping when we reach the door that goes back to the hallway that leads to the ballroom.

"You will say nothing about this," Evan says, his hand digging into my arm. "If you utter one word — to anyone — your friend Jenna, and that man she was with tonight, will end up like my mother."

No. Jenna and Martin are like family to me. If he cared about me at all, he wouldn't harm them. What am I saying? He killed his own mother. Why would I think he wouldn't kill the people closest to me?

"Tell me you understand," Evan says slowly.

I nod. "I understand."

"Good." He smiles. "Let's return to the party. I'd like to make a toast."

We go into the ballroom, and it's as if nothing has happened. No one seems to know about Vivian. Maybe the police haven't identified who she is yet. She didn't have any identification on her.

Evan tells the band to stop playing and takes the microphone. "Can I have your attention, please?"

The room quiets down as everyone focuses on Evan.

"Thank you all for coming tonight," he says, a big grin on his face. He puts his arm around me, and I instantly tense up. "Grace and I feel fortunate to have so many of you here to celebrate our engagement. I want to take this time to make a toast to—"

"Wait!" I grab the microphone from Evan, finding a strength inside me I didn't know I had. "I can't do this."

"Grace!" Evan whispers, trying to take the microphone.

I turn to face him. "I can't do this, Evan. I can't marry you."

The people around us gasp, but I keep my focus on Evan.

"I haven't been faithful to you," I say, deciding I need to take the blame for this, or it won't work. Evan needs to be seen as the hero. I need to be the villain. It's the only way I'll get out of this without putting my friends at risk.

"Grace, stop this," Evan says through gritted teeth. He looks like he's going to kill me, but if he tries, he'll have a whole room full of witnesses.

"It isn't right for me to go through with this when I haven't been faithful to you," I say, stepping back so Evan can't take the microphone. "You've been so good to me, and I feel terrible for what I've done." I sniffle and wipe my eyes. "You deserve someone so much better. And I know you'll find her someday."

Evan's staring at me in utter shock. He didn't think I had it in me to do something like this. I didn't either. I acted out of pure survival. One of the perks of growing up poor is always having to struggle. You learn to do whatever's necessary to survive. That's an advantage I have over Evan. He never had to work for anything. Never had to struggle. Never had to fight to survive.

He lured me in with his money. Lied to me. Tried to control me. He thought he'd trapped me. That I was his forever. But he forgot who I was before he met me. I almost did, too.

Until now.

It's over. The engagement is off. Evan won't try to get me back. A man with his money and good looks would be a fool to take back a woman who cheated on him. And Evan wouldn't stand to be seen as a fool.

I drop the microphone and run out of the ballroom as everyone watches in shock, too stunned to make a sound. I fling open the door and see two police officers standing there.

"Miss," one of them says. "Is this the engagement party for Evan Sinclair?"

"Yes." I wait for them to go past me into the ballroom, and then I smile. "But the party just ended. And the engagement is off."

CHAPTER 39

Three Months Later

"Can I get a refill over here?" a man at the counter yells.

I grab the coffee pot and make my way down to him, filling his empty cup.

"Do you need anything else?" I ask in a cheerful voice, hoping it'll earn me a little extra on the tip. But given how rude he's been, he'll probably leave me nothing.

"Give me a blueberry muffin," he grunts. "And hurry it up! I ain't got all day!"

"Coming right up!" I say, racing off to get it.

I've been back at the diner for a few months now. Some days, it seems like I never left. I wish I never had. I still have nightmares about what happened the night of the engagement party. I'll see Evan pushing Vivian to her death and wake up in a cold sweat. Even when I'm awake, I'll see that scene in my head and feel like I'm reliving it. It was a horrible night, one I'll never forget. But at least it ended with me getting my freedom back.

After I called off the engagement in front of everyone at the party, I took a cab back to Evan's apartment, quickly packed a bag, left my ring on the dresser, and drove back to New Jersey. I called Jenna on the way there and told her I needed a place to stay and that I'd explain when I got there. I ended up telling her the story I told everyone else. I couldn't tell her what actually happened, knowing if Evan found out, he'd come after her.

"You're supposed to be on break," Jenna says as I put a blueberry muffin on a plate.

"I'll go after I give this to the guy at the counter."

Jenna takes the plate from me. "I'll do it. Go take your break."

"Thanks!" I smile at her and head to the break room.

Collapsing on the couch, I put my feet up and get out my phone. I do a quick search for Vivian's name but don't find anything new. Her death was ruled a suicide, but I keep hoping the police will find evidence showing that Evan did it. Like maybe they'll find out there were cameras on the roof and uncover video of Evan shoving his mother to her death.

It's wishful thinking, I know. I'm sure it'll never happen. Evan will get away with it, just like Vivian got away with killing Lori and Dana. What a messed-up family. Rich people always look so perfect from the outside, but the reality is they're just as screwed up as everyone else.

My phone rings. My heart nearly stops when I see Evan's name on the screen. I haven't talked to him since our engagement party. I thought for sure he'd show up at my apartment after that, or at the very least call and yell at me for what I did. But it never happened. He never showed up. Never called. As the weeks went by, I wondered if I'd ever hear from him again.

"Hello?" I say, answering the call. I should've ignored it. Why didn't I?

"Hello, Grace," Evan says in his smooth, deep voice. "How have you been?"

"What do you want, Evan?"

"There's no need to be unpleasant."

I don't respond.

"Fine, I'll get to the point. I'm calling to make sure you're clear on our arrangement."

"What arrangement?"

"Regarding what happened that night. The terrible tragedy that took my mother's life."

"I already told you I'd keep quiet," I snap.

"Yes, well, I wanted to make sure you weren't having second thoughts."

"You didn't give me that option after you threatened to hurt my friends." I pause. "Were you just saying that to scare me? You wouldn't really do it, would you?"

"You already know the answer to that. It's why you haven't told anyone."

"So you're saying you'd hurt them if I—"

"Goodbye, Grace."

I look at my phone and see he hung up. Why would he call me out of the blue and remind me to keep quiet? Are the police investigating Vivian's death? Maybe my fantasy will come true, and Evan will get charged with killing his mother.

My phone rings again. I don't recognize the number.

"Hello?"

"Hi, is this Grace?"

"Yeah, who's this?"

"Andrea. You don't know me, but you know my fiancé. Evan Sinclair?"

Fiancé? Evan's engaged? Again?

"You're marrying Evan?" I ask, confirming I heard her right.

"In three weeks. I can't wait! He's such a great catch!"

"Three weeks," I say. My heart rate kicks up a notch. "Wow, that's soon."

"Yeah, but I love him, so why wait?"

I said the same thing. I can't believe how stupid I was back then.

"Anyway," she says, "this may sound kind of strange, but I wanted to know what happened with you and Evan. He won't tell me. He says it's disrespectful to talk about his ex with me, but I really want to know. I can't imagine why anyone would give up a guy like him."

That's why Evan called me. He knew this woman was going to contact me and ask why I called off the engagement. He was warning me not to tell her the truth. I'd love to be honest and save her from what I'm sure will be a horrible life with Evan, but I can't risk it. I can't risk him hurting Jenna and Martin, or me.

"Evan's a great guy," I say, almost choking on the words. "But I wasn't ready to get married. I was seeing someone else when Evan and I were engaged, which proved to me I needed more time to be single."

"No wonder he didn't want to tell me," she says in a sad voice. "Poor Evan."

"But now he has you, so it all worked out. Is the wedding in New York?"

Why am I asking her this? Why do I care? I should just end the call.

"San Francisco," she says. "He left New York months ago. You didn't know?"

I assumed he did, but I didn't know for sure.

"We didn't stay in touch," I say.

"Yeah, that makes sense," she says with a nervous laugh. "Well, that's really all I wanted to ask."

"Hey, before you go, how did you get my number?"

"I found it in Evan's phone. I knew your name was Grace, and you were the only Grace is in his phone, so I figured it was you."

"Did you tell Evan you were calling me?"

"No. He'd be upset if he knew. He doesn't like it when I ask about you, so it's best if we keep this a secret. That's not a problem, is it? I mean, I assume you don't talk to him anymore."

"No. Never. I'm surprised he still has me in his phone."

"I was too. I was going to ask him about it, but then he'd find out I was snooping in his phone. Well, I should go, but thanks for clearing that up. And I guess I should thank for you not marrying Evan, because now I get to!"

"Congratulations. I'm sure you two will be very happy."

"Thanks! Bye!" She ends the call.

That was strange. Why would this woman care why Evan and I broke up? Is she having doubts about him like I did?

I have so many questions, but I need to forget about it. That's not my life anymore. Evan is my past. I don't want to even think about him anymore.

My phone chimes with a text. I look and see it's from Evan. I'm very pleased. Your performance was excellent. Mother always did like you the best. Too bad things didn't work out with us.

My performance? Was Evan listening in on my call with his fiancé? How else would he know what I said to her? Did he somehow bug my phone? He had access to it when we were living together. Maybe he did something to it so he could listen to my calls. I don't know what that would be, but I'm not a tech person. Evan's a genius with tech stuff.

I toss the phone on the table and back away from it, my entire body trembling. As soon as my shift ends, I'm going to the store and buying a new phone. And I'm blocking Evan's number so he can't call me again. I'm officially done with him. I'm never talking to Evan again.

He's someone else's problem now.

THE END

THE JOFFE BOOKS STORY

We began in 2014 when Jasper agreed to publish his mum's much-rejected romance novel and it became a bestseller.

Since then we've grown into the largest independent publisher in the UK. We're extremely proud to publish some of the very best writers in the world, including Joy Ellis, Faith Martin, Caro Ramsay, Helen Forrester, Simon Brett and Robert Goddard. Everyone at Joffe Books loves reading and we never forget that it all begins with the magic of an author telling a story.

We are proud to publish talented first-time authors, as well as established writers whose books we love introducing to a new generation of readers.

We won Trade Publisher of the Year at the Independent Publishing Awards in 2023 and Best Publisher Award in 2024 at the People's Book Prize. We have been shortlisted for Independent Publisher of the Year at the British Book Awards for the last five years, and were shortlisted for the Diversity and Inclusivity Award at the 2022 Independent Publishing Awards. In 2023 we were shortlisted for Publisher of the Year at the RNA Industry Awards, and in 2024 we were shortlisted at the CWA Daggers for the Best Crime and Mystery Publisher.

We built this company with your help, and we love to hear from you, so please email us about absolutely anything bookish at feedback@joffebooks.com.

If you want to receive free books every Friday and hear about all our new releases, join our mailing list here: www.joffebooks.com/freebooks.

And when you tell your friends about us, just remember: it's pronounced Joffe as in coffee or toffee!